RUNAWAY

BOOK ONE OF THE LANIS CHRONICLES

V. BRICKER

K. NOBLES

BRICKER
NOBLES

Cover Illustration by Audrey Hotte
Editing by Ash Works
Proof by Holloway House

ISBN 978-1-963455-06-9 (paperback)
ISBN 978-1-963455-07-6 (hardcover)
ISBN 978-1-963455-08-3 (ebook)
www.brickerandnobles.com

To Rhett and Dan,
who enrich our lives just by being in them.

CONTENTS

Acknowledgments

First and foremost, we would like to thank our amazing friends and families, who were always very encouraging even when we doubted ourselves. It took over ten years to write this book and get it into your hands. So many people helped us, not in just the creation of the book, but by supporting us when we needed a break, a drink, or a shoulder to cry on.

We would also like to thank Brock, Robin, and Rhett for their help during the editing process when we really didn't want to work.

PROLOGUE

A warm evening breeze sighed through the courtyard, bringing with it the smell of warm, delicious sweets baking in the ovens. Sophie tried not to wipe her palms on her skirt as she knelt on the soft, woven rug her father had laid out for her. She was nervous and found it hard to sit still as the man in black robes settled across from her on a rug of his own. Although she was only seven, she could tell just by looking that his robes were finely made, even if she didn't know what they were made of. The dress she wore was of the same material. She was only allowed to wear it when special guests were visiting.

Sophie knew that the man was here because of her, because she'd done something very strange a few weeks ago. She'd been playing with her younger brother on a day like this one, a hot, humid day in the late spring. She and Aluemos were playing in the fountain near the garden to try and fend off the heat. Papa let her splash around in the fountains as long as they didn't have any visitors. Otherwise, she had to act like a lady.

She had waded into the water, soaking the bottom of her dress, and climbed up the pair of marble fish that were the centerpiece of the fountain. Water flowed out of the open mouths of the twin fish and glittered in the sunshine as it fell into the pool. Sophie reached out her hand in an attempt to catch the sunlight. She knew it was impossible, but she loved the way the water sparkled through her fingers like liquid gold. With her short arms, she couldn't quite reach the cool water and stretched her hand out as far as it would go. She bit her tongue and scrunched up her face as she reached for the sparkling liquid. *If only it would come to me!*

As soon as she'd thought the words, the water had slowed its descent and started drifting toward her, floating in little rivulets in midair.

Sophie had shrieked in delight. "Ali! Look!" The boy looked up from his splashing and laughed, pointing at the floating water. When she raised her hand, the water had followed her movements, swaying this way and that. Her brother clapped, and they giggled as the water fell into the pool and began to flow from the fish's mouth once again.

Grandfather had been walking in the garden, as he often did in the afternoons, and had seen what she'd done.

Now, the man in black robes was here to talk to her. Sophie didn't quite know what to make of him. She'd heard her parents arguing about it the night before. Hiding by the door, she hadn't been able to make out what they were saying, but Mama had been crying.

"Comfortable?" the man in black robes asked. He'd introduced himself before dinner. What had his name been? *Iseul*, she thought. *What a weird name.* He'd asked her questions as they ate. How old was she? What did she like?

Did she know anyone who could use magic? Did she know what a wizard was?

What a stupid question. Of course she knew about the wizards of Zo'rahn.

The wizards were the ones who ruled in Zo'rahn, the country where she lived. Everyone who could use magic was what Papa called *the nobility* in Zo'rahn. She had learned from her tutor that the country was broken up into provinces, each ruled by a Vizier, with smaller areas managed by a Vasalii. Her family lived on Vasalii Erol's lands. Well, Papa said the grounds were technically theirs, but that her grandfather paid a levy, whatever that was, to the Vasalii. She had met a wizard only once before, a tall man who had come to buy something from her grandfather.

Papa explained to her once that he and Grandfather were merchants, people who bought things far away and brought them back to Zo'rahn to sell for a better price. That's why their house was so big and how he could give Mama nice things. The wizards liked nice things, too, so they would come and buy things from them.

Iseul had also asked about her hair. Everyone always asked about her hair.

Remembering that the man expected a response, she ducked her eyes in embarrassment for her daydreaming and nodded.

Iseul chuckled. "Don't be afraid, little one. This won't take long." He reached into his robes and pulled out a stick, a silver box, and a piece of parchment and set them between their mats. Iseul was a tall man, older and fatter than Papa, but not as old as her grandfather. He had the typical Zo'rahni coal-black hair and olive skin. He also had a neatly trimmed goatee and smiled at her whenever he caught her eye. He seemed like a nice man.

Sophie looked at the items, then up at him quizzically.

He smiled again and gestured at them. "Pick one. Then we can start."

Looking at the three objects sitting between their mats, Sophie's eye was drawn to the silver box. It was perfectly square, the lantern light gleaming off an intricately inlaid design on its surface. She stared at it for a moment, then tore her eyes away from it. It was beautiful compared to the other items, but Grandfather had said that Iseul was going to test her. Was this part of it? Did he expect her to choose the box first? Was it a trick?

She reached out, but at the last moment decided to pick up the stick instead of going for the box. It seemed like a less obvious choice, and she didn't want to fail the test within the first few minutes. When she looked up at him, Iseul nodded at her and gestured for her to continue.

Settling back on her mat, Sophie brought the stick closer, examining its length. It was smooth and slender, sloping down to a point at one end. There were carvings in the dark wood, symbols she didn't recognize. Running her thumb over the carvings, she asked, "What do these mean?"

"They are called runes," Iseul began in a soft and patient tone, sounding much like her tutor when explaining how something worked. "And that is called a wand. Each rune carved on that wand represents a different type of energy. Energies weave together in different and complex ways to create the spells that wizards and other magic users cast, whether they are implementing runes such as these to guide them, or casting from their power within. By carving runes on an object such as this, a wizard can press some of their power into it to create a tool that can be used by anyone with the gift, assuming they can figure out how to use it."

Sophie's eyes were wide as she stared at Iseul. She had never heard magic explained in such a way. "What does it do?" she asked, voice quiet.

"That is for you to figure out," he said with a sly grin. "I can't just give you the answers."

Right. This was a test. Sophie looked back down at the wand and frowned. She rolled it between her fingers, carefully studying each rune. One rune near the base of the wand looked familiar to her and she bent closer to examine it. It seemed a little like the symbol for fire that she'd been forced to memorize in lessons. An image of a dimly glowing flame appeared in her mind, flickering softly like that of a candle, or the lanterns placed around them.

The tip of the wand abruptly sparked, making Sophie jump. She yelped and dropped it, as if it were a snake about to strike, losing her balance and falling back onto her bottom.

She picked herself back up a moment later, her cheeks hot, and tucked a few loose strands of hair that escaped her bun back behind her ear. She eyed the wand suspiciously, but it had ceased whatever it had done and just lay where it had fallen on the ground, looking like a stick once again.

Iseul wasn't smiling anymore. He looked... *surprised*. Was he upset with her? Was he going to tell her parents she failed the test?

"I-I'm sorry," she said quickly, looking down at her hands. "I didn't mean to break your stick." She glanced back at the wand still lying there innocently.

He blinked at her words and shook his head slowly. "No, you didn't break it." He inhaled deeply, and then the smile was back, only now it seemed somehow different from before. "Why don't we move on? Go ahead and pick another item."

Sophie reached out and tentatively picked up the silver box, as though it, too, might bite her. If what she thought was a stick was dangerous, then the box must be even more so, even if it was pretty. Now that she could look more closely, she could see that it was inlaid with a delicate floral design curving around the edges, flowing and scrolling over the surface. She followed the pattern with her fingertips. It was so beautiful.

She didn't see any seams, but tried to pry it open anyway. Her fingers slipped on the cold metal, but it wouldn't budge. She shook it, but felt nothing within the box. Was it empty? She held it up to her ear and shook it again. It sounded empty.

"What is this one?" she asked.

"It's a bit different from the last one," he said smoothly, seeming to expect her questions. "The box will react to your focus and imagination. The very basis of magical practice is the ability to shape what you imagine into reality. If you believe the box should open, and focus that desire on it, it *will* open. It's as simple as that. Now, close your eyes."

"Why?" Somehow, she didn't believe it was that easy.

His smile fractured by a degree, but he recovered it quickly. "Closing your eyes will help you concentrate, especially since you don't know how to focus correctly yet," he said patiently.

Sophie looked back at the box in her hands. She still couldn't see any way to open it. She stared at the swirling designs and sighed, closing her eyes.

"Good. Focus on the weight of the box in your hands. Picture it in your mind."

She did as he instructed and she saw the silver box in her mind, much as she had the flickering candle flame had when she'd studied the rune on the wand.

"Can you see it?"

She nodded.

"Now, I want you to focus on the box. Imagine the designs on it, every little detail. Fill in what you can't picture."

The image of the silver box in her head gained a little detail, becoming more vibrant as she imagined it. The floral pattern sharpened into focus as she concentrated, trying to remember every line and curve. Sophie imagined the silver twinkling as it had in the lantern light, and she gently ran her fingers over its surface. The replica in her mind's eye moved and shifted along with the real one in her hands.

"Concentrate on the box," came Iseul's calm voice. "How would you open it?"

"I *can't* open it," she mumbled.

"Focus, Sophie. How would you open it, if you could? How do you think it *should* open?"

She thought of the inlaid floral design on the box. The object in her mind gained even more detail, mirroring what she remembered about the item she still held. She smiled. If she could imagine it opening any way she liked, why couldn't it bloom like a real flower?

Sophie imagined the sides of the box peeling away layer after layer, shimmering as the metal moved and formed into the shape of petals, flowing away from the box's center. In her mind, a small butterfly no bigger than her thumbnail rested in the middle of the metallic flower, pale luminescent wings twitching in the slight breeze.

"Is it open?" Iseul asked. His voice sounded far away, a muted quality to it, as if he were in a different room.

"Yes..." The butterfly flicked its wings when she spoke.

"Close it again. Focus on reversing the exact way you opened it."

She did as he instructed. It took her some time to get the box closed in her mind again, trapping the butterfly inside.

Iseul had her repeat the process three times. Each time, the process was smoother. The box-flower would open slowly and close slowly, folding its petals back in on itself and enclosing the insect within.

"Once more," he began again, "but this time, I want you to push the image away from you, down your arms, and into the box in your hands. Make it bend to your will."

She wasn't quite sure what he was talking about. How could she make the box do what she wanted? Still, she tried to do as Iseul said, focusing on making the object in her hands into what she saw in her head. She opened her eyes and stared at the box still resting in her palms and willed it to open, for it to unfold like the beautiful flower in her mind. *It should open*, she thought. *It was a flower.*

She almost jumped off the mat when the designs on the box suddenly started to shift and move. She fumbled the box, almost dropping it on the ground, but barely managed to keep a hold of it.

It started blooming exactly as she had visualized. The sides fell away, and the top of the object curved and writhed into the shape of a bud, even as silvery petals pulled away from the center. Sophie's eyes widened as she watched the box transform into the silver flower she'd imagined. Even absent the butterfly, it was amazing to watch. Was this magic?

"Interesting," Iseul murmured.

"How did it do that?" Sophie whispered, examining the silver flower closely.

"You did that. The box is just a tool. Using magic means shaping the world around you, bending it to your needs, and using your ability to create your own reality." He waved his hand over the flower and it shuddered, the petals beginning to fold back in. Within seconds, it had returned to its original, cube-like state.

She looked up at him incredulously, her fingers tight around the box. "Does that mean I used magic?"

"In the most basic sense, yes. You exerted your will on the box, and it changed shape to your wishes. You made that flower bloom." He chuckled to himself. "Most just imagine the lid opening."

"Oh," she said. Did she do it wrong? Was she failing the test? "Do I need to imagine it doing that then?"

Iseul shook his head. "No. What you did was just fine." He looked down at the parchment. "There is one more item left. I don't think it's necessary, given what you've already done, but I would like to see what you can do."

What she could do? She didn't feel like she was doing anything. She was just imagining things. What she *did* feel was tired, like she had been outside playing for hours. Sophie stifled a yawn and looked down at the parchment. It looked like the same writing paper she had used dozens of times to practice her scripts. She picked it up and unfolded it. It was blank.

Sophie glanced up at Iseul, but he made no indication of noticing the issue. She turned the paper over and held it up to the lamplight, but still couldn't see anything on it. It seemed like just a regular sheet of paper. But that didn't make sense. It had to be special in some way, just like the other items were.

After the relative ease of using the previous items, she spent what felt like forever trying to get the paper to do *something*. She tried rubbing her hands over it, folding it in different ways, even closing her eyes and imagining it folding into different shapes. Nothing seemed to work. She asked Iseul what it did, but he was not forthcoming, merely smiling and telling her to keep trying. Perhaps it really was just a regular piece of paper. She flicked it away from her in frustration, and it drifted to the ground. Iseul still said nothing.

"I don't know what to do," she admitted, folding her arms over her chest and glaring at the parchment sourly.

Iseul smiled apologetically. "Unfortunately, I'm not able to help you with this one. It is something you have to figure out on your own."

"Does it even do anything?" she growled.

"Yes," he admitted, "it does," and said nothing further.

Sophie scowled down at the parchment. It had fallen not far from where she had dropped the wand. She was overcome with the irrational urge to set the paper on fire and snatched up the wand, thought of fire, and smacked the tip on the parchment.

The wand sparked as it had before, but instead of catching on fire, the paper began glowing softly. Writing appeared across the sheet. She couldn't read very well yet, but still picked up the paper and held it up in awe, the wand cast aside and forgotten. The script was delicate and flowed from one line to the next, as if she was watching an invisible hand write it. The symbols were strange to her, but the words glided together seamlessly.

Eventually, the glow faded and went out as the writing reached the end of the page.

"What does it say?" she asked, her frustration with the paper forgotten.

"It's the first page of the first chapter from *Theorems on Ritual Magic*." He pulled the parchment out of her hand and looked it over, then glanced at her, his eyebrows raised. "You have successfully activated all three items. We're finished here."

She grinned and felt her chest swell. That must mean she passed the test. Papa was going to be so happy with her.

Iseul looked at her thoughtfully for a few moments. "Fetch your parents, child. I need to speak to them."

Sophie nodded and stood. Her legs felt a little numb after kneeling for so long, and she stumbled before catching her balance. She turned from Iseul and sprinted across the courtyard, up the stairs, and to the front door, pulling it open. "Papa! Papa!" she called as she raced into the foyer. "I'm finished!"

A tall, lanky man with graying hair and an angular face stood by the stairs. He turned to frown at her as she ran inside. He'd been speaking quietly with another man, also tall, and with similar features, but with hair as dark as the night sky. Both men wore long-sleeved, belted *shoen*, a formal tunic, the older man's with gold and red embroidery and the younger's with blue and silver. The long garments went to their knees, and they both wore cream-colored trousers under the shoen, with sandals to match.

Sophie skidded to a halt in front of them and bowed, out of breath. "Grandfather. Father."

Papa looked concerned but smiled when he saw her. Grandfather, however, wore the same expression he always did when he looked at her, like he'd eaten a sour grape.

"I've completed the test," she said much more calmly.

Grandfather hated when she spoke casually in front of him, and she didn't want to get Papa into trouble. "Iseul wishes to speak with you, Father." She looked up at him. "Where is Mother?"

He glanced at her grandfather briefly, and for a reason she couldn't fathom, his expression deepened from concern to worry. "Your mother was not feeling well. She is resting." Before Sophie could ask what was wrong, her father shook his head and said, "She'll be fine." He held out his hand to her and smiled again, but it seemed forced. "Was the test difficult?" he asked gently.

She skipped forward and took his outstretched hand, ignoring the look her grandfather was giving them. Her hand could only hold three of her father's fingers. She shrugged, trying not to let her nervousness show under her grandfather's critical gaze. "No, not really. But it was weird. The things he has are odd."

He frowned slightly, and it was difficult to tell what he was thinking. Was he mad at her? "Come," he began, leading Sophie back to the front door, her grandfather following close behind. "Let us see what the wizard wants."

By the time he had finished administering the test, the sun had dipped below the horizon and a chill was settling into the late-summer air. Iseul scratched his goatee thoughtfully, still looking down at the three items laid out in front of him. The child had managed to activate all of them without too much prompting from him. While that wasn't unheard of, it was exceptionally rare in one so young. Typically, a child's magic did not manifest until their twelfth year, right at the start of adolescence. As far as he knew, a situation such as this had not happened with a child outside of the magical families for at least a century, maybe longer. She had the potential to be a powerful wizard one day, with the proper training.

Zo'rahn was divided into seven provinces, and the lands inside those borders into seven different territories. While Vasalii Erol ruled this territory, the lands inside the province were controlled by Vizier Lau'ren Tashiir. Seven Viziers made up the Ruling Council of Zo'rahn, and all of the regions within a province owed their allegiance to a Vizier. Iseul was part of Vizier Lau'ren's household and, as such, was required to offer the girl's adoption to the Vizier first.

Iseul hoped that the Vizier would overlook the child's mixed blood and take her into his household. The mother was obviously a foreigner, probably from a country on the continent to the west, Morigael or Tanalin, judging by her accent. The girl had inherited her mother's physical features, most notably the vibrant red hair and stormy gray eyes.

Yes... Iseul thought, *I think I can convince the Vizier to take her.*

Iseul picked up the testing items and put them into an inner pocket of his robes, then stood as the door to the main house opened. Sophie walked back outside, her tiny hand holding onto her father's, the grandfather, Fahren, trailing behind them.

He'd almost waited until next season to come and investigate the claim filed by Fahren, the patriarch of the Karr merchant family. His records indicated that the Karr family had not produced a magically gifted child in the past, and he'd been busy with other testing requests this season. The detour had proven well worth the trip.

The two men approached him and bowed deeply, but

the mother was nowhere to be seen. *Just as well*, he thought. She'd seemed hostile around him and must not have grasped who he was and the importance of his visit. He was surprised that someone of such low birth, never mind a foreigner, would have been allowed to marry into a prominent merchant family like the Karrs. By her mannerisms, she had not been of high station in her homeland, nor had the marriage added to the family's reputation or wealth. Such an action by the son and heir must have been quite an insult to older members of the family.

"*Alheim*, Nadil," he said, greeting the girl's father by name. "The testing is complete, and I am pleased with the results. Your offspring will bring you great honor."

Nadil bowed again, less deeply than before. "Thank you, Wizard." He straightened and patted his daughter's head affectionately. "My child bestows much joy on her mother and me. We are very proud that she can bring further honor to our family."

"Do you understand what comes next?" Iseul asked.

The young merchant looked troubled but nodded. Every Zo'rahni child was tested at some point in their life. No doubt Nadil was remembering his own experience. "I know what would happen if she were older," he said as he looked down at his daughter. "But she's only seven. Surely, she's still too young..." Nadil hugged his daughter a little closer to him as he spoke, and Iseul could hear the desperation in his voice.

Iseul pursed his lips. He had witnessed countless reactions over the years from parents of children who were chosen for the adoption process. Most were delighted when their child was chosen, but there had been trouble in the past as well.

The girl clung to her father's hand and watched him

with her large eyes. Iseul had a sinking feeling in his stomach that this was not going to be an easy acquisition.

"I need to send a few messages to the Vizier before the negotiations can begin. Would it be intrusive to ask for lodging for myself and my entourage until the proper arrangements are made?"

Nadil opened his mouth to answer, but Fahren spoke over him. "It would be our pleasure to see to your needs," he said, bowing politely once more. "You and your retinue are welcome in our home as long as it pleases you."

"Excellent. I will need some privacy to conduct my business then."

After a few brief pleasantries, he left the company of his host, and a servant took him to a suite of rooms in the east hall with a common area, study, and sleeping quarters. The rooms were richly furnished with items that he recognized as Omeran in design with their almost-white-colored wood and silk tapestries of red and gold from Alkhazai. The dark-eyed woman bowed to him and left.

Iseul sighed and stretched. He was tired from the day's travel, but there was still much work to do before he could rest for the night. He needed to send a message to the Vizier and inform him of his delayed return. It was possible that the negotiations could continue for up to four full days, at which point law dictated an agreement must be reached. Iseul fished a slender stone tablet with a wax face out of his robes and set it on the table in the study. Then he took off his robe of office and hung it on a hook. His formal duties were completed for the day, and though he still had work to do, his dark-green tunic and black breeches would suffice.

A light knock at the outer door echoed throughout the chamber.

"Enter," he commanded, searching through the inner pockets of his robe, his back to the door.

The door opened and closed with a soft click. He looked over his shoulder at a young woman with dark hair cut at shoulder length, wearing violet-dyed robes. The young woman was Mari, his apprentice. She bowed to him. "Master," she said politely. "I am assuming by our lodgings that the child shows talent."

"That is an accurate assessment," he said, turning back to the robes and finally finding what he was searching for, a slender stylus that was a companion to the tablet. Iseul motioned for her to follow him into the study. "The child successfully activated all of the test items." Mari's brows rose at that. "Contact the Vizier and inform him of the child's potential and of her... unique heritage." He set the stylus on the table next to the tablet.

If Mari had any thoughts about that last part of the message, she gave no sign. Mari dipped her head in a shallow, but respectful bow and sat at the small writing table. She dutifully began carving Iseul's message into the wax. As Mari scribed the message, the letters began to sink into the wax and disappear.

CHAPTER
ONE

Vibrant oranges and reds faded to violet as the autumn twilight approached over the capital city of Tanzar, the largest and busiest in all of Zo'rahn. It was a night like any other, warm with a cool breeze sweeping in off the sea, the smell of salt in the humid night air. People walked home after a day of selling and buying in the bazaar, and lamps started lighting all over the city. The whitewashed walls and domed roofs of homes gleamed in the fading sunlight.

Sophie sat in a cushioned wooden chair by the only window in her room, staring out at the soft glow as lights winked on in homes. Her room was on the third floor of the main house, which allowed her a view over the walls. Normally, at this time of night, Sophie would have her nose buried in a book, devouring anything from magical theory to an essay on the uses of calendula root. Study was a large part of her responsibilities as an apprentice mage, but it was also one she had developed a keen fondness for over the eleven years since she had been adopted.

She turned her attention from the sunset to her room.

It was small and sparsely furnished, as most rooms for apprentices were, but this one looked exceptionally empty. A single glass orb with a dim orange flame floating at its center hung from the ceiling, illuminating what was left of her belongings. The bookcase stood with only a few tomes, a fine outline of dust where her other more treasured books had been earlier in the day. A dark-blue traveling cloak hung on a peg by the door. It matched the dress she wore, long-sleeved and simple with slits in the sides to make movement easier. She tucked a loose strand of her bright red hair back behind her ear and inhaled deeply.

On the floor below the cloak, a worn leather pack rested against the wall. It was tied shut, and although she knew most of her small library and other personal effects were inside, the bag looked only half full. Atop a narrow desk in the far corner sat an untouched bowl of stew from the midday meal. Anxiety had strangled her hunger.

A soft knock on the door drew Sophie out of her thoughts. She eyed the door apprehensively and, after a moment, murmured, "Come in."

The door creaked on its hinges to reveal a young man a few years older than she was, with black hair and a handsome, angular face. He wore long black robes with rich purple lining and embroidery. He quickly walked into the room and shut the door quietly behind him. The lock clicked and he murmured a few words under his breath, too low for Sophie to hear. She felt a light snap of energy, then Zephan turned to face her with a forced smile plastered on his face.

Zephan had been Sophie's best friend since her first day at the estate. Four years her senior, he had been kind to her when few of the other children were. She had been different with her red hair, lighter skin, and gray eyes, an outcast as soon as she arrived—a half-breed.

She gave him a tired smile and stood as Zephan approached, concern evident in the lines of his face. "Are you all right?" he asked. "You're looking a little pale."

She shook her head. "I'm fine. It's just…" She gestured around the room and emotion welled up in her. Was this really happening? "I don't know." Looking up into his face, she felt her eyes begin to water. "I don't know if I can do this."

A pained expression passed over Zephan's face. Taking her hands in his, he looked down at them, brushing his thumbs over her knuckles. "He won't just let you leave. You know what will happen if he catches you. You'll be stripped of any status in the family and enslaved, if he's feeling generous." Sophie tried to pull her hands back and turn away, but Zephan's grip tightened. "Do you understand what's at stake?"

"Of course I do," she started heatedly, "but I have to go." She didn't know if she wanted to cry or scream. Apart from the few brief years with her birth parents, this was the only home she'd ever known. Was she really choosing to leave everything behind? This was where she had been taught to use her abilities, the magic that gave her life meaning.

And then there was the Vizier. Could she turn her back on him?

The memory of the exhilarating rush of vitality and awareness was followed closely by a sickening feeling that made her stomach clench with fear and revulsion. Who knew what would happen or what she would become if she continued down that path?

Zephan watched her closely but did not speak. He knew her well, and knowing he would always be there for her was a huge comfort. She focused on that and was able to turn her rising anger and fear into resolve.

Sophie shook her head and pulled her hands out of his. He let them go without protest, looking at his empty hands before dropping them. "Zephan," she began, her voice stronger than before. "I can't go on as if nothing happened. I wouldn't be able to live with myself."

"He won't just let you leave," Zephan repeated, but the heat was gone. "You're the only one who can use that... that thing."

"Then it shouldn't be used ever again," Sophie said firmly.

"Sophie..." Zephan began, sounding exasperated. The ghost of a smile played at the corners of his mouth.

"I can't help him anymore." Her eyes began to water again, but she refused to look away. "Please, don't try to convince me otherwise. It's hard enough without that."

Zephan averted his eyes and cleared his throat. His face began to flush, and he blinked rapidly, but his voice was surprisingly steady. "You should keep your spells simple in the city. The saturation of magic here will make you harder to track, but once outside the city walls, use your spells sparingly." The shift in topic startled her. "Remember that power draws power. Magic used can be traced."

He reached into an inner pocket of his robes and pulled out a rolled-up piece of parchment. He beckoned for her to follow, then walked over to the writing desk and unfurled the parchment, laying it flat. Sophie peered at the drawings on the rough surface and realized it was a detailed map of Tanzar and the surrounding countryside.

"You should head out the southwest gate." He indicated the spot with his index finger. "It's the smallest of the seven gates, and there are fewer guards posted there, so it shouldn't be difficult to slip past them. The shortest route is through the bazaar. Most of the shops will be closed by now. Try your best not to be seen. Once outside the city, follow the river until you reach the forest. That should take a few days." He tapped his finger on the thick blue line that flowed off the map. "Once you reach the forest, head south along the tree line. Eventually, you'll reach an overgrown wooden archway. Be careful not to miss it, I've been told it blends in with the trees there. Take the path that runs through it and into the forest."

Sophie tried to speak, but Zephan stopped her with a shake of his head. "Please, just listen. I don't know where you are going or why you are going this way. It's best that I know nothing." He rolled the parchment back up. "Follow the path until it forks, then go left. Bring a lamp or a torch. No spells. The light might draw attention, but it's better than twisting your ankle."

"The path will eventually lead to a clearing. Someone will meet you there. You might have to wait for a while, but show no signs of threat when confronted and ask for Vyraeli. Anai live in that forest, but my contact assured me that they won't harm you if you don't use magic against them." Zephan frowned, worry still marring his features. "I wasn't given much detail about what happens after that, but this Vyraeli person will make sure you get to your final destination." He handed her the map. "Did you get all of that?"

"I think so." Closing her eyes, she recited the directions back to him. "Southwest gate. Follow the river to the forest. South to the arch and take the path. Left at the fork. Vyraeli." Sophie opened her eyes and gave him a frown of her own. "Who did you get this information from, Zephan?"

"Someone who I used all of my favors to get a meeting with," he said, smiling sheepishly. "Don't worry. These people have a reputation for helping those who wish to leave Zo'rahn." She eyed him suspiciously, and he sighed again. "There aren't a lot of options, Sophie. It would be easier to pay for passage on a ship out of the docks, but any captain could just hand you back over and double their profits." He ran his fingers through his hair in frustration. "No, there are too many things that could go wrong. Going by land will take longer to get you to wherever you are going, but I think it has the greatest chance of success."

Sophie wasn't wholly convinced, but she trusted Zephan. The Vizier wouldn't expect her to travel overland, but she didn't like not knowing what her final destination was. "I don't like this. I want to be prepared."

He shrugged, looking a little flustered. "I'm not supposed to know, I guess."

Sophie sighed and carried the rolled-up map over to the traveling pack by the door, stuffing it inside. The pack looked no fuller than it had been before. Zephan was the one who'd given it to her. It wasn't a normal bag. It had been enchanted to hold more than it looked like it could. Not a lot more, but it was enough to hold the food, clothes, and books that she'd packed.

Zephan had helped her every step of the way with this. He'd had the contacts, he'd told her what to pack, and he was even supplying the map. It was hard to imagine herself even getting this far without him.

"Zephan..." She hesitated before continuing, attempting to control the feelings of excitement and dread rising in her chest. "Will you come with me?"

He looked startled at first, like the thought hadn't crossed his mind. Then he looked away from her, his expression distant. She shivered, the look reminding her unnervingly of the Vizier. "I don't think that's a good idea," he said flatly, avoiding her eyes.

Heat crept up her cheeks. She understood why he didn't want to go with her. This was her problem, not his, and he had worked so hard to finish his training. "I'm sorry," she said with a sad smile. "It's just frightening to be doing this alone."

Zephan looked back at her and his expression softened. "I know it is. You're probably better off without me anyway. Besides, someone has to stick around to steal tarts when the cook's not looking. She wouldn't know what to do if there were suddenly extras lying about."

She sighed and shook her head. She appreciated his attempt to lighten the moment with humor. With the over-whelming feeling that she was taking the first step down a road from which there was no return, she put on her cloak, then picked up the pack and slung the straps over her shoulders.

"I guess this is it then. I'm going to miss you. You've always been there for me, and now I don't know if or when I'll see you again." Her voice broke on the last word, and she had to clear her throat. Zephan was her friend, her best friend, and she would likely never see him again. "You've been a really good friend to me, and I want to thank you for—"

Before she could finish, Zephan closed the distance between them and wrapped his arms around her. He rested his chin on top of her head. "I'll miss you more than you know."

She felt her resolve break. When she finally pulled back, there were wet spots on the front of his robes. "Sorry," she said again, but Zephan waved her apology away.

"Thank you, for everything." She looked up into his dark-brown eyes one more time, smiled, and stretched up on her toes to kiss his cheek. Then she turned from him and opened the door, feeling the tiniest snap of energy as the muffling charm that Zephan had placed on the room broke. Sophie closed the door behind her and turned down the hall that would lead her down the stairs and to the kitchens. From there, she would leave through the servants' entrance.

As much as she wanted to, she didn't look back.

CHAPTER
TWO

The sun had fully set by the time Sophie made it to the road. The twin moons, Aeris and Thaera, lit the cityscape with their pale glow. Lights from the buildings in the city pierced through the darkness like thousands of tiny stars in a sea of dark masses. Traveling to the city proper from the manor was a far walk without the assistance of magic or animals, but Sophie found it peaceful.

Her Vasalii, the title bestowed upon the head of a magical family, was also one of the seven Viziers of Zo'rahn. These Viziers were the rulers of Zo'rahn, so it was no surprise that they lived on lavish estates in the heart of the richest area of the territory they governed, areas reserved for only the wealthiest and most influential people in the country.

It hadn't been hard to slip past the guards. She had simply waited for the guard rotation to leave a small section of the wall unwatched and climbed over, using a little magic to aid her. There were wards on the walls to prevent infiltration and alert the soldiers to the presence of an intruder, but since Sophie was a member of the family, she had a talisman that allowed free access through the protective barriers around the main houses.

Once she was far enough away from the manor, she tossed the talisman into the bushes by the road.

Now that she was on her way down into the central part of the city, she was mostly alone. Most of the locals who lived in the area were inside, probably eating dinner with their families, and wouldn't venture out onto the public road until morning. Sophie could see a few people in the distance, walking the same route she was. It wasn't unheard of to have a servant sent down into the city around this time to collect something that had slipped a wealthy wizard's mind during the day. As she thought that, she spotted a large wagon much farther down the road that was probably delivering something of the sort. Cricket chirps echoed through the trees, and the tall grass to either side of the cobbled-stone lane swayed lazily with the breeze.

Looking down at the city, Sophie felt a twinge of sadness. The capital was her home. Was she doing the right thing? The path ahead of her would be dangerous, but she would be able to make her own decisions and do what she thought was necessary. Here, she had been just another apprentice, but her magical education was extensive, and she was sure that any other country would deem her a full wizard. Her Vasalii would try to find her, but if she could just make it out of the country, he would be limited in his actions outside of Zo'rahn. He also wouldn't want the other Viziers to know what he was working on and why she had left, so she didn't think that he would come after her with all of his considerable power and influence. The best thing was to get as far away as she could as quickly as possible.

The problem was she had no idea where to start. In theory, it should have been as simple as leaving under cover of darkness and traveling by sea, but as Zephan pointed out, that was a foolish idea. Sophie had no experience in this area. She'd rarely left the estate and had never been out of the city on her own. Zephan was the one who had arranged everything. When she had first confided in him about her plans to leave, he'd immediately objected, but, over time, she convinced him that this was the only option. She'd had to wait weeks until he had returned with news of a way out. Sophie trusted Zephan, but she wasn't sure about whoever these people were that had agreed to help her.

Sophie passed a low wall separating the inner ring of estates from the rest of the city. Past the wall, buildings were closer together and the architecture was simpler. Living closest to the center of the city would be the middle class of Zo'rahn: merchants, artisans, and craftsmen. Signs outside the structures proclaimed what the people inside did and what services they could provide.

The road continued south for a short distance before it came to a fork. The left went toward the docks, which was the opposite direction of where she wanted to go. The main road was to the right. That way would be the fastest but would also be the one with the most traffic and would increase the chances of someone she knew seeing her. With her fairer complexion and red hair, she would be noticeable even with the hood of her cloak covering most of her face. What she needed was to look a little less like herself.

Looking around to make sure that no one was watching, Sophie ducked down a narrow alley between two buildings. There was trash heaped in piles next to doors on the sides of the buildings. Once far enough out of sight from the road and hidden by the shadows, Sophie swung the travel pack off her shoulders and set it on the ground. She opened a side pocket and pulled out a small tin filled with a fine white powder. She unscrewed the lid and took a small pinch of the powder and rubbed it on her face. Then she lowered the hood of her cloak and let her hair down. She took another pinch, rubbed it into her hands, and ran her fingers through her hair.

Closing her eyes, she focused on the powder while visualizing the effect she desired. With a small effort, she pushed her magic into it, bringing it to life. Her face and scalp tingled for a moment before a sensation like cool silk brushed against her skin, and she knew the magical effect was in place.

It was a subtle, simple spell, but very effective. The powder wasn't actually necessary for the magic to work, but it helped. As she'd learned when being tested all those years ago, being able to focus on a physical component saved the caster some of the energy required for the spell. It also helped to ease the strain on the mind, which translated into the spell being easier to cast. Sophie could manage that raw, brute-force type of magic if she had to, but preferred to use physical aids if they were available. It made her spells more accurate and less costly.

She opened her eyes and watched as the strands of her long, red hair darkened until they were a glossy black. The skin on her hands gradually turned a rich bronze. There was a small silver hand mirror in her bag, and when she took it out to look at herself, the dark, muted eyes and sharp features were strange to her. The new face wasn't pretty or ugly, but as plain as she could have imagined it. An average-looking Zo'rahni woman, which was exactly what she wanted to look like at that moment. Just another young woman heading home after a day of work or running errands.

After another moment examining herself, she quickly placed everything back into the bag and lifted it onto her shoulders again. Sophie stopped at the edge of the alleyway to peer around, but there wasn't anyone nearby, so she stepped back out and continued down the main road.

It was still early in the evening, and the hustle and bustle of the city did not end at nightfall. The closer she got to the merchant district, the more people she began to see out on the streets. As she passed, most people didn't even glance at her. For the first time since coming to Tanzar, Sophie felt truly invisible.

She'd practiced that spell at the estate, but never out in the general public. Now she wished she had. Foreigners were rare in the city, and half-breeds even more so. Even after eleven years of living here, she was still gawked at and spoken down to. Now she passed by the populace without a second glance, let alone the animosity to which she had grown accustomed.

As she continued to walk, she noticed that a few people did seem to be looking at her a bit longer than she would have liked. At first, she was afraid the spell had failed but, after a while, realized that it wasn't the usual stares. A few men smiled at her, and Sophie realized she was grinning. She attempted to school her face back into a neutral mask, but it was difficult. The result was an amused smirk that she couldn't get rid of, but she hoped the expression was less memorable and out of place than beaming at everyone she looked at.

The road she was on would pass through the bazaar and, eventually, all the districts of the city. It was lined with shops, food stalls, taverns, and brothels. If she could have cut through the less-crowded streets and alleys she would have, but she'd spent the majority of her time on the estate and didn't know the roads well enough to circumvent the crowd. It would look extremely odd for her to take out a map every other street. There was also the risk of someone noticing her glamor. More-experienced wizards could sense a spell if they were close enough, and ranked wizards could nullify magic from a distance, but as long as she poured a little energy into maintaining the spell as she went, it shouldn't draw too much attention.

It wasn't long before Sophie came upon the bazaar. Located in the heart of the merchant district, the bazaar was easily the busiest part of the city. Both wooden and stone stands, all covered by colorful awnings, lined the wide street. While there were still quite a few people around, it wasn't nearly as crowded as it would have been during the day. This was where most of the community purchased and traded goods. Farmers would bring in crops, pay a modest rental fee, and sell their wares at one of these stands. Silks, pottery, and foreign goods were brought up from the docks every morning by merchants, who, in turn, sold them to the public. Every time she had ventured to the bazaar on her free days, there had been entertainers performing in and around the stands and shops. Patrons were encouraged to sit on the rugs provided and enjoy the shows, as long as they purchased food and drink from the vendors.

Now, late buyers hurried home with baskets full of food and dry goods. A few merchants could be seen closing up their shops for the night, tying down cloth overhangs, and packing up their wares. Men were loading leftover crops into carts and preparing their horses for the ride home. Few spared her more than a glance as she passed them.

As she approached a tavern near the middle of the bazaar, two of its patrons stepped out of the front door and into the street. Sophie would have thought nothing of it if their bright robes hadn't caught her eye. She realized almost immediately that they were wizards. Worse, she knew them. They were former apprentices of her Vasalii who had recently gained rank.

Fantastic. It was just her luck that she would come across someone who could not only sense the glamor around her but identify her.

The two men stood in the street, talking. Huan was short and stocky with a square face and cropped hair, and Thaksin was lean with a hooked nose and a pointed beard. Both wore the blue and purple silk robes of a first-rank wizard. These two men were part of her adopted family, and she had no doubt that if they were to recognize her, they would ask why she was out so late.

Sophie had the urge to turn and walk quickly away, but she thought that would look suspicious. The best thing to do would be to just walk right past them. She reminded herself that the spell she was using was simple enough that they shouldn't be able to detect it with the latent magical energy that already drifted about the city unless they were close enough to touch her. She was just another citizen walking home. Quickly. Walking home quickly.

She averted her eyes and focused on a point on the ground ahead of her, then crossed to the other side of the street. That shouldn't be so odd. People did that to her sometimes when walking by. People weren't necessarily scared of the magical families, at least nothing she'd read or heard had indicated that, but they also didn't want to become a grumpy wizard's collateral damage.

Thaksin's voice drifted to her from across the road, and

Sophie couldn't help but listen. "—assignment in Nemethy you've been so quiet about?"

"Just research. Gathering samples and writing reports. The Vasalii is interested in some ruins there." They walked at a leisurely pace, not bothering to speak quietly.

Sophie risked a glance at them. There was a slight red tinge to their cheeks and sleepy droop to their eyelids. Both moved with a barely noticeable stagger to their gait.

"Hmm..." They passed her and continued walking up the main road. "What about the, ah, residents?" Thaksin stroked his beard absently.

Huan chuckled. "I can handle a couple of dirty Anai." He suddenly stopped and looked around. "Did you feel that?"

Sophie's heart skipped a beat and she held her breath.

"Feel what?" Thaksin said, pausing beside the other wizard to look around as well. "I don't feel anything."

Please don't look at me, please don't look at me. Oh Samar, let them not notice me, Sophie recited in her head as she forced herself not to bolt. She stared fixedly on a spot ahead and kept walking, careful not to change her pace too much.

"I thought I felt something..."

"Sounds like you've just had too much to drink. Come now, if we hurry, there should still be some food left when we get back." Thaksin continued walking

Huan said nothing, but after a moment's hesitation, the heavy footfalls of his sandaled feet retreated in the opposite direction, back toward the estate.

Sophie continued to stare straight ahead and barely breathed until she rounded a corner. She leaned against it and waited for the pounding in her chest to subside. She hadn't even made it out of the city yet and had almost been caught. She breathed deeply, trying to calm herself.

Sneaking around like this was not something that had been in her training.

She took one last breath to steady herself. Once she was out of the city, it would be much easier to move around, but she would still have limited use of her magic. She knew it would take a couple of hours to reach the gate, and as it got later, there would be more patrols roaming the streets. It wouldn't be long before the Vasalii discovered she was missing, so she had to move quickly.

Gathering her courage once more, Sophie murmured another prayer to Samar and hurried toward the southwest gate.

As Zephan had predicted, there were only a few guards stationed at the gate. Since this entrance to the city wasn't one of the major routes, it was just wide enough for a cart or two to pass through side by side and only a couple of feet taller than a man. The wall itself towered over the nearby buildings. She estimated it was about thirty feet high, with the gate opening cut directly out of the stone.

Sophie sat on a bench near the bank of the River Shar, deep in thought. The gate was closed for the night and only opened to let out farmers from the surrounding countryside. No foot traffic was passing through at this time. Only two men were guarding the gate, leaning on the wall to either side of it, spears in hand. She couldn't think of a way to get past the guards without them seeing her. It was possible to make herself all but invisible, but the gate would need to be open for her to slip by, and there hadn't been anyone trying to leave in the last hour or so that she'd been watching.

Going over the wall wouldn't be as easy as it had been back at the Vizier's estate. This one was much taller and would require more energy. Magical energy lingered after using it, and the stronger the spell, the longer it stayed. The energy from simple spells dissipated within a few hours, but the power used for stronger spells could last for days. That lingering energy was like a signature, and everyone's was different. Anyone accustomed to her style of spell-casting would be able to track her by the magic she used. If she tried to put the guards to sleep or otherwise disable them, the energy used would light up the spot like a beacon to anyone who knew how to look.

But what good was a wizard without magic? Sophie wasn't very strong physically, and she wouldn't be able to hold her own in a fight. She didn't know anyone outside of the family, and other than Zephan, no one could be trusted. Sophie watched the reflection of the moon, Thaera, swaying back and forth on the surface of the water. She was just an eighteen-year-old girl. What could she do?

The wind picked up and blew a couple of leaves into the river, distorting the moon's image. They twirled about in the water for a moment, then the current picked them up and carried them off toward the sea. Her eyes scanned the water's surface, then idly followed the river's path from the wall.

Sophie blinked and leaned over, looking into the shadows at the base of the wall. There had to be a way for the river to flow under it. Maybe she could swim through. She wasn't the best swimmer in the world, but she wouldn't drown either. There had to be an opening under the wall to let the water pass through.

After glancing at the gate to make sure the guards weren't looking in her direction, Sophie slowly approached the bank. The water was low at this time of year, low enough that she could walk along part of the riverbed. She carefully climbed down to the water's edge and ducked so that the top of her head wasn't visible above the rocks lining the riverbank. The ground was muddy, and the cold water and dirt of the river seeped over the sides of her sandals. She leaned down and unbuckled them, slipping her feet out and gingerly stepping into the mud. She cringed at the squishy feeling between her toes, but it was a small price to pay. She would need the sandals for the rest of her trip and didn't want to risk losing them in the mud. For lack of any better options, she rinsed her sandals off in the river and tied them to her pack to dry. Remembering the books she had packed, she decided it would be better for her belongings if she didn't have to swim.

Sophie slowly navigated through the rock and muck. It was more difficult than it had seemed from the dry, even stone and grass above. It was slow going. The mud sucked at her feet, and she had to move carefully to avoid making noise. Once, her foot hit a sharp rock and she almost cried out and lost her balance, but she caught herself at the last second. Sophie regained her footing and stopped to listen, heart pounding in her ears, waiting to see if the guards had heard her. When no one called out after a few moments, she let out the breath she hadn't realized she was holding and started moving again.

By the time she reached the wall, her heart was still pounding in her chest from exhaustion and fear, and beads of sweat ran into her eyes. Using the back of her sleeve, she wiped her face, fighting to control her breath. She steadied her shaking hands on the cool stone of the outer city wall.

As she expected, there was a shallow opening at the base of the wall, maybe twenty feet wide, allowing the water to pass freely underneath the stone above. Thick iron bars, vertical and evenly spaced cross the entire opening, must have been intended to prohibit passage. Perhaps a small child could squeeze through the gaps between the bars, but she doubted that she would be able to. The river was low enough to see where the first three bars connected with the ground below, the dark water hid the others. If one of them were loose, she might be able to get past.

She tried each bar. They were firmly set.

Because that would be too easy.

Sophie gave herself a chance to think. There were many spells she could use to shrink herself, bend the bars, or tear through the wall completely, but they all would leave a large mark here and it was likely the guards would notice someone force-blasting through the wall. But it was either this or through the gate. "Something simple," she whispered to herself, repeating Zephan's warning.

If she couldn't loosen the bars, maybe she could remove one. Sophie reached into her belt pouch and pulled out a small bottle filled with a green liquid. She removed the stopper and stuck her index and middle fingers into the bottle, swishing them around to coat them in the liquid. She chose the bar closest to the water's edge and smeared it around two points: one right below where it met with the rock of the wall, and the other just above the waterline. When those two points were covered all the way around in a thin line, she rinsed her hands in the river. Sophie concentrated on the physical component of the spell and pushed some of her magic into it, focusing on the effect she wanted.

The chemical composition of the liquid changed, turning from a base to an acid. She pushed more energy into it, and the substance began to hiss and bubble as it ate through the iron. She pushed harder. There would be evidence that someone had gone under the wall, but the signature would be weak. Hopefully, they wouldn't notice it. Sophie suppressed a cough and took a few steps back as a reddish smoke rose from the metal and dissipated immediately in the air.

When she judged the metal to be brittle enough, she put both hands on the iron bar and pressed her weight against it. With a grinding *snap*, the bar came free. Not waiting to see if the guards heard the sound of the bar breaking, she hurriedly scampered through.

Sophie ran along the muddy riverbank as best she could, trying to get away from the wall and out of sight. She risked a glance over her shoulder but could see nothing but shadows and the outline of the wall in the silvery moonlight, like a long-tailed beast that loomed over the countryside.

When she was a good distance from the gate, she stopped to wash the mud off her feet and strap her sandals back on. Sophie giggled as the nervous energy she'd been feeling all night was replaced by excitement that ran through her like a wave crashing against the shore. She threw her arms up and twirled in a circle, staring up into the stars with a broad grin. She couldn't help it.

She was one step closer to freedom.

THREE

S ophie rolled over, muscles sore and joints stiff. With a groan, she forced herself to sit up and stretch, then wiped her face, her sleeve coming away with sweat and dirt. She looked around blearily. Blankets were spread around and under her, tangled from her tossing and turning throughout the night.

The sun was already high in the sky. It must have been close to midday. She'd walked through the night until she could no longer stand. By the time she'd finally settled down behind a clump of bushes by the riverbank, a thin band of light had appeared on the horizon.

Sophie sighed, wishing for nothing more than a bath. Washing her face in the river would have to be enough.

Within a few minutes, the blankets were put neatly back in her pack and she made her way to the river. As she ambled down to the water's edge and dipped her hands beneath its gently rippling surface, she couldn't help but marvel again at what she'd done. Yes, she left behind the world she'd grown up in—not to mention a promising future as a wizard in a powerful family—but what would the cost of that future have been? A seductive power that she'd almost lost herself in, a magic that would consume her, that would make her—

Sophie abruptly shook her head, clearing her thoughts. Focusing on the past would not help her with the problems that lay ahead. She had to keep moving and couldn't let her mind get caught up in those memories.

The water felt good against her skin and helped to clear away the last traces of sleep and half-remembered dreams. She took her sandals off and let her feet soak in the cold water while she ate a few pieces of dried fruit and cheese. Then she fastened the shoes back on her feet and stood up to look around, getting her bearings by daylight.

At night, it had been hard to tell, but the dark shapes in the distance were now clearly mountains. At their base, she could almost make out the deep greens and reds of the forest canopy. Sophie had been walking for the past four days, resting by daylight and walking mostly at night. This far from the capital, there were only sparsely placed villages and farms, but she still tried her best not to be seen. That had been more difficult on the first day. Sophie had never traveled outside the city on foot, and, judging by the number of new blisters on her feet, her sandals had not been made for walking long distances. Sleeping on the hard ground was also something she decidedly never wanted to experience again once this journey was over. The food she'd packed was simple and magically preserved so that it wouldn't go bad, but she was tired of dried meat, cheese, and fruit. She longed for a soft bed and a hot meal.

Along with the items she'd packed, she'd found two pouches full to bursting, one filled with coins and the other with small canisters of spices. After adding up the coins, she was staggered by the amount. There was enough to buy a small kingdom. Zephan must have slipped it into her bag without her noticing. Sophie smiled to herself. He was still looking out for her, even if he couldn't be there with her.

It would take at least another day of walking to reach the forest, and then she would need to find the arch that Zephan had described. *Head south along the tree line. Eventually, you'll reach an overgrown wooden archway... Take the path that runs through it into the forest.*

Sophie was desperate to get this long walk over with. If she started now, she thought she might be able to reach the tree line before nightfall.

Steeling her resolve with the hope of sleeping in a real bed that night, Sophie slung her pack over her shoulder and continued following the river west, toward the mountains. There was no road here, not even a footpath, so her progress wasn't as quick as it could have been on even ground. While she realized she was less likely to stumble upon anyone unexpectedly, roads were a necessary byproduct of civilization, and their absence reminded Sophie just how far she was from anything familiar.

The day turned hot, making the humid air almost unbearable. With the sun shining down on her, it didn't take long for Sophie to become uncomfortably hot, and soon she was wiping more sweat from her brow. If she could've used magic, she could clean her clothes, make herself practically invisible, and bathe in the river. She could have conjured something more comfortable to sleep on or made the ground softer. But if she used magic here, in the middle of nowhere, it would certainly be traced, and she would be right back where she started. But that didn't make the thought any less tempting.

She arrived at the tree line a few hours before sunset. It was surprising to her how distinctly the tall grass ended and the trees began. It didn't seem natural. The valley was suddenly cut in half by the wall of massive tree trunks that rose high enough to block the sunlight and cast deep shadows within a hundred feet of the forest. The late-afternoon light had difficulty penetrating the thick canopy. Only the first few feet of the woods were visible from the outside, leaving the rest obscured by shadows and foliage.

Sophie had heard stories of men and women entering the forest and being attacked by shadows that seemed to melt into the trees. An exaggeration, she was sure. Someone accustomed to using the terrain in their favor would be able to pull off such an illusion as that, she reasoned, but the thought still made her shiver. Never having met an Anai in person, she didn't know what to expect.

Non-human races were considered an oddity in Zo'rahn. On the rare occasion that one was seen, it was usually as some traveling merchant's slave or in a menagerie.

There were Anaiian courts to the south and the far west that traded with other countries. From what she had read about them, they were reserved but generally had peaceable intentions. Perhaps their smaller numbers and being so removed from others of their race made these Anai more hostile. The dark woods loomed ominously in front of her, and she faltered.

They know I'm coming. It will be fine. It might not be safe, but she continued on anyway.

Deciding to keep a cautious distance from the forest, Sophie began walking parallel to the tree line. She watched the trees as she walked, looking for any sign of movement, but the coming darkness and thickness of the brush prevented her from seeing anything, save for vague shapes behind the trees.

The forest was vast and stretched in front of her as far as she could see. Sophie knew that it spanned the entire mountain range, starting near the northern coast of Zo'rahn and south for hundreds of miles. If she got lost within its borders, there was a good chance that she would not come back out again.

By the time Sophie found the old wooden archway that Zephan had described, it was well past dark. She had almost walked past it but noticed the irregular shape out of the corner of her eye. She was tired of walking, and her stomach was cramping. The food she had wasn't enough to sustain her with all the energy she was expending, and she mentally debated finding a place to sleep for the night, but the inviting thought of sleeping indoors pushed her to continue.

The archway blended into the trees around it. It wasn't nearly as tall as the surrounding trees, but it was still enormous. Vines twisted around the sides, and leaves sprouted from the branches growing at the corners. Moss draped over the top of the arch, giving the illusion of a curtain. It appeared to have grown out of the ground and was formed while keeping the roots intact. From what she could tell, it was very, very old—an archway of living wood.

What caught her eye was the carvings. As she drew closer, they became more distinct. She could see them at the top where the moss did not cover the wood and extended down the sides of the structure.

Forgetting her fear for a moment, Sophie reached out and gently moved a few of the vines to reveal shapes etched deeply into the wood. It was hard to see in the dark. If she had a little more light, she might be able to read what was there.

Sophie barely caught herself before muttering the

beginnings of a light spell, quickly dispersing the energy with a flick of her wrist.

She shook her head to clear it. "What am I thinking? I *must* be tired." For Sophie, magic was like breathing, a necessity. It was part of her.

There were many times in the past few days when she had been tempted to use it, and others when she had almost cast a spell unconsciously—starting a fire to keep warm on a chilly night, regaining some strength and fore-going sleep, healing the aches and pains of her body or at least making them less noticeable. After honing her talent for her entire life, not using it was the hardest thing she had ever done. She could feel it under her skin, itching to be released. So far, she had stopped herself every time, but it was becoming more and more challenging to remember not to use it.

Aeris and Thaera were both out and mostly full, but the light couldn't penetrate the forest canopy any better than the sun had. Magic or no, she needed light. She was more likely to break her ankle stumbling blindly through the woods than to be harmed by anything else. Fortunately, she had prepared for this.

Sophie set her pack on the ground and reached inside, pulling out what appeared to be a brass lantern, only it had no wick, oil, or holes for ventilation. There was a small lever on the bottom of the housing. Sophie pushed it up a notch, and a little golden flame sputtered to life behind the lantern's windows. The lantern had been enchanted to hold firelight, and while technically the object itself was magi-cal, its energy field was self-contained and would leave no trace of its use. The flame floated in the center of the glass panels, emanating a dim glow, no more than that of a single lit candle. She pushed the lever up another few notches until the flame glowed as bright as a torch. She held up the lamp, illuminating the carvings closest to her on the archway.

The carvings looped and curled in intricate designs up one side of the arch and down the other. Unable to help herself, Sophie traced a few of the runes with her fingers. They looked familiar, but she couldn't read them. The script was similar to Anaiian and could have been an ancient dialect. Each symbol was inscribed perfectly and as pristine as it probably had been the day it was made. From what she could see, she guessed that someone with great skill had carved these runes.

She sighed and let the vines slip back into place. These carvings were intriguing, but not the reason she was here, and it probably wasn't the best idea to linger.

The path that began at the archway was rough and narrow, just big enough for two people to walk shoulder to shoulder. Judging from the grass and the roots growing in the middle of the path, it was not traveled often. The only difference between the ground here and the ground around the trees was the distinctive lack of rocks and bushes. Thin beams of moonlight pierced the forest canopy here and there, but even with the lamp she held, it was impossible to see more than a few paces from where she stood.

The forest was quiet and black, the trail disappearing ahead as if into a yawning mouth. She shivered at the thought and stared into that darkness with a dizzy feeling, as though she were looking down from a great height. From this point on, she knew her freedom and safety were in the hands of others.

With a last glance back, Sophie took a deep breath and started down the path.

FOUR

Navigating the forest felt like something out of a nightmare. The path twisted and turned through the trees, often lost among the roots that snaked out from their trunks and crawled through the grass. When the path temporarily disappeared, Sophie panicked and frantically searched for it, only to find that it continued a few feet away. She had to pick her way over roots and growth, running into the trunks of large trees multiple times while she watched her feet. Grass and twigs crunched beneath her sandals, and the sound echoed through the forest. Once or twice, an owl hooted somewhere in the distant darkness, but the other animals, if there were any near her, remained silent.

Progress was slow. The lamp only illuminated a small circle around her. Her vision into the forest was obscured by low-hanging branches that grasped at the edges of her cloak, forcing her to free herself before continuing. The footing on the path was dubious at best, and Sophie had to be careful where she stepped.

Occasionally, something would move somewhere in the

trees, making the bushes sway in their wake. Sophie would search for the source of the movement, but darkness met her wherever she looked, and what little she might have distinguished was ruined by the brilliance of her lamp.

It was difficult to keep herself from speeding along the path as fast as she could. As far as she could tell, there weren't any animals around, but all the same, she'd felt eyes on her as soon as she passed beneath the archway. It could be that her mind was playing tricks on her, but her instincts were screaming that she wasn't imagining it. There was something out there, following her movements.

Sophie lost track of time in the darkness of the forest. The sky wasn't visible from where she was, and it felt like she'd been walking for hours. Her stomach growled in hunger, and her legs increasingly felt as if they were made of stone, each step harder to take than the last. Sophie yawned and rubbed her eyes but forced herself to continue. She didn't dare stop. The thought of sleeping in the forest, alone and vulnerable to whatever had been following her, scared her enough to continue putting one foot in front of the other.

The trail finally forked at a thick trunked tree, and Sophie took the left path as Zephan instructed. She glanced down the other way, but it twisted into the brush and vanished.

She was so intent on her walking that she didn't notice the path had begun to widen. She blinked heavily, and her eyes stayed closed. One foot tripped over the other, and she stumbled to one side, immediately awakening from her daze as gravity sought to pull her down. Sophie threw out her hands, catching herself on the trunk of a tree and nearly dropping her lamp, then shook her head to try to clear her senses. With a soft groan, she looked around blearily and only then realized that the entire forest around her had changed.

The canopy of leaves that had been impenetrable above her head before was not as thick as it had been, and blue-white patches of moonlight filtered through the trees. The branches curved overhead in a uniformity that was hard to believe came naturally. The tree trunks were so tightly woven together that it would have been difficult to slip between them. The result was that the rocky trail through the forest floor had become a tunnel, partially illuminated by moonlight.

Sophie looked over her shoulder. The tunnel continued behind her and as far back as she could see. When had it started?

She saw movement out of the corner of her eye and whipped around. Holding up the lamp, she searched between the trees and squinted into the darkness beyond her little tunnel. "H-hello?" she called, voice high and cracking. "Is someone there?"

Silence answered her. A slight breeze ruffled the leaves above her before it lightly caressed her face, the first she had felt since entering the forest. Sophie waited for a few moments, then tentatively took another step down the path.

A low, feminine voice echoed through the tunnel, making it difficult to pinpoint the source. "You are a long way from home, wizard."

Sophie jumped and dropped the lamp, startled. It bounced once on its side and rolled away from her, the light distorting the shadows around her. Her eyes darted down the path and between the trees, looking for the source of the voice, but was met by more darkness. She raised her hands instinctively, her mind screaming at her to cast a shielding spell as she turned in a slow circle.

"Who are you?" Sophie called out, taking a step toward the fallen lamp while her eyes continued to search the forest.

A musical laugh flowed through Sophie and made her shiver. "What is it you seek, little one?" the voice asked, ignoring Sophie's question.

Sophie put all the will power she could muster into lowering her hands calmly and slowly. If whoever this was meant her harm, it would have been easier to attack her while she was falling asleep on her feet, not after she was alerted to their presence. She knelt and picked up the lamp, once more trying in vain to pinpoint where the voice was coming from.

Sophie stood up straight and tried to project confidence. When she spoke, her voice was surprisingly steady. "I seek the aid of one who is called Vyraeli."

The forest seemed to sigh with her answer, a swirling breeze blowing loose strands of her hair.

"Why do you seek Vyraeli?"

"I was told that she could help me," Sophie said, then added in a pleading tone, "Please, I need to speak with her. She is the only chance I have."

The breeze died abruptly, and the whole forest seemed to hold its breath. Sophie continued to scan the trees, looking for any sign of movement. After what seemed like an eternity, the air moved again, and there was a rustling of leaves to her right. Sophie jumped back and watched in amazement as, with the deafening crunch of a thousand snapping branches, the wood bent and parted, making a new passageway through the trees.

A tall, lithe Anai woman stepped out onto the path,

dressed in dyed cloth and leather. Sophie would have placed her as middle-aged if she were human, but with graceful features that no human could ever possess. Green and orange leaves were tangled in her long, dark hair. In the lamplight, her bronze cheekbones seemed unnaturally high, and Sophie could make out the tips of the telltale pointed ears peeking out from beneath her hair. The woman carried a staff of cream-colored wood twisted into the shape of an owl at its tip.

With a wave of the woman's hand, the pathway closed, tree trunks settling back into their regular positions, another roaring series of creaks in the otherwise still forest. Sophie reached out with her senses, feeling the Anaiian magic wash over her. It was so different from her own, more wild and primal. The butt of the woman's staff hit the ground sharply as the magic from her working faded.

"Then speak, traveler."

Sophie felt muscles that she didn't even know she was tensing relax. The woman's voice was the same that had echoed through the passage. This Anai, while still intimidating, wasn't as imposing as the disembodied voice had been. Taking a deep breath, she bowed politely and asked, "Are you Vyraeli?"

The Anai nodded once, and Sophie continued.

"My name is Sophie. A friend of mine arranged for my passage outside of Zo'rahn and instructed me to seek you out here."

The Anai woman watched Sophie, her gaze intense. Her eyes flicked down her clothes, then back up to her face, expression foreign and unreadable. Sophie felt her cheeks warm. Being on the road for the past few days left her clothing tattered and dirty. It didn't make for a good first impression.

Vyraeli continued to watch her as Sophie fought the urge to fidget. She forced herself to look into those cold, dark eyes that were inspecting every inch of her.

Finally, the Anai broke the silence. "You're younger than I expected. Tell me, are you strong, wizard?"

The question caught Sophie off guard. Strong? What did she mean? Was she speaking of physical strength, or did she want to know how good she was at magic? "Um," Sophie began, unsure of how to answer. "I know a fair bit of magic, but I'm still technically an apprentice."

Vyraeli began to pace around her, moving like a cat stalking its prey. "How old are you, girl?"

"Eighteen," she answered, standing still as the Anai paced around her, trying to think non-threatening thoughts.

The Anai completed her circle and reached out a hand. Sophie barely stopped herself from moving away as Vyraeli gently took a strand of red hair between her fingers and examined it. After a few seconds, she nodded to herself and let the hair fall back into place. "Your friend has some very interesting contacts. Why would a wizard want to leave Zo'rahn? You're practically royalty here." She tapped a finger to her lips as her eyes flicked over Sophie again. "Tell me, what are you running from?"

Sophie swallowed. She had just met this person. There was no way that she could tell her why she was running from the Vizier. What she knew could be dangerous, and the fewer people she told, the better. "I..." Vyraeli was watching her closely. She couldn't outright lie, but she didn't have to tell her everything.

"What wizards do here... I don't want to be a part of it anymore. My master doesn't care about anyone other than himself and the family." She averted her gaze from the older woman's. "I want to be free, and this is the only way," she finished, feeling that she had not done a very convincing job.

Vyraeli stared critically at her for a few long moments, then sighed. Sophie could tell that the woman suspected there was more, but she didn't push. Vyraeli's expression softened.

"You're in a terrible state, child. A hot bath and some food would do you a world of good." Sophie thought she saw the barest hint of a smile before the Anai turned her back on her. She started walking down the path and beckoned for Sophie to follow. The Anai looked over her shoulder, eyes gleaming in a patch of moonlight.

"You don't need that," she said, indicating the lamp. "There is more than enough light to make our way through the trees."

Sophie doubted that she would be able to navigate in the dark but was hesitant to contradict her new host. She switched off the lamp and stowed it back in her bag. Vyraeli nodded and continued walking.

It took a few minutes for Sophie's eyes to adjust to the darkness, but it was easy enough to follow Vyraeli as she passed through stray beams of moonlight. Without her lamp to blind her to what was beyond its light, the forest was a completely different place. Small animals and reptiles skittered across the moss-covered forest floor. The pale tendrils of moonlight filtering through the canopy were just enough for her to see where she was placing her feet.

Every so often, she caught a glimpse of something moving in the trees from the corner of her eye, a quick shadow that was gone when she looked for it, the gleam of moonlight on metal that disappeared within the trees.

With a shiver, she realized that this path was perfect for

an ambush. Arrows could be shot from behind those trees into the narrow tunnel, and the shooters could fade back into the forest. No wonder no one had ever found where the Anai of this forest lived. Then again, someone like Vyraeli could manipulate the shape of the trees to lead travelers in circles so that they might never find their way out.

With a chill, she stared straight ahead, walking quickly to keep up with the Anai, unable to shake the image of a target between her shoulder blades.

Vyraeli glanced back and smiled at the expression on Sophie's face. "Don't worry," she said warmly. "No harm will come to you. You are my guest now."

CHAPTER

FIVE

Elasariin was unlike any other place on Lanis. According to the history books, the Anaiian city was built centuries ago by a tribe of Anai that decided to stay in the old forest in Zo'rahn, despite the rest of their kind moving across the sea to form the Anaiian Court of Nemethy. Wooden platforms crafted into the trunks of trees rose a hundred feet above the ground, blending in with branches and leaves to form a living foundation. Wood and rope bridges connected each platform to the others. Small buildings were erected in a cluster around each trunk, each platform holding five or six dwellings.

The main way into the city from the forest floor was to climb the long spiral stairway carved into the trunk of the largest tree in the center of Elasariin. The city was easily defensible because of its remoteness, and the Anai had lived here peacefully for ages. The only occasional enemies were their Zo'rahni neighbors, but none had ever breached the city. It was the safest, most serene, and tranquil place to live in the world.

At least, that's what Eolisti's mother had been trying to convince her of her entire life.

To Eolisti, Elasariin was a never-changing, monotonous collection of treehouses she had seen every day as far back as she could remember. There was no excitement, no adventure, no fun. It was the same day in, day out. The city was small compared to what she'd learned of human settlements, with only several hundred Anai living in the treetops. A select group of the more senior members of the community, the High Council, made all the major decisions for everyone living here. The rest of the Anai just followed along like a hoard of mindless sheep.

Eolisti was in the prime of her youth. She should have been out traveling the world on an adventure and making a name for herself, but her mother never let her stray very far from the city, not even into the uninhabited areas of the forest. The other Anai her age were able to come and go as they pleased, but no, not her. Her mother kept her right where she wanted her—home, safe, and bored.

It wasn't that she couldn't protect herself. Eolisti had taken up the sword at a young age, and after years of honing her skills, she was one of the best swordswomen in Elasariin. She knew the practice was just meant to keep her busy, but was it her fault that she wanted to put her skills to use? She knew sparring wasn't the same as a real battle, fighting for your life and vanquishing foes.

She couldn't even argue with her imprisonment or appeal to a higher power. Her mother was the city shaman and a member of the High Council, and the only one fully trained in magic in Elasariin. If she pulled a few strings to convince the Council to keep her daughter here, who was going to say otherwise?

Eolisti grumbled to herself, shifting in her seat high up

in the branches of the tree in the center of the city. She watched the stairs leading up into the city with undisguised anticipation and pushed a couple of leaves out of the way to get a better view of the archway at the top of the spiral stairs. Was it her fault that she was reduced to hiding in the trees anytime there was even a hint of the unusual just to catch a glimpse of excitement?

No, it was not.

Whispers had rippled through the city earlier that evening. A human had entered the forest. These days, it was rare for humans to get anywhere near the forest, let alone wander into it. What was even more interesting was that the human seemed to know how to reach the city. When humans did show up, her mother, being the youngest and most capable on the Council, usually parleyed with them. Eolisti had even gotten to talk to a few of them.

The humans coming here were usually runaway slaves of the wizards in Zo'rahn, seeking aid from the Council to travel across the mountains safely. Eolisti didn't know the details of why the Elasariin Anai helped them, but she knew that her mother and the Council were involved with some sort of organization. It was unclear what exactly they did, but she had never seen them turn the human slaves away. This human must be another slave if she knew how to find them.

Four days ago, her mother had received a message in the middle of the night. Eolisti had been asleep in her room when a cawing had woken her. After realizing that the noise was coming from inside the house, Eolisti had jumped out of bed and quietly snuck into the hall and down to the doorway that led to the kitchen. There was a soft murmur from around the corner and the flap of wings. She'd risked a glance and found her mother tying a green ribbon around the leg of a raven. A rolled-up parchment lay in front of her, a message from whomever had sent the bird. Fearing being caught, Eolisti had tiptoed back to her room and, when settled in bed again, lay awake thinking.

Something was happening, and this time she would not be left out.

Movement from below shook Eolisti out of her thoughts and back to the present. She could see the top of her mother's head ascending the stairs. Eolisti leaned forward, gripping the branch so hard her knuckles were white. There was someone with her. A coppery red headscarf came into view as a human trailed behind Vyraeli. *No,* she thought, *that's hair.* She'd never seen hair that color before.

It was difficult to see the newcomer's face from where she was positioned. The person appeared to be female and looked very different from an Anai. Her figure had accentuated proportions, versus an Anai whose shape was typically willowy, and her movements were clumsy where an Anai's would be graceful. But she wasn't like the humans that Eolisti had seen previously. The woman held herself differently than those who'd come here before. So, if she wasn't a runaway slave, who was she?

Eolisti's mother turned and said something to the woman, and then they started heading toward the Council building, the largest structure in the city.

She waited until they disappeared before climbing out of the branches. Her hands were trembling and her heart raced. She had to know who that human was and why she was here. This person looked so different from any other human who had come here before. Maybe she was royalty in disguise.

A wide grin spread across the Anai's face. This was the most fun she'd had in ages.

Casually, Eolisti strolled from the center platform across the bridge that led to the Council building. There weren't many others out at this time of night. All the children had been put to bed, and most of the other Anai didn't give her a second glance. Eolisti was usually out all times of the day and night, running errands for her mother, or doing what the townspeople dubbed "causing mayhem."

Whatever. They wouldn't know how to have fun if it struck them on the nose, which it might have. A few times.

She walked around to the back entrance of the Council building, where the caretakers and staff would enter and leave. After checking to make sure all was clear, Eolisti pressed her ear against the door, listening. She couldn't hear any sounds from within. With the barest push, the door swung inward. Luckily for her, locks were rarely used in Elasariin.

The door opened into a dark hallway leading off to the left and right. Doors lined the hall, small meeting rooms for the Council members' private conversations. Guest rooms would be closer to the kitchens, which would be to the right, near the front of the building. There shouldn't be anyone working at this time of night, but the caretaker and his family lived here, and it wouldn't have been the first time she'd been caught wandering the halls of the Council building at night.

Best not to let anyone know I'm here then, she thought as she looked down both hallways then stepped inside, closing the door silently behind her.

Light from outside filtered down through skylights in the ceiling, broken only by the branches and leaves from above. Even in shadow, Eolisti had no trouble navigating the familiar place, following the sounds of movement coming from the kitchens. She treaded lightly, carefully testing each floorboard before putting her full weight on it. These buildings were old, and the last thing she wanted was the creaking of wood to announce her presence. It was slow going, but it kept the planks from squeaking too loudly. She wasn't afraid of getting caught. Being known as a troublemaker made her immune to criticism, but it was so much easier to get things done if no one knew what she was doing until after the act was committed. It seemed like her mother was always scolding her for one thing or another, so she'd rather apologize after the fact instead of asking permission to do this or that.

When she reached the end of the corridor, Eolisti paused to peek around the corner. A dim yellow light shone through the crack underneath a door on the right wall, the entrance to the kitchens. This door was larger than the others, and the fading varnish signaled its frequent use. A low murmur of voices carried to her ears, but she couldn't quite make out what was being said.

Her heart beat loudly as she tiptoed down the hall, pausing only briefly at the kitchen door. Shadows moved against the sliver of light shining from beneath. She could hear the voices better here, but they were still too muffled by the door to make out the conversation. She could try to listen at the crack to hear what was being said and risk someone opening the door on her, or she could keep going.

After a moment's hesitation, Eolisti decided to move on. The human wouldn't be in the kitchens anyway. She could feel a broad smile spreading across her face as she tiptoed away. Too easy.

It was a few minutes before Eolisti found another door with light shining from under it. Creeping close, she listened but couldn't hear anything. Was the human in there? She wouldn't make much noise if she was by herself, of course, but wouldn't she at least be changing, washing up, or moving around? Well, at least the silence meant that her mother wasn't in there. If she had been, Eolisti was sure she would've been questioning the human.

"What *are* you doing?" asked a small voice from behind her.

Eolisti's heart almost flew out of her chest as she jumped, rolling forward into a low defensive stance.

A young Anai girl stood in the middle of the hall facing Eolisti, the light of the moons making her hair shine with a silvery glow. She was holding a wooden tray with a lidded bowl and a piece of brown flat Anaiian bread, called *bära*. The girl was short for her age, with the top of her head coming just under Eolisti's breast. She wore long green skirts with a white apron over them and slippers.

Eolisti knew her. She was the caretaker's daughter, Aerynis. *Damn.*

Aerynis raised a thin, pale eyebrow, waiting for Eolisti to answer her question.

Eolisti straightened and cleared her throat. "Good evening," she said in the politest voice she could muster.

The girl rolled her eyes. "Why are you sneaking around here, Eolisti?"

Eolisti's temper flared, but she managed to rein it in and smiled sweetly. "I heard we have a guest in the city. A human." She glanced down at the tray of food. "Is that for her? What's she like? Where did she come from? How did she get here?" Eolisti bit off a dozen other questions before they escaped her lips. She could barely contain her excitement.

Aerynis's eyebrows climbed further up her forehead

with each question. "I don't know anything, Eolisti. I haven't even seen her yet."

Her eyes flicked down to the tray of food.

"As you can see, I was on my way to offer her some food." Aerynis shrugged, then narrowed her eyes at Eolisti. "Even if I'd already met her, what makes you think I'd tell you? You're not even supposed to be here. Does your mother know you're here?"

When Eolisti didn't answer, Aerynis sighed and rolled her eyes again. "I have work to do. Now get out of my way."

She moved to step around her, but Eolisti blocked her path. She reached down and snatched the tray out of Aerynis's hands before the girl could stop her.

"Hey!" Aerynis squeaked in surprise and reached out to take the tray back.

Eolisti held the food over her head and smirked down at her. "I'll take it from here." She turned on her heel and looked over her shoulder at the other Anai's incredulous face. "Well? Get lost."

"*Mifela*," Aerynis said under her breath.

"What was that?!" Eolisti growled, but by the time Eolisti turned back around, Aerynis was already halfway down the hall. How dare she call her a *mifela*. That little brat would get it. *Later*. She reminded herself. *There are other matters to attend to*. She needed to hurry before her mother got wind of this little encounter. Aerynis was probably on her way to tell on her right then.

She turned back, balanced the tray on her hip, and rapped on the door three times.

No answer came right away. She heard no movement from inside the room. Eolisti was beginning to wonder whether this was the right door or not when a soft "Come in" came from inside.

Eolisti pushed the door open, and light poured out into the hall. This guest room was just like the others she had seen before. Simple, with a yellow curtain dividing it down the middle, a small bed and a table with two chairs on one side, and a chamber pot and a large wooden tub on the other. A lamp with a small flickering flame rested on the table, casting a dim golden glow over the room. There was a window on the wall next to the bed, open to let in a slight breeze. The walls were plain, and the room held no decorations. It was used for functionality. Visitors to Elasariin didn't tend to linger.

The young human girl sat on the bed, hugging her legs to her chest. Now that she could get a closer look at her, the girl really was different from any of the humans Eolisti had encountered before. Her hair, the color of her skin, the shape of her face, her eyes—everything else was different. Eolisti knew that there were other lands where humans dwelled, over the mountains to the west and across the sea, and she knew of the countries stretching over two continents. Those of fairer complexion to the north and darker to the south. She had seen a map of Lanis before, but those places seemed so far away. Her mother had told her before it was extremely rare for any of the western humans to travel this far east unless they were being sold as slaves.

But she didn't look like a slave. She looked well-nourished, and her clothes, filthy as they were, were much too fine to belong to any but the most highly placed slaves. Her eyes also didn't have the distant look that many of the others coming through Elasariin had.

The girl looked about the same age as Eolisti, though she knew that humans aged faster than Anai. *She's pretty for a human*, she decided, *but not as pretty as me*.

Eolisti tried to give the girl a friendly smile. "Good

evening! My name is Eolisti." She held up the tray for the human to see. "I have some food for you." Eolisti walked over to the table and put the tray down, tossing some of her dark hair over her shoulder.

The girl watched Eolisti with her big gray eyes. She didn't speak, and Eolisti felt the corner of her mouth twitch as she tried to keep the smile on her face. How long was she going to stare at her? She had the sudden urge to wave her hand in front of the girl's face to see if she would respond, but suppressed it. That might offend her.

"Sophie," the girl said finally, her voice shaking slightly. "My name is Sophie."

Eolisti nodded and then gestured at the food. "Hungry?" she asked with that smile still plastered on her face, setting the tray down on the table.

Sophie watched her like a frightened animal for a few more moments, then unfolded herself and stood. "Thank you," she said softly, finally averting her eyes and fixating on the tray of food instead. She sat down on one of the chairs and lifted the lid on the bowl. Eolisti leaned over to see what she had been given. *Makile* stew. Of course it was. The food here didn't vary much. It was all so boring.

The girl looked at the stew for a moment, then picked up the spoon and took a sip. It was too bland for Eolisti's tastes, but the girl apparently didn't mind it. She ate with a gusto that Eolisti imagined could only come from days without substantial food. She hadn't even asked what was in it. "It's better if you eat it with the bread," Eolisti suggested, staring at her in astonishment.

Sophie nodded and dipped the *bära* in the stew.

Eolisti sat down across from the girl as she ate but waited until she was finished before speaking again.

"So, how did you come upon our little city, Sophie?" she

asked, trying to keep the tone conversational. Eolisti was bursting with questions, but she knew from experience that people usually got upset if they were bombarded with inquiries while they ate.

Sophie glanced at her warily and did not answer immediately. Eolisti's foot twitched, wanting to tap impatiently. Instead, she kept that friendly smile on her face. Sophie swallowed her food and said, "A friend of mine directed me here. I walked for four days from Tanzar through the countryside, and then through the forest."

"And you weren't afraid of entering the forest at night?"

She gave the Anai an almost sickly smile. "Of course I was afraid, but I had to do it. I'm more afraid of what I left behind."

"What *did* you leave behind?"

A pained look came across the girl's face. She set the bread down and folded her hands in her lap. "I..." She paused, considering her words carefully. "I just needed to get out of there." It looked like she wanted to say more but remained silent.

Eolisti nodded. Even though she knew that wasn't the whole story, Eolisti knew how it felt to really need to leave somewhere. She had that feeling every day. "I've heard some stories about Zo'rahn," she admitted when Sophie provided nothing else. "Are you Zo'rahni? You don't look Zo'rahni. Are you a slave?"

Sophie looked both surprised and relieved at the sudden change of subject. "Yes, I'm actually half. My mother was from Morigael. My father is Zo'rahni. I've been told I take after my mother more than my father." She allowed herself a small smile. "I don't remember them that much. I was taken away from my family at a young age. But no, I'm not a slave." She suddenly looked up, eyes wide, clearly afraid she'd said too much.

It took all the will power Eolisti had to not roll her eyes. "Relax," she said, forcing that unthreatening smile on her face again. "I'm not reporting anything you say to anyone. We're just chatting." She placed a hand over Sophie's and changed her expression to worry. *Eyebrows raised. Relaxed facial muscles.* "It seems like you need someone to talk to," Eolisti said in a gentle, calming voice she'd heard her mother use when trying to calm frightened deer.

Sophie smiled sadly at Eolisti. "Thank you." The girl was silent for a time, and Eolisti had the impression that she was deciding whether or not she could trust her. Apparently deciding that she could, Sophie continued speaking. "I'm not a slave. Technically, I'm an apprentice wizard and not old enough to apply to become ranked yet."

"What do you mean by 'ranked'?" Eolisti asked. It seemed they finally stumbled onto something interesting.

Sophie's expression changed, and her voice took on an airy quality. "Being ranked means that you have taken the testing required to be recognized as a fully-fledged wizard of Zo'rahn. Normally, that means you are over the age of twenty and have completed two years of apprenticeship to a wizard of fourth rank or higher. There are seven ranks," she explained, seeing Eolisti's confused look.

"Each rank above the first requires both a test of skill and an assessment of your achievements in magical studies. Some apprentices are quite powerful but hold back on testing to the next rank to sharpen their talent, even if they are old enough. Once you make rank, it becomes very competitive."

"Sounds boring." The words left Eolisti's mouth before

she could even think about stopping them. "W-what I mean," she stammered at Sophie's look of shocked indignation, "is that it sounds like a lot of book work. You must want to get out and travel and explore. Experience the world around you, not just study."

"Well, some study is like that, but others are less so. We are always trying to push the boundaries of the world around us with magic. Sometimes, that requires us to do fieldwork. Zo'rahni wizards are sent all over Lanis on missions researching and looking for artifacts and other magics that have been lost over time..." She trailed off at this, a troubled look clouding her face.

Whatever Sophie said about the study of magic, it still sounded incredibly dull to Eolisti. If all of the Zo'rahni were like this, why were her people so wary of them? They didn't sound formidable at all. Eolisti wasn't stupid. She knew magic could be extremely dangerous and had seen her mother use it to deadly effect on intruders before, but how dangerous could a girl like this be? She was the exact opposite of what the Anai had expected from a wizard of Zo'rahn.

"Are most people in Zo'rahn like you? You seem very, uh, different from what I've heard of your people."

Her cheeks reddened. "Well, no. Not really. Most of the wizards in Zo'rahn conform strictly to tradition. We are trained to be better than those around us. Stronger. Deadlier." She met Eolisti's eyes and shook her head, smiling ruefully. "Not 'we.' Not anymore. They."

Eolisti only half-listened as Sophie spoke. She didn't sound very interesting, but Eolisti's mother went out to meet this girl herself, so she had to be a person of some importance. The amount of secrecy was strange, too.

Usually, the entire city would be preparing days before humans arrived, and she did make the trip here from Tanzar by herself and unscathed. There had to be more to her than met the eye. Eolisti just needed to figure out what was so special about the girl.

Sophie was still talking softly when another noise from the hall caught Eolisti's attention, the low thumping of approaching footsteps. Eolisti jumped up, startling Sophie into silence, and walked across the room. She pulled back the curtain and dragged out the large wooden tub, taking a bucket out of it. "You look like you could use a bath," she said hurriedly, glancing back at Sophie and smiling apologetically as the door slammed open, startling the poor girl again.

In the doorway stood Vyraeli, with clenched jaw and furrowed brow directed at her only daughter. "*I see you've met our guest,*" she hissed scathingly in Anaiian. Aerynis's blonde head poked out from behind Vyraeli, a smug look on her face. That little traitor.

"Mother." Eolisti smiled sweetly and gestured to the tub, speaking in the human tongue. "I was just preparing a bath for her. She looks so tired. I think it would help her relax before sleeping. Don't you agree?" she asked innocently.

Eolisti held her breath, bucket in hand, as the anger on Vyraeli's face slowly turned to wry amusement. Sophie looked back and forth between them, but Eolisti, determined not to be thrown out, kept her eyes on her mother.

Finally, Vyraeli sighed and closed her eyes. Her fingers twitched at her side, and Eolisti knew she wanted to massage her temples and ask the gods to give her strength like she did whenever Eolisti misbehaved. She opened her eyes and smiled woodenly. "Aerynis, please fetch some water from the kitchens so our guest can wash. You," she glared at Eolisti. "Sit."

Eolisti shrugged as Aerynis approached and snatched the bucket from her in much the same way that Eolisti had snatched the tray from the girl earlier. When Vyraeli wasn't looking, the young Anai stuck her tongue out at Eolisti. Eolisti's temper flared, and she briefly considered trying to trip the brat, but reminded herself that that would be stupid and only get her into more trouble. The moment passed, and Eolisti walked over to the table and sat in the chair as Vyraeli instructed. She folded her arms over her chest and leaned back. There would be time for revenge later.

When Aerynis closed the door, Vyraeli's gaze shifted from Eolisti to Sophie.

"My daughter is right. A hot bath would help you sleep. Our Council will meet on the morrow to discuss how to handle the special circumstances that your position requires. You must understand that we don't normally deal with people of your station and will need to make adjustments to our usual arrangements. We'll inform you when everything has been agreed upon and assign you what we call a Vendarii, a protector. This person will be one of our trained warriors and will be able to escort you to your next destination. You will be provided with the essentials for your journey." She turned to Eolisti and narrowed her eyes, a wicked grin spreading across her face.

"Since my daughter seems to have taken to you, please feel free to have her fetch anything you need."

Eolisti eyed the older Anai suspiciously, but said only, "Of course, Mother."

With that, Vyraeli took her leave. Eolisti waved at her as her mother stepped aside to allow Aerynis entry with a bucket of steaming water, then closed the door behind her.

"Well, Sophie," Eolisti took the bucket from Aerynis and poured the water into the tub. "Let's get you cleaned up."

CHAPTER
SIX

It was well after midnight before Eolisti was able to return home. She'd been fulfilling the tasks set forth by her mother and taking care of Sophie. The girl had asked for just a few small things, her clothing needed to be cleaned and she'd wanted some tea before going to bed. But Vyraeli had also left a list for her. Once Sophie had fallen asleep, Aerynis had happily presented Eolisti with it when she tried to leave.

She'd taken Sophie's sandals and dropped them off at the cobbler's house with a note to see if the shoemaker could use them as a guide for making some sturdier footwear. Then she was to deliver messages to each Council member at their residences to inform them of the arrival of the human, reserve horses with Ilas Balrie, the quartermaster, for when Sophie left the city, and deliver a request for supplies to Ristell Fendar, the old Anai who ran the general store.

Eolisti was met with the grumpy faces of each person she'd awoken to deliver her mother's orders and was almost shouted at by the quartermaster, who pointed out repeatedly that it was far too late for any decent Anai to be calling on him. By the time she had finished with the list, she was thoroughly annoyed and beginning to think that humans were far more trouble than they were worth.

Eolisti yawned as she crossed the bridge leading to her house. She thought she could get in a few hours of sleep before dawn, then try to find out when the High Council meeting was scheduled.

As she approached her house, she noticed someone waiting by the door. It was difficult to make out who it was in the dark, but there weren't many people who wandered around the city this late. She assumed it might be one of the other Council members' assistants. When she was close enough for the person to hear her footsteps, the visitor turned, and she recognized him.

He was half a head taller than she, with straw-colored hair that fell to his shoulders and a round, kind face. When he saw her, a wide grin stretched his lips, making him look handsome and even younger than he actually was.

"Eolisti," he said, raising a hand in welcome, "you're back late."

"Myrin." She returned the gesture and the smile. "I could say the same of you. Why are you here?" She looked down. There was a letter clutched in his hand. "Council business?" she asked, trying not to sound too eager. Myrin was the assistant to Alewin Haerell, a member of the Anaiian High Council. Maybe he could tell her when they would be meeting.

His smile turned wry. "If it is, you know I can't talk about it, especially not to you. This message is for Shaman Vyraeli, and for her eyes only, Eolisti," he added, noticing her eyeing the letter.

"But you must know something, Myrin. Alewin trusts

you, and you know he's very hard to please, so you must do your job very well." She batted her eyelashes and flashed him a knowing grin that promised more than her words conveyed. She leaned into him a little and looked up into his eyes. His face was heavily shadowed in the near darkness, but Eolisti thought his cheeks turned faintly pink.

Myrin looked away from her and cleared his throat. "I really can't talk about it, Eolisti. You know how Alewin is. He'd be furious if he found out I even spoke to you tonight."

Eolisti pushed out her lower lip in a slight pout. "I live here, too, so I don't know what else he would expect. I promise I won't say anything. Alewin would never know I saw you tonight." She widened her eyes significantly and took a step closer to him. "Please," she said, putting as much need in the word as she could manage. "She's my mother. I just want to know what's going on. I'm worried about her."

That did it. Myrin closed his eyes and let out a resigned sigh. "Swear to me that you won't tell anyone."

"I swear it," she replied, trying to keep the triumphant grin off her face.

"And you won't act on anything I tell you?"

"Of course not," she said innocently.

Myrin ran a hand through his hair and groaned. "Fine, fine." He handed the letter to her. Her mother's name was inscribed on it with narrow, neat writing and sealed with the image of a willow tree stamped into greenish-gold wax the color of autumn leaves.

"Don't open that, but it says there will be a meeting of the High Council at dawn." He leaned in closer and lowered his voice, almost whispering. "Apparently, there's a human in town. But this one is different from the ones that usually pass through. She isn't a slave. She's a wizard of Zo'rahn. A

Nightingale operative requested an immediate extraction from Zo'rahn through the pass. Between us, Alewin is furious that Vyraeli accepted without consulting the Council first. He thinks the wizard is a spy."

Eolisti nodded conspiratorially, but she seriously doubted that Sophie was a spy. She was far too skittish. "Why would the Nightingales request the extraction? Is she someone important?" The Nightingales must be the organization that the Council worked with. She thought she'd heard the name before, but couldn't be certain.

He grimaced and pulled back. "I don't know, but she wouldn't be here if she was a nobody. The Nightingales wouldn't work with a Zo'rahni wizard unless it was absolutely necessary." Eolisti opened her mouth, but Myrin cut her off. "That's all I know, Eolisti," he said and looked around like a nervous cat. "If I'm much longer, Alewin will wonder where I am. We can talk more tomorrow if you'd like." He gave her a watery smile, glancing at the bridge leading away from her home.

Eolisti didn't have to fake the yawn she gave. "Maybe. You should get going before someone sees us. I'll give my mother the message." She waved at Myrin as he hurried off over the bridge she had crossed minutes before.

The High Council was meeting at dawn, huh? Eolisti allowed herself a small smile as she opened the door to her home. That would give her time to get a few hours of sleep before finding a good hiding place to watch.

But when she lay down in her bed, she found that she couldn't sleep. Her mind was racing. That human might be her chance to get out of the city. Sophie was going to be assigned a Vendarii to guide her through the mountain pass anyway, so why couldn't it be she? Eolisti knew how to fight, and her mother had shown her how to hunt and track. The mountain pass wasn't that far from the city, four or five days on horseback. What else was there to know?

That settled it. She would have to find a way to be assigned as Sophie's Vendarii and guide her through the mountains. She'd only be gone for a couple of weeks. Better yet, if she proved herself, she could start being assigned other missions by the Council.

Eolisti sat up, grinning. Sleep was fleeting in the face of her excitement. Dawn was only a few hours away, and she couldn't risk missing that High Council meeting. She leaped out of bed, dressed, and began pacing her room, thinking. It would be best to get to the Solixium before anyone else arrived. If someone were to see her there, they would surely eject her before the meeting started. High Council meetings were considered sacred. Only Council members and the Council scribe were allowed to be in attendance.

They would meet, usually for hours, and would announce whatever they had decided to the rest of the city afterward. The High Council consisted of ten of the most revered and experienced Anai in Elasariin, Eolisti's mother included, and they made decisions on all manner of issues, from the mundane to the extraordinary. Well, Eolisti had never seen anything extraordinary come from the Council, but she supposed it was possible. Normally, they decided things like when or how often scouts would be sent out to the surrounding lands.

She *had* to be there. She *had* to make sure she was chosen. There were a few spots she thought would be good to hide in, and then when the Council was deciding whom to send with the human, she could reveal herself and make her case. Her mother wouldn't be too happy with her, but as long as she could convince the Council to send her, Vyraeli would follow what they decided.

This will work. She thought to herself excitedly. *It has to.* With a spring in her step, Eolisti grabbed a piece of *bära* out of the kitchen and left her house for the second time that night.

The forest was quiet. The birds and animals were asleep, and few Anai were out in the hours before dawn. Even so, Eolisti took care to hide as much as possible, creeping from one building to the next and slinking across bridges when she had to. It would be just her luck for someone to spot her and report her to Vyraeli. It wouldn't have been a long walk during the day, but under the circumstances, the trip to the Council building took her much longer than she had planned.

The Council met in a place called the Solixium. The Solixium was built on the branches of the enormous old willow tree that towered above the Council building. She liked to think of it as the oldest, tallest tree in the forest. There was no way that it was *actually* the oldest tree in the forest, but she had had the idea when she was a child, and it stuck with her. The Council building was where the High Council worked during the day and had individual meetings, but the Solixium was where they convened.

Like most of the city, the branches of the willow had been woven together into a net-like platform surrounded by a feathery curtain of willow leaves. It may have been several trees at one point, but whatever magic her ancestors wielded had molded them into one. Eolisti had been up there a few times before and found it to be a beautiful and surreal place. The area inside the Solixium was wide enough to hold many more Anai than just the High Council and was thought at one time to have held a council of over one hundred. Anai from all over Lanis would come to convene in Elasariin, even representatives from Drushald and Nemethy. Over the centuries, Eolisti's people had either moved on or perished at the hands of encroaching humans. Even with all its beauty and serenity, it always felt like a lonely place to Eolisti, a reminder of what once was.

When Eolisti arrived, there were already ten chairs set in a wide circle in the middle of the Solixium. Did they leave them there after the last Council meeting, or had someone set them up before she arrived? She looked around but didn't see anyone, so she continued to creep around the edge of the platform. There was an area at the north point of the platform where a few larger branches grew inside the curtain, creating an area that was just big enough for her to sit behind without being seen. Hopefully, she would still be within earshot of what the members were discussing.

It was surprising that, as far as she knew, no one had ever thought of spying on the Council from there before. They could know everything that was going on, and what decisions were being made, before anyone else did. Eolisti allowed herself a satisfied grin before climbing into the small pocket and settling down.

The meeting wouldn't begin for a few more hours. How would she make her case to the Council? She was old enough, but untested. She needed to be given an assignment at some point, so why not this one? She could take one human girl into the mountains, no problem. Her mother would be against it, but she could be overruled by a majority. Maybe. Eolisti hadn't spied on them before, and she didn't know how the Council came to their decisions. Did they vote on it as she imagined?

Eolisti yawned and laid her head against the wood of the willow's branches. Now that she was sitting there waiting, the lack of sleep was finally catching up to her, and her mind began to wander. It would be great to get out of this boring forest and into the world beyond it. She could meet other Anai that lived in the Anaiian courts. She could travel across the ocean to distant lands. Maybe she could even fight monsters and save a country. She would have to return after taking the girl across the mountains, of course. She knew that. But just that one journey could open up more for her. It could convince her mother that she was not just a child and that she could handle herself. She could finally start to live her own life.

Eolisti smiled sleepily. Perhaps she would close her eyes for a little while. There was plenty of time before the meeting...

"Preposterous!"

Eolisti started awake, smacking the side of her face against a knot in the branch her head was resting on. She clamped a hand to her mouth to keep from crying out. She held her breath, listening to see if someone heard her, but the conversation didn't pause.

"Bringing one of *them* into the city, after everything they've done to us?" The voice was angry.

"The last time I checked, we have never been attacked by a child." Vyraeli's voice was cool and controlled.

"She knows where the city is! She could tell the other wizards!" said the same man. Eolisti recognized the voice now. Alewin. His tone boiled with anger and indignation. "Do the rest of you actually agree with Shaman Vyraeli? Why should we help her? Will you take responsibility if a Zo'rahni army shows up at our doorstep? Will you tell the others that they will have to die because of your—"

"Be very careful with your next words, Councilman." Her mother's voice was like ice, and it sent a chill down Eolisti's spine. "The High Council has already made its decision. We help the girl escape Zo'rahn and turn her over to the Nightingales, as we would for any other person, human or otherwise, who seeks our aid. Your concerns have been addressed thoroughly by this Council." There was a creak of wood, and her voice dropped to a low enough whisper that Eolisti had to strain to hear her next words. "Accept defeat gracefully."

"Enough," said another firm female voice. "We will not squabble among ourselves like humans. The High Council moves as one." There was a pause before she continued. It was as if everyone there was holding their collective breath.

"The issue has been settled." The woman went on, after allowing her words to echo throughout the chamber. "The mage will be escorted through the mountains and delivered to the checkpoint in Bardov. After that, the monks will decide the best way to get her across the Silver Sea and into Morigael. Shaman Vyraeli, I assume you have already taken care of preparations?"

"Yes, *Omalonne*," her mother said, mollified.

"Very well then, I suggest that she depart the city as soon as possible to avoid any further unrest. She was seen entering, and by now, word of her arrival and"—she sniffed disdainfully—"*occupation* will have spread. We are already going to get complaints for the next week at least. Let's not do any more damage than has already been done."

The woman could only be Lethena Thestara, the Speaker for the High Council. She was considered an elder in the city, though Eolisti was sure she was no older than two hundred years. Lethena was tall and willowy, with hair the color of birch wood, and pale, luminous skin. Despite her age, her face was without wrinkle or blemish. The older Anai did not originate from Elasariin but had come here over a century ago from the Anaiian Court of Nemethy in the land to the west. She was also one of the strictest people Eolisti had ever met, and she had never liked Lethena much. One would think that since Lethena was from somewhere interesting, she would understand Eolisti's need to entertain herself in such a boring place.

Then again, now that she thought about it, she didn't like anyone on the Council, besides her mother, and the feeling was mutual. She didn't cause nearly as much trouble as they said she did, she just liked to have some fun, and the High Council hated fun. Her kind of fun anyway.

"It sounds as if everything is in order," Lethena continued. "Shaman Vyraeli, we will leave the rest up to you, unless there is anything else to add?" They were all silent. "Then, this meeting is adjourned." Wood creaked, and a general murmur ensued between the members as they stood and began leaving the Solixium.

Wait, what about the Vendarii? Had they already assigned one while she had drifted off? *Dammit!* She had gone to the trouble of getting there early, only to fall asleep during the crucial part. Granted, bursting out of her hiding place and shouting "Me!" while they were discussing who was going to be Sophie's Vendarii hadn't been her greatest plan, but at least it had been something. Eolisti raked her fingers through her hair. That girl was her ticket out of here! What would she do now?

Eolisti waited as the footsteps died out, and the voices faded away. She sighed and pulled a few strands of her dark hair free of the entangling branches before crawling out from behind them. Morning sunlight shimmered through the great willow's leaves, casting the meeting place in golden feathered glitter. As she stood and brushed herself off, someone cleared their throat. Eolisti whirled around.

Vyraeli stood near the entrance to the Solixium, arms folded over her chest and a stern look on her face. Eolisti winced, knowing that a scolding was coming.

Her mother just stared at her as she approached. Eolisti tried to smile at her as if she had just noticed a friend in passing. "Good morning, Mother," she said in the sweetest tone she could manage. "Did the meeting go well?"

The Anai woman didn't speak.

Eolisti grew increasingly uncomfortable under that gaze. She grasped for something to say, anything that wouldn't incriminate her. "I wasn't spying!" she finally burst out. "I just wanted to know what was going on. You always keep me in the dark and when something interesting happ—"

"When something interesting happens, I take care of it, like I'm supposed to," Vyraeli interrupted, her voice holding little warmth. "And you, my dutiful and loving daughter, do as I say so that I may carry out my work."

"You didn't say I couldn't listen to the Council meeting," Eolisti grumbled.

Vyraeli's eyes flashed with sudden anger. "Must I dictate your every action, every courtesy of our people? Are you telling me to control every aspect of your life lest you get yourself into more trouble?"

Eolisti flushed, and her temper rose to meet her mother's. "You have no idea what it's like to be stuck here! People don't like me, Mother! Every time I turn around, another Anai is waiting for me to make a mistake so that they can say I did something wrong, so why not meet those expectations?" She groaned in frustration. "I'm useless anyway! There are Vendarii years younger than me who have already been sent out on missions, and others who have ventured out into the world. All I do is run errands for you! Am I really so untrustworthy that I can't do anything else?"

She took a few deep breaths to calm herself as her words echoed around the Solixium. The following silence was deafening. Vyraeli stared at her with wide eyes.

"I do know what it feels like," Vyraeli began softly, all the anger melting from her voice. She took a step toward her daughter. "Perhaps it is time for you to take on more responsibility. You've trained enough."

Eolisti's breath caught. Could her mother be saying what she thought she was saying? Could she dare to hope?

Vyraeli held up a finger, suddenly stern again. "Not *this* mission. This is far too dangerous for your first time out of the city. The next time we have an escort mission, you can accompany the Vendarii and learn from them on the job. Then, provided you do well, we can start sending you out on your own. How does that sound?"

The Anai frowned but nodded at her mother. Eolisti knew that she was ready to be a Vendarii now and that she could escort Sophie through the mountains. But she also knew that if she contradicted her mother, she would be in even more trouble, and she might not let her go on any mission. Ever. Eolisti nodded. "Fine," she said grudgingly.

Vyraeli smiled and leaned forward to kiss Eolisti's forehead. "Now, go tell Taenaran that he will be escorting our guest to Bardov. Yes, the Council chose Taenaran," she said in amusement to Eolisti's look of indignation. "He's been a Vendarii many times and is one of the most experienced hunters we have."

"But he's just a woodcutter! Didn't he retire a long time ago? He hasn't been on a mission in ages!"

"Regardless, who the High Council sends is not subject

to your scrutiny Eolisti. Now"—she pushed her toward the entrance to the Solixium—"go tell him to prepare. We'll talk more about your future assignments later. You still have a few things to learn."

Eolisti left the Solixium, a frown marring her features as she thought. Vyraeli said she would be able to go the next time a Vendarii was needed to leave the city, but who knew when that would be? It could be months from now. What could Taenaran do that she couldn't? She knew that she was no doubt better with a sword than he was. And too dangerous? They were just going to Bardov. It was only a week's ride away. All they had to do was make their way out of the forest and follow the road. How dangerous was that? Besides, Sophie was probably the most interesting person that had ever passed through their village. A Zo'rahni wizard had never been here before.

No, she wouldn't let this opportunity slip through her fingers. The question was, how would she make this work?

SEVEN

The day after Sophie arrived in the Anaiian city turned out to be another long one, and even hours later, she was still confused by everything that happened.

It began with the Anai, Vyraeli, coming to see her in the morning. Sophie had barely woken up and dressed when there was a knock at her door.

The shaman had brought her breakfast, more of that strange bread and a kind of rice porridge that was sweet. She had explained that Sophie would leave the following day. Another Anai, what she called a "Vendarii" named Taenaran, would be accompanying her through the mountain pass that led to Bardov.

Sophie had studied maps of the area surrounding Zo'rahn, and from what she could recall, Bardov was a small trading town nestled in the mountains to the southwest that split Omer, Alkhazai, and Zo'rahn. Situated in the only land passage between the three countries, it was perfect for travelers and merchants alike. The land was technically in Omeran territory, so the town followed

Omer's laws, though it was somewhat isolated from the rest of the country. She recalled that the books she'd read suggested that it had initially been an Anaiian outpost centuries ago, but other than that, she knew nothing else about the trading town.

Sophie had thanked Vyraeli for all her help, and the Anai instructed her to be ready to depart the city at dawn, then left Sophie to finish her breakfast. She'd found herself looking out the window of the small room often, trying to observe the goings-on of the city. There were more Anai in Elasariin than she had expected and was curious to know more about them. The only relationship her people and the Anai had was one of small skirmishes and guerrilla warfare, so most of the Zo'rahni assumed that few Anai remained in the forest.

What she really wanted was to explore the city. Few humans had been here before, and the thought of being able to directly observe a culture that she'd only read about in books made her giddy. There seemed to be a system in place for receiving outsiders, but the few interactions she'd had with those helping her, with the exception of Vyraeli and her daughter, felt forced. She'd gotten the feeling that she wasn't welcome here, only tolerated because of her situation. In the end, it was just as well her stay here would be a short one.

Besides, she wasn't very good at meeting new people.

After midday, while Sophie was seated by the window reading a book, the Anai from the previous night knocked on her door. Eolisti looked to be about the same age as Sophie, though it was difficult to tell exactly. Anai lived longer than humans, so they also aged more slowly. She was beautiful, with a sheet of silky dark auburn hair and bright green eyes. Eolisti was slender like most Anai, but her proportions were slightly more robust than her fellows.

There was little in the way of greeting before Eolisti thrust a bundle into Sophie's arms and said, "Put that on and follow me."

The bundle turned out to be a gold and white cloak with an embroidered willow tree on the back and a deep hood. "People here aren't used to humans," Eolisti explained. "They're nervous, so it will be easier to move around the city if you wear that."

When Sophie asked where they were going, Eolisti waved off the question. "There's been a change of plans. We need to get you ready to leave now. Come on. We haven't got all day." Eolisti gave Sophie a reassuring smile and beckoned her to follow.

To Sophie's surprise, the cloak seemed enough to ease the Anai around her as she followed Eolisti. Surely, it could not hide that she was human. She sensed no such illusions in it. But the Anai barely took note of her as they passed, and some even nodded to her, thinking she was one of them.

In the dappled sunlight, Elasariin was even more fascinating than she had first believed. The entire city was housed in the treetops, and the platforms built around the trunks allowed for dwellings and walkways high up in the trees. Older platforms appeared to be shaped from the branches, probably with the same kind of magic she'd seen Vyraeli use when they'd first met. The newer platforms were made of wooden beams, but as the trees had grown, the wood merged into the bark, making it impossible to tell where plank ended and tree began.

Elegant rope bridges woven around exquisitely carved wooden slats connected the platforms. When she looked more closely at the rope beneath her fingers, she noticed that some of the fibers were green and sprouted tiny leaves that trembled in the soft breeze. She realized the whole village was *alive*, and the effect of it all was breathtaking.

Sophie made the mistake of looking over the side of the bridge they were crossing. Her stomach lurched, and she stared down at what she guessed was over a hundred feet to the forest floor. She clutched the ropes and took several deep breaths before she could stand straight again.

When she looked up, Eolisti was already at the next platform looking over at Sophie, her lips pressed tightly together. Sophie walked steadily toward Eolisti, trying not to think of how high up they were or how flimsy those bridges suddenly felt.

"Are you all right?" Eolisti asked when she had made it across. Sophie steadied herself with a deep breath and nodded.

"Well, try not to stop again," the Anai scolded. "We're nearly there. I don't want to be held up."

Sophie found the abrupt change in Eolisti's tone strange, but continued to follow as they made their way to the spiral staircase that she had climbed the night before.

When the two women finally reached the bottom, Sophie resisted the urge to sink to her knees. Her thighs burned, and while the descent hadn't been nearly as painful as climbing up those stairs, she still had no desire to ever repeat the experience.

Sophie looked around. The forest was completely different during the day. In the dark, it had been a terrifying landscape full of shifting shadows, but during the day, it seemed almost peaceful. Eolisti led her around the big tree that held the staircase. "Just a little farther," she murmured.

Eventually, the trees gave way to a clearing where thick rays of sunlight were able to burst through the canopy. Three dusky brown horses were tied to a tree branch, two saddled and the third carrying supplies. Eolisti approached the horses and waved for Sophie to follow.

"I'll be taking you to Bardov," she said as she picked up a belt with two leather pouches and a sword, and began strapping it on.

"It will be about a week's ride, but we have plenty of supplies. You can go ahead and tie your bag onto that horse." Eolisti pointed at the third horse.

Sophie approached the mare cautiously. Her family had horses when she was a child, but she hadn't had much to do with them in the past eleven years. The mare nickered at her, and Sophie jumped. The Anai sighed and took Sophie's pack out of her hands, securing it with the rest of the supplies.

After helping Sophie onto her horse and mounting her own, Eolisti looked around the clearing intently.

"Let's get going. Don't worry," she added, seeing the look on Sophie's face. "Your horse will just follow mine."

Eolisti clicked her tongue, and Sophie clutched the mare's mane as it started forward.

They rode the rest of that day, breaking through the tree line just before dusk. Sophie heard before that a rider had to be careful handling horses in rough terrain, but their procession was sure-footed, and the horses seemed to have no trouble navigating the roots and underbrush. She didn't know much about horse riding, but she had the impression that Eolisti was moving them quickly. They rested for food and water only once on that first day of travel, and only for an hour or so.

She was surprised by Eolisti. Sophie had expected the

Anai to question her during their time alone on the ride as she had the night before, but since the start of their journey, Eolisti remained silent, focusing on everything around them. The farther they rode from Elasariin, the more comfortable she seemed to get, but she still didn't talk much.

However, this silence didn't last once they made camp. As soon as they had settled down for the night, the Anai was even more talkative, if that were possible, than she had been back in the city. She asked Sophie if she had ever been out of Zo'rahn before, which she hadn't, and about her life with the wizards. Sophie had spoken no more than a few sentences before Eolisti launched into stories of her own childhood, typically with her performing various feats that ended with her doing physical labor as punishment. Mostly, she complained about how boring Elasariin was, which was hard to believe, but Sophie thought it best that she not voice that opinion.

She liked hearing about how the Anai led completely different lives from her kin. The way Eolisti described it, their society sounded less governed by laws and more by the needs of its people. The thought of living like that helped keep her mind off the slow, gnawing feeling in the pit of her stomach. Up until this point, she had known every step she would need to take. Now, the weight of the unknown threatened to drag her down. Her freedom rested entirely on the shoulders of an Anai who she'd met less than twenty-four hours ago.

The next day was filled with more riding. They were going faster on the road than they had through the forest, not having to dodge roots and branches. Eolisti seemed less tense and their pace felt more relaxed. She wasn't looking around at sounds that Sophie couldn't hear, and seemed to be enjoying the ride much more than she had the previous day. She still didn't talk much and kept glancing down at the map she clutched in her fingers, but she smiled more, and they rested every few hours.

Sophie's feeling of unease only increased as they followed the road south. The tree line was visible in the distance on their right. The closest farms were miles from where they were, but it would be easier to spot them here than in the forest. Traveling through the woods might be slower but being out in the open was dangerous.

"No way," Eolisti said when Sophie suggested this to her.

"But what if we're seen?" she pleaded. "I know there aren't a lot of people this close to the forest, but there are some. They could send a message—"

"To who? Guards that we could spot from miles away?"

"No," she said, trying to be patient, "to mages that can make themselves unseen and sneak up on us while we're sleeping. There are wizards stationed in most towns and magistrates that ride the countryside. Not to mention the ones that are probably out looking for me. I was only an apprentice, and they have access to magic that I don't. Aren't you afraid that they'll head us off when this joins up with the main road?"

Eolisti looked momentarily stunned but recovered quickly. "The time that we save taking the road is well worth the small chance of being seen," she said confidently. "Besides, do they know that you came to us for help?"

"Well, no but—"

"Do they know that you went to the forest?"

"No, but—"

"Then stop worrying about it." Eolisti smiled over her shoulder. "Look, I'm your Vendarii. Do you think the High

Council would've let me escort you to Bardov if they didn't think I could do it? I've never been spotted before, and this is the best way to get to the pass."

"You've done this before?" Sophie asked, feeling somewhat relieved that the Anai had experience taking this route.

"Yes. Trust me, I'll get you there safely." The Anai turned back around, scanning the landscape. "We'll make camp soon. The sun is going down and there's no use pushing ourselves through the night. There are some trees over there," she pointed to an area in the distance just off the road. "We can camp there."

Sophie squinted and could barely make out the dark clumps that Eolisti was pointing at. She would never have known those were trees from here. Was an Anai's eyesight better than a human's?

By the time they settled down, there was only the barest hint of purple on the horizon. They didn't have a fire since there would be no way of masking it outside of the forest. Sophie sat on a blanket laid over the grass, thankful that she didn't have to be on the horse any longer. She never realized that horseback riding could be so taxing. Unlike the first part of her journey, her feet weren't sore, but her thighs and back were. She learned the first night on the road that sleeping on the ground did nothing to alleviate the pain.

Having noticed her stiff movements, Eolisti tossed her a saddlebag and told her that there should be a tin of salve that would help her muscles relax. Sophie opened it to find an assortment of canisters and bottles. Curious, she lifted a medium-sized bottle from the bag. There was writing on— no, *in* the glass—but as she was unfamiliar with the Anaiian language, she was unable to decipher its meaning.

She uncorked it and lifted it to her nose, and instantly recognized the sharp scent of hair dye.

When she'd first gone to Tanzar as a child, she had tried to dye her hair in order to fit in better with the other children. The substance had burned on her scalp, and, in the end, her hair had turned a ghastly gray-green color that made the others ridicule her even more. To make matters worse, her hair had started to break and fall out after a few days, and, ultimately, she'd had to shave her head to not look like some diseased urchin.

She felt her cheeks burn at the memory. A quick glance at Eolisti's back told her that the other woman had not noticed her discovery of the bottle or her odd reaction. The salve forgotten, she quickly stuffed the bottle to the bottom of the saddlebag, set it aside, and tried to look nonchalant.

Eolisti sat down on her blanket and opened a pack containing dried fruit, cheese, and bread and handed Sophie her portion. Eolisti seemed fine with the long ride, hardly seeming tired when they stopped. Perhaps she was used to these kinds of conditions on her trips outside of the Anaiian city.

Sophie accepted the food gratefully and immediately began eating. She didn't really care for the Anaiian bread. Zo'rahni bread was seasoned with cumin and basil, so the Anaiian fare was bland in comparison, but Sophie was hungry enough to eat just about anything. Even though they were only two days out of Elasariin, she already missed being in any kind of civilization.

Eolisti stared at the bread with faint disgust. "I'm so tired of eating this. Couldn't you make food? I would love something hot."

It took her a moment to realize what the Anai meant. "That's not really how magic works."

"Why not?" Eolisti looked up from her food after giving it another disgusted look.

"Magic doesn't allow you to create something out of nothing. I can condense the moisture in the air to make water, change the chemical composition to transmute one item into something else, or use energy to impose my will on reality. Magic is very useful in many circumstances, but I don't have anything that I could use to make a new meal with. I would need the basic ingredients to even— Are you listening to me?"

Eolisti was staring off into the darkness with a vacant, glassy expression before jumping at Sophie's words. "Yeah, yeah. Creating stuff, ingredients, reality. Got it." She stood up and stretched. "So, what you're saying is that if I go kill something, you can cook it?"

"W-what?" Sophie stammered.

"You know, make with the fire! I doubt anyone would notice if it was just long enough to cook something." Walking over to the horses and grabbing her bow and quiver off the one she'd been riding, Eolisti surveyed the countryside around them and touched the sword at her belt. "I might be able to find some rabbits, or maybe a deer." She looked over at Sophie and laughed at the look on her face. "I can skin it and everything, you just cook it."

Sophie was feeling a little sick again. "I can't cook the meat since I can't use magic."

"Why not? Isn't that the *one thing* you do?" she asked with an eyebrow raised.

Sophie flushed. "I *can* call up fire, but magic used like that can be traced. It releases a signature in the area that dissipates over time."

"Uh-huh," Eolisti said, half listening again. "So, what's the problem?"

Sophie felt her temper flare. Eolisti's mother was a shaman. Did she not know anything about how magic worked? She tried to keep her voice level. "The *problem* is that if I use magic in an area that is as sparsely populated as this one, other wizards anywhere close to here will be able to sense the energy that I use. They would come and investigate since there isn't supposed to be anyone in this area to begin with."

"Soph—"

She cut Eolisti off. "It's not like I don't want to use magic. Learning magic has been my life. I just can't use it, or someone will find us. I'm not sure what the Vizier would do, but—"

"Be quiet! I think I heard something," Eolisti whispered urgently as she scanned the darkness around them, her hand twitching toward the sword at her belt. "We're not alone."

EIGHT

Eolisti gestured to her, and Sophie stood up, moving closer to the Anai. Looking out into the night, all Sophie could see were vague, black shapes barely outlined in the light of the waning moon. It was impossible to discern what part of the terrain the sounds Eolisti heard were coming from and what might be out of place.

There was a soft snapping sound, and something passed within a few inches of Sophie's cheek, faster than she could see. Eolisti grabbed her arm and pulled Sophie behind her. "Move over to the horses and get my shield. Go now!" she hissed and gave Sophie a small push backward.

Sophie turned and scrambled toward the horses as Eolisti slowly backed up. As she reached for Eolisti's shield on the lead horse, another arrow came out of the darkness and barely missed her outstretched hand. The startled horse reared as the arrow bounced off the shield, and Sophie snatched her hand back.

"I wouldn't try that again if I were you," a deep raspy voice called out from behind her.

Sophie whipped around to see three figures materialize

out of the blackness. There was a spark from the figure on the far left and a flare of light as the end of the torch he was holding ignited. The three figures were all men, tall and muscular, with dirty clothes and worn faces. All of them looked like they were of Zo'rahni descent. With only the torchlight, Sophie would have put their ages between thirty and forty. It also looked like they hadn't shaved or washed in weeks, giving them a rough, menacing appearance—that, and the fact that the two men on the sides had their blades drawn.

"Well, well," the man in the middle said, the same voice that had spoken moments before. They stopped just out of sword reach from Eolisti, who had already drawn her weapon while Sophie's back was turned. "An Anai and a foreigner. We don't see many of your kind around here." He looked pointedly at the horses. "Where are you ladies off to with all those supplies?" He smiled, but it didn't touch his eyes.

Eolisti glanced back at Sophie then to the man. "We're just passing through," she said firmly. "Please leave us in peace."

The man chuckled and the other two followed suit. "Seems to me the only people who would be traveling this road with so many supplies would be escaped slaves."

"I'm not a slave," Eolisti said in a flat tone.

He looked her up and down. "Maybe you're not. Sometimes, we see Anai come out of the forest. But she most certainly is." He tilted his head toward Sophie, and she took an involuntary step back. "She looks like some rich merchant's slave. I bet there's a hefty reward for whoever returns you to your master."

Sophie shook her head frantically and Eolisti said, "That's not happening. Leave. Now. We don't want a fight."

All the mirth drained from the lead man's face. "I don't think so," he said as he reached for the weapon at his belt.

At that moment, Eolisti struck. She lunged forward before the man's sword was halfway out of its sheath and swung at his chest.

He had been expecting this and threw himself to the ground as the other two men turned on her, slicing with their weapons.

Eolisti was faster. She propelled herself forward and leaped over the prone man, rolling and coming up with her sword ready. There was another snapping sound, and she dodged to the right as an arrow hit the ground where she'd been standing a moment before. Eolisti looked over her shoulder and cursed as the swordsman without the torch rushed her.

While the Anai fought, Sophie scanned the landscape. There must be an archer out there somewhere. Her eyes fell on the torch held by the remaining swordsman who had not yet joined in on attacking Eolisti. They were all humans and they were unlikely to be able to distinguish friend and foe in the dark. Their backs were to her, focusing on the Anai. If she could put out the torch, the archer might not be able to shoot accurately at them. Hopefully, that would be enough to give Eolisti time to take out the others.

But how could she put it out without magic?

Steel rang as Eolisti parried another blow. She pressed him and the man staggered back, then she dropped and kicked his legs out from under him.

The man who had been speaking before joined the fray as Eolisti bore down on his companion.

Slowly, Sophie reached for the waterskin on the horse so as not to draw their attention. Her hands shook violently as she tried to untie the waterskin. Behind her, she heard Eolisti laugh as one of the men grunted in pain.

After what seemed like an eternity, the knot finally came loose, and Sophie pulled the waterskin free. There was a sharp yell, and she spun around to see one of Eolisti's attackers stumble and fall, blood oozing from a deep gash in his leg. Eolisti rolled and dodged another arrow, then came up to block a strike from the other man.

Sophie took a deep breath. It was now or never. She couldn't let Eolisti get hurt on her behalf. While the Anai seemed to be holding her own, the longer they fought, the more likely it would be that she would be stabbed or shot with an arrow. It was her fault that Eolisti was in danger in the first place, and it would be her fault if Eolisti was injured or killed. She couldn't just stand around and do nothing. The man with the torch still had his back to her, and Sophie's heart leaped as he raised his weapon in one hand, preparing to join the fray.

This is stupid! This is stupid! She told herself as she screamed at the man and threw the waterskin with all her might. He turned just in time to receive it fully in the face with a satisfying slap.

"What the—?!" he hissed out as Sophie, eyes squeezed shut, threw herself on his arm. She clamped onto it tightly, adrenaline and fear giving her strength, and kicked out with her feet. They connected with something soft, and the man's flailing ceased as he let out a hoarse cough. There was a clatter as his muscles relaxed and the torch fell to the ground.

Sophie opened her eyes just in time to see a fist come down at her. He connected hard with the side of her head, and, for just a moment, there were stars in her vision.

The next thing she knew, she was on the ground and

looking up at the sky, dazed. The man was doubled over, holding his stomach and retching into the brush at his feet. Sophie moaned as her head throbbed painfully.

Once he righted himself again, the man loomed over her with a furious expression. Sophie was still reeling from the blow to her head and could only stare up at him with wide eyes as her heart pounded in her chest.

"Little bitch," he growled. "You'll regret that." The flickering torchlight cast deep shadows across his face, making his expression look monstrous, inhuman. If he attacked her, she'd have to defend herself. She'd been struggling to keep herself from not uttering a single spell, but in the end, she would have to use it anyway. She had no skill in physical combat. The only way she could defend herself was with magic.

As he raised his sword, Sophie stilled her mind, locking away the panic and drawing energy from her fear and anxiety. Magic fed upon the user's power, power that was made stronger by emotions, and, right now, Sophie was feeling a lot of it. Everything seemed to slow as her mind raced. This could land them in serious trouble, even more than they were currently facing, but she would not allow herself or Eolisti to be hurt because of her inaction.

The blade came down at her. Her lips parted, but before she could utter the spell, a rock the size of her palm struck the man's head with a sickening crack. His swing went wide, and he looked surprised for a moment. Then the sword tumbled out of his hand, and he fell bonelessly to the ground.

Eolisti stood a few feet away, arm outstretched in a throwing motion. "What are you doing?! Don't just sit there!"

Sophie stared at her. Hadn't she just seen what

happened? But of course, she hadn't. She'd been fighting the entire time. Sophie tried to get up, but her head spun dangerously. Deciding that it was best to stay seated, Sophie looked around for the torch. It was close by on the ground, the dry grass around it starting to singe and burn. Quickly, she reached over and grabbed the blanket she'd been lying on earlier and smothered the fire. The smell of singed wool filled her nose. Even getting on her hands and knees made her nauseous, but she was able to put it out.

Sophie sat back and took deep gasps of the chill air, trying to still her head and stomach. Steel rang on steel, and now only moonlight illuminated the two figures dancing with their blades in the night.

CHAPTER

NINE

Back and forth they went. Eolisti lunged and her opponent jumped back. He swung and she spun gracefully out of his reach. It was almost like watching a performance, actors missing each other by inches to the cheers of spectators. Now that arrows were no longer flying at her, Eolisti looked more relaxed and focused.

Sophie stayed seated on the ground next to her singed blanket, unable to tear her eyes off of the duel. Eolisti feinted right, then turned and landed a kick in his side. The man, the same one who encouraged them to surrender, moved with the blow to reduce its impact and then jabbed his blade at the Anai in retaliation.

The strike grazed her shoulder, and Eolisti took the opportunity to close the distance. She stepped forward and elbowed him in the chest, making him stagger back. Then, she kicked hard at his knee. A crunching sound echoed throughout the night and he screamed in pain. In a panicked rage, he brought his sword down, but Eolisti ducked to the side and punched him hard in the face with her sword hand. That, combined with his crippled knee, sent him toppling to the ground unconscious.

Eolisti sighed and sheathed her sword. She winced and shook out her hand. "Like punching a rock," she mumbled to herself, then turned to Sophie, a wide grin on her face. "That was fun, wasn't it?"

Sophie blinked. Fun? *Fun?!* They almost died and Eolisti thought that was fun?! Was she insane?

The look of disgust must have shown on her face because Eolisti burst out laughing a moment later and said, "Calm down. Our supplies are still intact and we're both fine. What's the big deal?"

"*What's the big deal?*" Sophie heard herself getting louder and higher pitched with every word. "I'm not fine! That guy"—she pointed to the man on the ground near them—"hit me on the head. I could have a concussion."

Both of Eolisti's thin eyebrows climbed her forehead. "But can't you heal yourself with magic? I've seen my mother do it."

Sophie rubbed her fingertips against her temples. "Magic isn't a solution for everything. Yes, I can heal myself to some extent, but not if the injury is bad enough. Head injuries are tricky, and concentration is a huge part of working magic. But that's not the point," she fumed. It was unlikely that she was injured beyond what a few hours of rest would fix, but she needed Eolisti to understand what could have happened. The Anai seemed to be treating the situation like a particularly vigorous training exercise. "That was dangerous. We could have been captured or killed before we even reached Bardov."

"That was nothing," Eolisti replied unperturbed and walked over to where Sophie sat, offering her hand. "That's why I'm here, to protect you."

Sophie glared at her hand, but after a moment, she took it. With Eolisti's help, she got to her feet. The nausea was fading, and though her head throbbed dully, it wasn't as painful as it had been a few minutes before. "Thanks," she said. "You're very good, you know, at fighting and all that." She sighed and gave the Anai a small, tired smile. "I guess it was a little exciting."

A shape moved behind the Anai. The man Eolisti had hit with a rock stood, blood streaming down a face contorted in rage. He held a dagger in his hand and brought it down at Eolisti.

Sophie acted without a second thought, gathering in her focus and releasing energy in an instant. A spark as bright as a roaring fire ignited just over Eolisti's shoulder, blinding her attacker. Sophie directed the heat away from her companion and back toward the man, blasting him in the face with superheated air.

Just as quickly as it appeared, the spark was gone. The man dropped his dagger and his hands flew to his face. He stumbled back, muffled screams coming from between his fingers.

Eolisti whipped around, drawing her sword and crouching. She paused for half a second, seeing the dagger on the ground, then lunged at him and drove her knee up into his groin.

The breath exploded from his lungs and he collapsed. He writhed in agony on the ground, one hand clutching his groin, the other still covering his face. The skin there was cracked and blistered from where the heat had seared it. Sophie felt a twinge of guilt, watching him lie there in pain and seeing the effects of her spell.

Sophie thought she heard the snap of a bowstring and instinctively raised her hand, drawing in her power again and forming it into a barrier. There was a flash of blue light, and the arrow that was speeding toward them stopped in midair, spinning slowly, as if it were suspended in water. She kept the barrier raised in case more arrows came at them, but no others followed the first.

The man on the ground stared at her with wide eyes through his fingers. "Witch!" he gasped, voice hoarse with pain.

"That's right," Eolisti said, earning a glare from Sophie, and prodded him with her foot. "Now, why did you attack us? And don't lie." She kicked the dagger away from him and placed the tip of her sword at his throat. "I'm tired and have little patience for fools tonight."

"Why should I tell you anything," he growled, looking up at Eolisti with narrowed eyes. "You Anai are savages. You'll just kill me anyway." He painstakingly got to his knees, Eolisti's sword following him as he rose. The man leaned forward, piercing his skin on the point and spat on her boots. A trickle of blood dripped down his collarbone and into his shirt. "Go ahead, bitch."

Eolisti's shoulders tensed at his words, and Sophie thought she really was going to kill him, but she only sighed and lifted her sword from his throat. His expression changed to one of uncertainty. "Not today," she said and brought the hilt of her sword down, smashing savagely against the same side of his head that she'd hit with the rock. He collapsed again. "I told you I don't have patience for fools."

She sheathed her sword once more and turned back to Sophie, looking mildly annoyed. "We're going to tie them up and start a fire. A campfire," she added as Sophie opened her mouth in horror. "To draw out anyone looking for you.

We'll go back to the tree line and watch to see if anyone approaches. Do you know how to use rope?"

Sophie shook her head and Eolisti rolled her eyes. "Fine, I'll do it. Just pack everything up." Eolisti walked over to the packhorse and took a length of rope, that had been neatly looped, off the animal. Sophie followed and began digging through her pack. The Anai stared at her. "What are you doing?"

"There's no point in letting him die when we went to all the trouble of keeping him alive." She pulled a small leather sack out of the bigger bag and went back over to the unconscious man.

Sophie knelt and examined him. There was a large gash in his head from the rock, but it wasn't bleeding much anymore. Most of the blood and vomit on his face had been burned away. He looked awful, but he was breathing steadily. From her perspective, it looked like Eolisti's blow did serious damage, but she'd only hit him hard enough to knock him out. He would have a colossal headache and a lump the size of an egg in the morning, but he would probably survive.

Opening the sack, she pulled out a small bottle of greenish paste, a roll of linen bandages, and a clean white cloth. Uncorking the bottle, she smeared the paste over the gash on the man's head.

"What's that?" Eolisti asked, leaning over Sophie.

"It's a paste made of ground yarrow leaves. It should stop the bleeding and keep his cuts from getting infected." She hesitated, then added, "I don't dare heal him with magic. The spells I used earlier could be tracked, but they were rather simple. Any hedge mage could cast them, given the chance." Seeing Eolisti's puzzled expression, she explained, "A hedge mage is an unsanctioned magic user, a highly illegal practice in Zo'rahn. So they have to avoid the attention of the magistrates." Turning back to concentrate on the man, she added, "It takes a lot more skill than they typically have to heal wounds. If I don't use anything complicated, they won't know it was a trained wizard." *Unless someone who knows me comes to investigate.* She thought with a chill down her spine.

She wrapped a bandage around his head and stood. "There. You can tie him up now." Eolisti raised an eyebrow, and Sophie's face suddenly felt hot. She looked away. "I'd rather not be hunted for murder, as well as running off, that's all."

Eolisti stared at her for an uncomfortably long time, then shrugged. "We use beeswax," Eolisti said offhandedly as she knelt to tie the man's hands and legs. "Elderberries work well too." Without prompting, the Anai launched into an explanation of plants and their medical properties as they worked, Sophie treating their wounds and Eolisti binding their hands and legs. Some of the plants that she listed Sophie didn't know, but assumed that they were just called by another name in Anaiian. She was surprised that Eolisti knew so much, but she must have traveled a lot being a Vendarii, and knowledge like that would be essential for someone who spent a lot of their time in the wilderness. Sophie only had basic medical knowledge. To be honest, she thought the study of medicinal herbs was a waste of time when she could heal with magic, but then again, she never thought she would be in a situation like this.

Sophie checked the other two men and bandaged them as best she could while Eolisti followed behind. Each had been hit on the head at some point, but they would all survive the night.

After the men were securely tied and gagged, Eolisti dragged them into a wide circle and then began gathering twigs and fallen branches. Sophie cleaned her hands on the cloth, put all her supplies away, then began folding their blankets neatly. She examined her blanket and sighed. It had a small hole burned into it and a large black stain from the torch. She would have to get a new one once they reached Bardov.

"Hey, since you've already magicked up the place, can you start the fire?"

Sophie waved her hand and focused. A spark flashed and caught on the kindling. Eolisti prodded at the fire while Sophie finished packing up their gear.

Eolisti left the dagger next to the fire then started examining the other weapons. "Garbage," she muttered. "I guess they weren't very good highwaymen, after all." After finishing with the campfire, Eolisti mounted her horse and led them back toward the tree line.

They found a spot under the thick brush where the campfire was still visible. Eolisti tied up the horses to a few trees a little way away, "just in case," and brought Sophie a couple of blankets, holding a long wooden bow in one hand.

"You go ahead and sleep. I'll keep watch over the campsite," she said, taking an arrow out of the quiver on her back and nocking it.

"Aren't you going to sleep?"

"I'll get a few hours in the morning and a few more when we stop at midday." Eolisti grinned. "Don't worry about me, Sophie. Just get some rest so we can get out of here quickly tomorrow."

Without further argument, Sophie laid the blankets down and made herself comfortable. Well, as comfortable as she could be on the hard ground. She knew she should do as Eolisti had said and get some sleep, but a tiny part of her had to admit that the attack had been... exciting. It wasn't just the danger of being hurt, killed, or captured. It was the thrill of letting out even just a trickle of the magic she'd been holding in since she'd left home. She even wondered to herself whether burning the bandit had just been an excuse to touch her power for a few more moments before sealing it away again. She tried to push those thoughts away, and calm herself with one of the exercises she'd learned long ago for clearing the mind, but she continued to shift and turn on her makeshift bed.

"What was your home like?"

The question was whispered so softly that she wondered for a moment whether she'd actually heard it or not. Sophie turned over to look at Eolisti and saw in the faint glow from their old campsite that the Anai was looking at her expectantly.

Sophie hesitated. Thus far she had kept key details about her life to herself. She realized it wasn't that she thought any of the Anai would betray her, but because part of her felt shame. Shame about what she had done before she decided to leave, and shame that by seeking refuge with them, she may have put them in more danger. She chided herself mentally for the latter. The Anai and Zo'rahni had always been enemies, and her presence didn't change that fact either way. Perhaps there wouldn't be any harm confiding in Eolisti.

"I lived in a big manor house in the middle of the capital city, Tanzar. My room faced west, and I had the best view of the sunset over the city every evening. There was a garden of sweet-smelling flowers below my room, and when the breeze was just right, it was like my room was filled with blossoms." As Sophie spoke, the memory of the sights and sensations of being back home flooded her.

"I actually loved going down to that garden when I first arrived in Tanzar. There were so many different kinds of flowers from all over the world, and each one had its own unique scent and beauty. I would spend most of my free time there until—" Sophie's throat closed at the memory, and emotions threatened to overwhelm her. She had not thought of that day in years. She swallowed hard but continued.

"I wasn't like the other Zo'rahni children. Most of the other apprentices wanted nothing to do with me at first. Some of them hated me and would go out of their way to make sure I knew I was unwelcome." She felt tears spring to her eyes, and her words became shakier. "About a year after I moved to Tanzar, a group of older apprentices found me in that garden and said the most horrible things about my father and mother." This time when she paused, she had to take a few deep breaths until she was able to go on.

"I told them they didn't know anything about me or my parents, and one of the boys shoved me into a bush with huge thorns." Sophie looked down at her palm and one of the nearly invisible scars she couldn't see in the darkness but knew was there. "I didn't go there alone anymore after that."

She closed her eyes and fell into silence as she realized that she'd strayed far from what she intended to share with the Anai. That was over half her lifetime ago. What had made her think of it, let alone talk about it now?

"People didn't like me much at home either," Eolisti said softly.

Sophie was somewhat surprised at the Anai's admission. Most of the time, she talked about the things she had heard about the world, or was asking questions about Zo'rahn, or how things worked. This was the most vulnerable thing Sophie had heard her say. Then she remembered how most of Eolisti's sorties ended, punishment. Wondering if the other woman would say more, Sophie waited in silence.

"You probably noticed how boring everyone is back in Elasariin. Most of them just want to stay cooped up, safe in our little forest, and do the same things the same way every day because *that's just how it is done*." Eolisti's voice took on a different tone as she mocked some nameless Anai, or, from the sound of it, *several* nameless Anai.

"I'm not like them. I want to see the world. I want to do more, to *be* more." Eolisti paused, seeming overwhelmed with emotions of her own. She had been getting louder as she talked, but when she spoke again, her voice was so low Sophie had to strain to hear.

"People don't like what they don't understand."

That simple statement resonated with Sophie. How much of the intolerance she had faced was because of that? It was a bit of a shock to realize that she and Eolisti had both experienced how that sort of ostracism felt.

"No, they don't," Sophie whispered back.

She was suddenly exhausted, and sleep was a welcome thought. She really was lucky to have Eolisti with her. Someone who knew what they were doing. And someone who understood something of what it was like to feel... *other*. Her eyelids grew heavy, and she wondered briefly who Zephan's contact had been. They must be important if the Anai trusted them. A spy, maybe? But for who?

Sophie closed her eyes, the questions that were running around her head fading until they were barely a whisper. Then, even that drifted away.

CHAPTER
TEN

After what felt like only seconds, Sophie was being shaken awake again. "Sophie, wake up," hissed a quiet voice in her ear. She blinked her eyes open slowly. Eolisti was leaning over her, sunlight giving her hair a golden glow. Was it already morning?

Sophie sat up and rubbed her eyes, yawning and looking around sleepily. They were still back in the trees and underbrush. Rays of bright sunlight filtered through the leaves and branches, and Sophie felt it warm spots on her face and arms. She was still so tired, but she must have slept for hours. "Is it time to leave?" she asked, stifling a yawn.

"Not quite," Eolisti said, tension in her voice. "There's someone at the camp."

At Eolisti's words, it all came flooding back. The fight the night before. Tying up the bandits to lure anyone else out. Sophie scrambled to her knees.

"Stay down!" Eolisti gasped and pulled Sophie back to the ground. "We're well hidden in the undergrowth, but they'll be able to spot your hair a mile away." Staying crouched, Eolisti moved forward, quietly pushing aside a branch in the bushes covering them. She motioned for Sophie to look.

The sun was low in the sky but very bright, reflecting off the rocks and making the ground sparkle with the morning dew. Sophie crawled over, looking through the gap that Eolisti had made. It took her a moment to spot the camp from the night before. She could see movement—three, no four people. The broader figures off to the side could only be horses. "They're leaning over the bandits, probably wondering what happened," Eolisti said, watching the figures. "There's a man in blue robes. The others are cutting the men free. Well, they're in no shape to fight, so why not?" she scoffed. "I think they are questioning them."

"Blue robes?" Sophie asked with a note of panic in her voice. Was it a magistrate? Or was it someone looking for her? Were they drawn to this spot by the magic she used, or did they just happen upon it? Would they be able to find her before the two women could sneak away? With blue robes, they could be from her family, but they also might not be. She had to be sure. "Can you see anything else about them, any distinguishing marks on the robes?"

Eolisti shook her head. "It's too far away to tell." There was more movement, and more figures rose from the ground. Eolisti squinted. "It looks like they are pulling the bandits to their feet, either they are still partially tied, or they are cowering from the robed person." She glanced over at Sophie, then gently put the branch back in place. "Time to go."

"Don't you need to sleep?"

A cocky smirk crossed Eolisti's face. "Anai don't need as much sleep as humans do. I'll get an hour or two when we stop at midday. Gather your blankets and get back to the horses. Stay low and make as little noise as possible. We'll travel in the trees today." She gazed back into the forest, searching. "They shouldn't be able to hear or see us from the road."

Sophie crouched low as she took a few steps back to where she'd been sleeping and gathered up her blanket, hands shaking, betraying her anxiety. Eolisti began spreading out leaves over where they'd rested. By the time the Anai had finished, Sophie could barely tell that they had been there at all. Eolisti gestured for her to follow, and they crept back to where the horses were tied. Sophie secured the blankets to the packhorse while the Anai saddled the other two.

There would be no way of hiding the presence of the horses since they had trampled the area and grazed on the grass. Eolisti caught Sophie's eyes, seeming to come to the same conclusion after gazing at their feet. She shrugged. "We'll go deeper into the trees. Hopefully, they won't want to wander too far into the forest. The road follows the tree line, and we can emerge in a day or so, once we get far enough away. We still have a few days to travel until we reach the pass, and I'd rather not double that time by having to navigate it through the forest." Eolisti helped Sophie onto her horse, then untied them from the tree and mounted her own. With a click of her tongue, she wheeled her horse around and headed back into the forest, away from the tree line.

The other two horses lurched forward and followed Eolisti's lead. Sophie looked back over her shoulder, watching the distant road for signs of the robed figure. Before long, she could barely see the sun peeking through the branches behind them. "This should be far enough," Eolisti muttered, pulling the harness to the left. They turned south again and continued their journey, hidden from sight beyond the forest.

Now and again, Sophie would see a flash of sunlight through the trunks and the yellowed grass of the Zo'rahni countryside, but it was too far away to make out anything happening beyond the trees. Multiple times, Sophie thought she heard the snapping of twigs behind them and whipped her head around, only to be greeted with the shady silence of the forest. Once, she even thought she heard voices but couldn't spot any movement around them. The Anai did not appear to hear these phantom noises, and after having her concerns dismissed for a second time, Sophie decided to keep these thoughts to herself. She must've been hearing things.

It was perpetual twilight in the forest. Sophie didn't know how long they had been riding, but it felt like hours before they stopped. As soon as Eolisti dismounted, she lay down on a small patch of grass and fell asleep while Sophie ate and tended the horses. She checked their hooves for rocks while eyeing them warily, gave them water, and let them graze on what little grass there was on the forest floor. Eolisti awoke a while later, scowled at the bread again, but ate, and then they were back on their horses and traveling through the woods.

They continued like that until nightfall, when the forest was black and seeing their footing was impossible. Sophie set up camp while Eolisti slept again and woke before Sophie lay down. She offered to stay up so that the Anai could sleep, but Eolisti just shook her head and laughed. "What are you going to do if someone comes for us? Scream? You're not supposed to use your magic, right? I'd rather put an arrow through someone's eye than wake up to a fight."

Disgruntled, Sophie laid out her blankets to sleep once again. She was beginning to feel useless, and the fact that Eolisti didn't trust her with the watch only added to her feeling of discontent. She knew that was unfair and that, between the two of them, Eolisti really was better suited to less rest, but being unable to use her magic was beginning to put her on edge, and she hated feeling like a burden. Once they were out of Zo'rahn and far from the Vasalii's spies, she would be able to use her magic again. He had no authority outside of Zo'rahn. Once they were in Omer, she would be able to show Eolisti what she could really do.

In the morning, Sophie packed their supplies and tended to the horses again while Eolisti took a brief nap. The day continued much like the previous one, stopping around midday for the Anai to sleep, then riding until nightfall. Eolisti set up her sleeping arrangements right after dismounting, only to wake a few hours later just as Sophie was lying down. Sophie didn't know how she was surviving on so little sleep. She estimated that the Anai was sleeping less than six hours a day, but still seemed bright and alert. She grumbled about food to Sophie, wishing for something warm to eat, but other than that seemed cheerful.

They emerged from the forest on the third day, following the same rest pattern as before and heading to the road. The road here was much more well-trodden than the western highway that Sophie had traveled when first leaving Tanzar. Farms were speckled across the countryside east of the road, and people could be seen tending to their fields in the distance. This far from Elasariin, there must not have been any issues with the Anai, and the people didn't fear living close to the forest.

Upon seeing the signs of increased civilization, Eolisti

began wearing a hood to cover her delicately pointed ears and advised Sophie to do the same, since most people would think she was a slave if they saw her complexion and hair.

Snow-capped mountains could be seen clearly ahead of them. When Sophie first entered the forest, they had been a gentle rise in the distance. Now they were stark against the early autumn sky. The forest was visibly thinning as the mountains encroached closer and closer to the road. The nearer they drew to the main highway running south of the capital, the more traveled the road was. People waved at them as they passed, and Zo'rahni children ran along with their horses for short distances. Eolisti said nothing to these people and only raised her hand in greeting, keeping her hood pulled low over her face at all times.

Two more days of travel, and the pair reached the southern highway. The hooves of the horses clopped on the paved stone thoroughfare, and they were able to ride more quickly than on the dirt road, regaining some of the time lost when traveling in the forest. Eolisti stared at the ground for a while before finally asking, "How did they do this?"

Still tired and sore from all the nights spent sleeping on the ground, it took Sophie a moment to register what the Anai had asked. Her eyes slid down to the precisely cut and placed stones below them as they moved steadily by.

"Magic," she said, then laughed, realizing how patronizing that sounded. "The road was designed and placed by masons and slaves, but for the road to stretch all the way to the mountains, there was a lot of magic involved in cutting, preparing, moving, and preserving the stone. This used to be the main trading route between Alkhazai, Omer, and Zo'rahn before seafaring craft allowed for much larger loads and easier travel. Roads were constructed to make the journey easier for traders as we received salt and precious metals from Alkhazai and cotton from Omer. This road cut off days of travel for merchants and was the main route for about three hundred years, but going up the mountain pass was time-consuming and dangerous for large caravans, so we turned to sailing. Now, this road is mostly used by citizens to reach the capital or by those needing to travel to Alkhazai or Omer who can't afford to travel by ship." She looked up and saw that Eolisti was looking at her over her shoulder with an expression of exasperation. Sophie's face heated and she looked over at the mountains. She must sound like a teacher lecturing a child. "That's just what I've read," she said quickly and fell silent again.

The Anai shook her head and faced forward again, riding on. Sophie caught a snicker from her, and she scolded herself. She wasn't a teacher giving a history lesson. Eolisti, whose people had been at war with the Zo'rahni multiple times over the past few centuries, wouldn't care why this road was built. She had just wanted to know how, that was all. No need for all the extra information. Sophie was just so tired that it was hard to think straight. If she could only sleep in a real bed, even for just one night...

"Hey, Sophie!"

Sophie jolted out of her thoughts and jumped so hard that she almost fell out of the saddle. Eolisti had stopped the horses and was turned in the saddle toward her, looking concerned. "I kept saying your name, but it didn't seem like you could hear me." Eolisti's green eyes flicked over her. "Are you all right? Your face is pale and looks like you're about to fall off your horse."

"Yes. I'm just tired," Sophie said, thinking about sleep again.

Eolisti's lips spread in a smile. "Me, too, but look." She pointed out in front of them. Sophie followed her outstretched arm and saw the road steepen, and the paving stones disappeared to be replaced by dark stone and gravel. Trees grew at either side for miles, thinning gradually until they became so sparse that they disappeared. The new road curved up and into the base of the mountains, snaking its way between them, like a stream flowing downhill. Tiny figures dotted the road, travelers making their way through the mountains. "Marik's Pass." Eolisti rubbed her hands together. "With a little luck, we'll reach Bardov tomorrow afternoon and have real food." Her eyes sparkled with mirth. "Do you think you can make it?"

Sophie was so relieved that she didn't know whether to laugh or cry, so she did a little of both. She was almost out of Zo'rahn. She was almost safe.

Sophie grinned through her fatigue. "Of course. Let's go."

CHAPTER

ELEVEN

Cold mountain air whipped through Sophie's hair, stinging her cheeks and forcing her to lean further into her horse's mane to shield herself. Its bite permeated the thick woolen cloak and clothes down to her flesh, making her shiver uncontrollably. She had never experienced a cold such as this, and all she could do was huddle in on herself as much as possible. Snow flew through the air, and the wind battered against bare brush and dead grass, blending in with the stone around them. Gone were the trees and their vibrant greens and golds. The land here was sharp and stark, contrasted by where white snow had gathered in corners and behind rocks. The sky above was a churning mass of dark gray clouds. There was a storm coming.

"We're almost there!" Eolisti shouted over her shoulder. Sophie could barely make out the words over the wind. "I can see smoke up ahead!"

They had been traveling up the mountain pass for two days. The air had steadily grown chiller after the first day, but Sophie had found it a pleasant change from the suffocating humidity of Zo'rahn. She had seen snowfall before, but in the capital, it would melt as soon as it touched the ground. Now, however, Sophie would have given almost anything to have the autumn warmth back and never see snow again.

She lifted her head and saw what Eolisti had moments before. The path turned around a corner ahead, but over the rocks, she could see dark smoke rising and then almost disappearing in the gray sky. They must be close then. Sophie let out a sigh of relief. They could get out of this cold before the storm hit.

Eolisti led them around the rocks and slowed as the path dipped down. The ground eventually evened out and created a valley nestled between two peaks. A short distance away stood a collection of stone and wood buildings that seemed to grow out of the frozen ground, lining the sides of the mountain. Their windows glowed with the light from within, and the smoke that they had seen earlier poured out of multiple chimneys. Just past the buildings and to the left, a steep path snaked up to a ledge that overlooked the village below, and Sophie could make out what appeared to be large stone buildings atop it. A few figures moved from building to building down in the valley, hurrying to get out of the cold.

More snow settled here than on the path, and the wind calmed somewhat as they descended into the valley, no doubt the worst of it being blocked by the mountains. Looking up, Sophie felt claustrophobic. The buildings were spread apart and there was room for expansion, but it felt as if the mountain might topple down on them. She thought briefly that it would be hard to live here with the mountain looming overhead.

Eolisti stopped and allowed Sophie to pull her mare up beside hers. She pointed to a two-story building close to the road. Wagon ruts and hoof prints led up to it and were lost in a multitude of traffic, making the snow dirty and muddy. People were going in and out the front door, and what could be a stable stood next to it. "Let's go there," she said, her breath puffing out in a white cloud. Her nose and cheeks were red. "I think that's an inn."

"I thought we were headed to the monastery," Sophie said. Eolisti had told her their destination the day before and, at that moment, Sophie felt they should just get the journey over with. She guessed that the monastery to Samar, the god of compassion and mercy, was the building on the cliff. It was impossible to see staring up at the rocks from the bottom of the valley, but the path leading up to it was still within view. If they stopped at the inn, Sophie wasn't sure that she would want to leave.

Eolisti scoffed. "Yes, but it's not the right time. We have to wait until later."

"Why?" Sophie asked, baffled.

Eolisti rolled her eyes. "There is a certain way that we have to do this. You can't just barge into a monastery while they are praying or whatever. We need to observe proper etiquette, or do you want to make all those monks upset?"

"No, of course not," Sophie said sheepishly. She didn't want to inconvenience them with her presence more than she already would. They were already doing so much to help her, and she didn't want to be rude.

"Then what are you complaining about?" The Anai pressed her heels into the sides of her mount and clicked her tongue. The animal leaped forward and trotted down to the village inn. "Come on! I'm freezing!" Eolisti called back to Sophie.

Sophie sighed. Eolisti knew what she was doing, right? Perhaps it was the cold, but she was feeling rather disgruntled with the whole affair. It just didn't sit right with her. She took a deep breath and reinforced her resolve. This had been her choice, but two weeks of hard travel had chipped away at her conviction. Maybe she would feel better once there was hot food in her belly. Sophie clicked her tongue and pressed her heels into her mare's sides, just as Eolisti had done. The horse moved to follow the other, the packhorse trailing behind.

As they approached the inn, a boy a little younger than Sophie, with light brown hair and eyes, greeted them. He was in the middle of leading another horse into the stables. Eolisti beckoned him to her and questioned him about the inn, asking what kind of food they were serving that day and how many people were inside. In the end, she gave him a small gemstone to feed and care for the horses while they went inside. The boy's eyes lit up as she passed him the stone, and he nodded eagerly, moving to help Sophie down from her mount. The Anai chuckled to herself and jumped down as he helped the mage.

As the doors to the inn swung inward, a burst of warm air hit Sophie in the face, making her smile despite herself. The smell of fresh bread filled her nose as she stepped inside, mouth-watering. The outside of the inn had been a mixture of stone and wood. On the inside, the walls were lined with dark, polished oak. The tavern was dim, lit only by oil lamps hanging from the walls and the fire in the hearth, but the atmosphere was lively.

Most of the fourteen round tables were filled with a variety of people with skin and hair of every color. Some were dressed like travelers and merchants, but other people looked like they might be farmers or live in the village. Several people were standing in groups closer to the fireplace with large mugs in hand, as though they were just in for a few moments to warm themselves before going back out to brave the storm. A few people glanced at them when they entered the tavern, then promptly went back to their own conversations. All kinds of people passed through Bardov, but she was so used to being stared at that Sophie was still surprised that they weren't even given a second glance. There were a few tables open, but if they did not seat themselves soon, there would be none.

Eolisti seemed to have the same thought and strode across the room, snatching up an empty table close to the fire. Sophie followed, unfastening the clasp of her cloak and hanging it over the back of a wooden chair before sitting down. She closed her eyes and leaned back, letting the heat from the fire wash over her and thaw her limbs. Her skin prickled as it adjusted to the difference in temperature. It was uncomfortable, but a welcome change from the stinging cold of the pass. Eolisti said something about getting food and Sophie nodded dully, only half hearing her words. A chair scraped on the floor and the general murmur of the gathered crowd seemed to grow distant as the prickling of her skin gave way to a tingling warmth.

Moments later, the chair scraped on the floor again, and the table shook slightly as something was placed on it. Was Eolisti back with food already? Sophie was having trouble telling how much time had passed. "When are we going up to the monastery? It's going to be today, right?" she asked, still resting her eyes.

"Excuse me?" said a deep, male voice.

Sophie jumped and nearly fell out of the chair, hitting

her knees on the underside of the table painfully. She inhaled sharply and looked up at a man that she had never seen before seated across the table, a bowl of steaming soup in front of him.

"Sorry," he said, and his mouth twitched. Sophie got a distinct impression that he was trying not to smile. "I would have asked to sit, but it looked like you were sleeping." He was an older man with dark eyes and hair streaked with gray. His clothes were leather lined with brown fur, and an eight-pointed star adorned the chest.

"Who—"

"Who are you?" said Eolisti in a cold voice as she came up behind Sophie, making her jump again. She held two bowls in her hands and a loaf of bread balanced precariously in the crook of her elbow. With a soft thump, she set down a bowl, brimming with the same steaming hot soup that the stranger had, in front of Sophie. The Anai narrowed her eyes at him dangerously. Sophie had seen that look before when the Anai had been about to draw her blade. "What do you want?"

"Peace," he said, holding both hands up to show he was unarmed, "and a chair by the fire to eat in. I find the cold far more unwelcome with age and need a place to thaw." The lines at the corners of his eyes crinkled as he smiled. He put his hands down and picked up the spoon sitting next to his bowl. "You two must not be from around here. My name is Joel. I work for the monks at the monastery up on the cliff."

Eolisti's suspicious expression melted away, and she sat down in the empty chair next to Sophie, placing the other bowl and the bread on the table in front of her. "Really?" she asked, tearing off a piece of bread and dipping it in her soup. "Are you heading back there soon?"

A bemused expression crossed Joel's face. "Yes... I've

finished my business in town and will be heading back up there after I eat. I'd rather not get caught in the storm, to be honest. It looks like it's going to be a rough one." He stuffed a spoonful into his mouth and swallowed. "Why are you not eating, girl?" he said, pointing the spoon at Sophie. "It's not bad."

"Oh, uh..." She was going to say that she wasn't hungry, but looking down at the bowl made her stomach rumble. She'd never seen a dish like this before, meat and vegetables swimming in a thick brown broth. It smelled of garlic and thyme. Copying Eolisti, she tore off a piece of bread that was warm to the touch and let it soak up the liquid before taking a bite. She was surprised at the pleasant flavor of the dish and eagerly took another bite.

"We'll accompany you then," Eolisti announced. "We were going to go to the monastery after we finished our meal as well."

"We were?" Sophie asked, another piece of bread halfway to her mouth.

"Yes," she replied with a hint of irritation in her voice and glanced at Sophie. "It'll be late enough. My name is Eolisti," she said to Joel. "And this is Sophie. We're expected there."

"Really?" Joel's eyebrows rose as he surveyed the two women. Sophie felt heat creeping up her neck and continued eating her soup in earnest. She wasn't sure what Eolisti was trying to do, but she didn't want to give something away. Besides, the soup was quite good. "The monks don't usually have overnight guests. Why are you headed there?" he asked.

"Wouldn't you like to know?" Eolisti said nonchalantly and raised the bowl to her mouth, slurping down the rest of the broth. When she finished, she put the bowl back on the table and wiped at her mouth with her forearm. "We don't know you. Our business is our own." The glare she gave was colder than the wind outside.

"All right, all right," he said with a grin. "I was just asking. A bit touchy, aren't you? You'll need to come up with a better cover story if you want people not to ask questions. You're in trouble, aren't you?" Sophie choked on her food, but Eolisti continued to glare at him. Joel chuckled. "Even a fool could figure out that there is more to the two of you than meets the eye." He placed his spoon on the table and crossed his arms over his chest, his eyes searching their faces. "Neither of you is from around here for one. We don't see a lot of Anai or girls with red hair passing through. Most people who travel this way are small-time traders that don't have enough money to go by sea or those who are truly desperate. Sometimes escaped slaves, sometimes poor folk looking for something better in another country."

He nodded at Eolisti. "Your armor is of good quality and that scabbard hanging off your chair is lacquered wood chased with silver. That weapon could feed this whole town for a week if anyone here could afford to purchase it. And you"—he nodded at Sophie—"have a finely made wool cloak with golden clasps and silk clothing. Neither of you looks particularly downtrodden, and you certainly aren't merchants. Someone might start to wonder why girls such as yourselves are traveling alone through the mountains."

"Stop calling us girls," Eolisti growled.

Joel barked out a laugh, causing some of the other patrons in the room to glance their way. "You're feisty. I like that. My sister always hated being called 'girl' when she was your age, too." He pushed out his chair and stood. "I'd be happy to take you up to the monastery if you're ready. Best to get there quickly, before dark sets in."

There were still some bits of meat and broth at the bottom of Sophie's bowl, but she put her spoon down sadly. The last thing she wanted to do was go back outside into the cold and snow. She sighed and, following Eolisti's lead, stood to re-fasten her cloak about her shoulders. The sooner they reached the monastery, she told herself, the sooner she could have a nice, hot bath.

Chill air slapped her in the face as she stepped out of the tavern's front door, making her gasp. It was darker than it had been before. The sky was a deep purple, and the storm clouds from earlier frothed even more menacingly. It must have been close to nightfall, but with the thick cloud cover, it was difficult to tell if the sun had already set or not. Everything was darker than it should have been, and the snow seemed to be drifting down much faster than before. Had they really been in the tavern that long?

"Hey, come on!" Eolisti called back to her, shaking Sophie from her thoughts. They trudged out through the snow, following Joel to the stables. The boy who'd taken their horses sat on a stool just inside the open door. A lamp sat next to him, and he was huddled under a blanket. Catching sight of them, he jumped up, looking confused.

"Dinn," Joel greeted the boy, smiling genially. "Can you fetch my horse and the ones that belong to these two ladies." He looked over at them and raised an eyebrow. "Unless you traveled on foot up the mountain."

Eolisti scoffed. "Of course not." The stable boy, Dinn, had already run off to fetch their steeds.

They waited outside for Dinn to return. After a few minutes, he came back with their riding horses, saddled, and ready to go. As Eolisti helped Sophie onto the back of her mare, the boy ran off again, this time returning with two more animals. One was their supply horse, the other a dusky brown stallion with a black mane and full saddle-bags. Joel took the stallion's reins from Dinn and flicked him a coin. He snatched the coin from the air and quickly bowed to Joel, who nodded back. Dinn ran off into the stables again, most likely to get out of the cold, Sophie thought, and Joel pulled himself up onto his saddle. "Shall we?"

Eolisti tied the reins of the supply horse to the back of Sophie's saddle, then mounted her own. They made their way through town and to the path that led up to the monastery. Sheltered as the path was by the mountain, the cold wind that had started to pick up was still throwing snow into their faces as they rode. Sophie gave up trying to pull the hood of her cloak over her ears, it just kept getting blown off. Navigating the road with the heavy snowfall was treacherous, but Joel seemed to instinctively know where he was going. A lamp was clipped to the front of his stallion's harness, and the light bobbed as the horse moved, illuminating the ground ahead of them. They rode slowly, Joel leading them around icy patches hidden by the snow.

It was a relief when they finally started up the path that climbed the cliff. It was steep, but wide and mostly shielded by the mountain. The wind blew the snow out into the valley, so there was little on the ground, and the wind quieted somewhat, not howling as loudly as when Sophie and Eolisti had been climbing up the mountain pass.

Eolisti pulled up beside Joel, and Sophie trailed behind them. "So, this monastery," Eolisti began, her voice echoing off the rocks around them. "it's full of monks, right? What are they like? Are they all humans? We're not in Zo'rahn anymore right, so what do they look like? Is it interesting to work for them?"

Despite her sleep deprived state, a thought occurred to Sophie while Joel seemed taken aback by Eolisti's barrage of questions. What she was asking didn't make sense to her. It was almost as if...

"You've never been here before, have you?" she blurted out, unable to keep the accusation out of her voice.

Eolisti looked over her shoulder at Sophie, her expression unreadable. "I never said I had."

"But I thought you'd done this before!"

She looked sideways at Joel. "Not this exact trip," the Anai admitted. "But I knew what I was doing. What's the big deal? We're here, aren't we?"

Sophie felt her face growing hot. Maybe it was because she was exhausted, but she was furious with the Anai for leading her to believe she had done this before. She knew she should be grateful. She'd arrived in one piece after all, but something about Eolisti's omission deeply wounded her. Eolisti had deceived her—*lied* to her. She glowered at the Anai until Eolisti turned back around and coughed.

Silence stretched out between the three of them and continued for some time. Eventually, Joel cleared his throat. Sophie, who had been watching the ground pass beneath her as she stewed, looked up. The large building that she had seen coming into the valley stretched out before her, windows lit from within and glittering in the night. It loomed over them, taller and more imposing than she could have imagined from the ground below them.

"Welcome to Ta'Shela," Joel said, smiling back at her and winking. "We've been waiting for you."

Torches bobbed as they grew closer and closer. She could see people carrying them and a door to the building opened, casting a long thin line of yellow light across the snow.

Sophie felt as if a large weight was being lifted off her chest. Despite what she'd been through and all she'd left behind, the sight of the monastery stirred something inside her. For the first time since she left home, she finally felt like she was safe.

TWELVE

The buildings that comprised Ta'Shela towered above Sophie. Looking up, she could barely make out the vague, dark shapes fading into the oncoming storm. The people carrying lights came closer, the flames flickering so hard in the wind that they threatened to go out. The storm buffeted them on the cliff much harder than it had in the village below, making their cloaks whip about wildly.

Joel brought the procession to a halt as they neared the largest structure. The men and women carrying torches rushed forward, huddled in on themselves to protect their bodies from the cold. Once they were closer, Sophie could see that they were dressed in thick, brown robes tied with rope at their waists. Were these the monks?

One man held his hand out to her, clearly intending to help her off her horse. She glanced over at Eolisti, who was waving away another trying to help her. The Anai scowled at him as she swung herself down from the saddle with ease. Not being as nimble as the Anai, Sophie took the offered hand and stepped down into the snow. Her feet sunk in a few inches before hitting the firm ground underneath.

The man nodded and stepped aside, gesturing toward the large wooden doors still standing open at the front of the building. Eolisti took the lead, and Sophie followed behind her. She glanced over her shoulder at their horses. The men and women were leading their horses off a different way, to another building that she was unable to make out in the dark and snow.

"Don't worry," Joel said from her other side, making her jump. "They'll take care of your horses and have your things brought inside."

As Sophie stepped into the building, she noticed that the doors were intricately carved with the image of the mountains surrounding Ta'Shela and the same eight-pointed star that adorned Joel's garments. The doors opened into a large foyer, dimly lit by what looked like hundreds of candles. Mosaic tiles of blue and gold covered the floors all the way to the altar across the room, glittering in the candlelight. The air inside was cool and damp, though it felt warm against her skin after the chill of the wind outside, smelling strongly of incense with a faint musty undertone. Murals lined the walls from the floor to the high ceilings, depicting the goddess Samar as a beautiful woman with long black hair, tending to those in need.

The entire effect was breathtaking at first glance, but upon closer inspection, Sophie could see that the monastery was aging faster than the monks could keep up with. The floors were clean, but the gloss on the tiles was worn down in the middle from years of foot traffic. The wooden pews were in need of new cushions. Peeling paint had been restored by an inexpert hand and was flaking off the edges of the murals. The color seemed muted, a pale shadow of the life they once contained.

An ebony skinned man with coarse, short-cropped hair and a kind face waited for them near the altar, smiling pleasantly as they approached. He was dressed in vibrant emerald-green robes with a gold sash tied around his waist. "Welcome," he said with a bow of his dark head. "I expect you've had a long journey. My name is Tamrat, and I am the Abbot of Ta'Shela." He looked at Joel. "Are these the young women that Shaman Vyraeli wrote about?"

"I believe so, Abbot."

Tamrat nodded and looked back at Sophie and Eolisti, still smiling. "Then I apologize for the necessity, but I will need some sort of proof that you are who you appear to be."

Sighing, Eolisti dug into a pouch on her belt and pulled out a smooth stone that she held out to Tamrat. Atop the flat surface was a willow tree carved into the stone and inlaid with gold.

The Abbot bowed his head to her. "Thank you, Vendarii. I'm sure that you understand that we cannot be too careful."

"Yeah, yeah," she said, stretching her arms above her head, the stone still gripped in her hand, and yawned. "Dangerous and whatever. Look, it's been a really long day, and we haven't had proper sleep in over a week. So, nice to meet you and all, but I'm ready to do some relaxing. A bath would be nice, too. Have you got running water all the way up here?" She looked around at the walls and floors and sighed. "Hmm, I guess not."

The Abbot looked slightly taken aback but quickly recovered. "Of course," he said, the look of calm serenity back on his face. "Joel, please show them to the room we have prepared. I will have Sister Sanea bring some hot water for you both to wash." His eyes met Eolisti's. "Vendarii, thank you for your service. There will be much to discuss in the morning." Tamrat turned toward Sophie and took a step to approach her. She resisted the urge to step back. She didn't want to be rude. "Please rest well. If there is anything you require, don't hesitate to ask."

The Abbot bowed his head, and Joel bowed in return. "Follow me," he said as he passed Sophie and Eolisti, walking toward a door to the right of the altar. The Anai followed Joel without a word to Tamrat, looking around with interest. Sophie bowed her head respectfully to the Abbot and followed after them. She looked over her shoulder to see him smiling at her with that same peaceful look on his face as he closed the door behind her.

They found themselves in a long hallway lit with lamps attached to brackets on the walls. Light flickered as they passed. *Oil lamps*, Sophie noted. The smell of incense wasn't as strong here, and the air was damp and earthy. The same dark stone that was on the outside of the building continued inside, and a multitude of doors lined the walls on either side. As they walked, they passed two more intersecting halls. Sophie tried to look down them. One appeared to lead into a large room, and the other turned a corner. They turned to the left only to be led down another hallway.

Eolisti sighed. "More walking. Just what I wanted to do." She sounded exasperated. "Where the hell are we going?"

"Your room is at the end of this hall." Joel looked at her and smiled apologetically. "It's not too far. It just seems like a long way."

When they finally reached the end of the hallway, there was a plain wooden door that Joel opened for them. Eolisti watched him suspiciously as she entered the room, Sophie following close behind. She pulled up short, joining Eolisti in staring around at their lodgings.

She had expected clean but well-worn furniture and a simple sleeping arrangement. What was in front of them was a lavish bedchamber, easily a quarter the size of the entrance hall they had just left, though not nearly as tall. Plush rugs were laid across the stone floor and curtains in oranges and golds lined the walls, hiding the cold stone. Oil lamps glittered from brackets suspended from the ceiling, filling the room with a pleasant glow that accentuated the colors. On one side of the room, a folding screen painted with gold flowers stood to give privacy for bathing and privy use. On the other side was a sitting area with a small bookshelf and stuffed leather lounge chairs. A four-poster bed, large enough for a family, was in the center of the room, with a tall wardrobe against the wall behind it. Sophie's bag and Eolisti's pack sat on the floor against the wardrobe.

The carpets under her feet were soft and the room felt warm and comfortable. It was hard to believe they were still in the monastery.

Eolisti whistled. "Is this where we're staying?" she said with a tone of excitement. "This room is bigger than my house."

Joel chuckled. "The monks believe in making guests as comfortable as possible." He lowered his voice conspiratorially. "I think they just want to impress people. They don't really get to indulge in anything, so they tend to make a big deal when they have visitors."

"I'm not complaining," Eolisti said approvingly. She moved around the room, inspecting every piece of furniture.

"Take this," Joel said to Sophie as Eolisti plopped onto the bed. He handed her a small silver bell. "If you ring this outside your door, one of the initiates will come to see to your needs. Someone will be close by all night."

Sophie took the bell and inspected it. The little piece of metal fit into the palm of her hand. Would someone really be able to hear this?

"Sister Sanea will be by soon with some hot water and snacks to hold you over until morning." He pointed at the folding screen. "There's a copper tub behind that screen. If you give her your clothes, she'll have them laundered for you."

"Thank you," Sophie said, as he bowed to her and left the room.

"I could get used to this," Eolisti said from her position on the bed. She propped herself up on one elbow and laughed. "Beats sleeping out on the mountain."

Sophie felt herself getting caught up in Eolisti's sense of awe before she was abruptly reminded of the Anai's deception. With a glare at her companion's back, she strode to the sitting area and sat down on one of the lounge chairs, saying nothing.

"Are you still upset?" When Sophie didn't answer, Eolisti sighed. "Look, I never said I'd been here before, but I still got us here safely. It's not like I don't know what I'm doing."

"You didn't have to trick me. You could have been honest from the beginning." She turned in her chair to face the Anai. "I was scared out of my mind, and you took advantage of that."

"You think you would have been less scared if you'd known? You think Taenaran would have done a better job than I did?"

Wasn't that who Vyraeli originally said was taking her? Sophie remembered the Anai's strange behavior on the day they left Elasariin, and a suspicion struck her. "You were never supposed to be my Vendarii, were you?" she demanded.

"Even if I wasn't, and I'm not saying that's what happened, I should have been!" the Anai said furiously, a flush creeping up her neck. "I got you here in one piece, and we barely ran into any trouble, just a couple of bandits. Haven't I proven that I'm good enough to be a Vendarii?"

Sophie raised her eyebrows. "Yes, you have, but that's *not* the point, Eolisti!"

"Then what *is* the point?" She blew a strand of hair out of her face and glowered at Sophie. "What's the big deal?" she huffed.

Sophie felt her anger rise. "Do you take anything seriously?" she hissed. "It may not seem like it, but the people who are chasing me are dangerous. Yes, you are a great warrior, but you apparently know nothing about wizards."

"You sound just like my mother. I know what I'm capable of. I'm ready to be a Vendarii. Why do I have to prove myself to everyone?" Eolisti sat up and folded her arms across her chest. She looked on the verge of tears.

"You never had to prove yourself to me! I trusted you! I had no choice but to trust you!" Sophie was shouting now, and her last words hung in the silence that followed. Both women glared at each other until Eolisti flung herself on the bed again, arms still crossed.

Sophie wanted to say more, about how her actions could have jeopardized her escape. She couldn't quite forgive the Anai, but reflecting on Eolisti's words, part of her could understand why Eolisti had acted as she had. She suspected that Eolisti had been trying to be a Vendarii for some time, but that she hadn't been given the chance. She wanted to prove to her people that she could be useful. That was a feeling Sophie was all too familiar with.

But she felt betrayed, misled by someone who she was beginning to think of as a friend.

Sophie looked away and plucked a book off the bookcase. *Omeran Folklore.* "I trust you. Please don't make me regret that."

The two women sat in tense silence for what seemed like hours until finally, Sister Sanea knocked on their door. She was a stern-looking woman, older, with her dark hair tied back in a bun. She wore the same green robes as the Abbot, though without the golden sash, and pushed a large cart into the room filled with steaming buckets of water and a tray of palm-sized pastries. They helped her pull the cart over to the copper tub and fill it with hot water.

Sophie and Eolisti took turns bathing, then gave their dirty laundry to Sanea. Sophie still had some clean clothes from when she'd stayed with the Anai and pulled on a light linen dress while Eolisti donned a long tunic to sleep in.

After Sanea left, the Anai crawled into the bed and mumbled "Goodnight." Within minutes, she was already sound asleep.

Sophie opened the book again, but her eyes couldn't focus on the words. She was tired but restless. There were so many thoughts and emotions running around in her head. If she lay down to sleep, she knew she would toss and turn all night.

She was relieved that she was finally out of Zo'rahn. A little of the urgency that had driven her this far was eased. Zephan's plan had worked. She wondered if he was all right and wished there were some way she could let him know that she was safe too.

Am I really safe though? She felt a pang of anxiety as darker thoughts raced through her mind. *Where do I go from here? It can't be as simple as this, can it?*

The monks had taken her in almost without question, much as the Anai had. Oh, they had been curious, but she had never felt like Vyraeli or even Eolisti's help was conditional. Distantly, she knew that she was still angry with Eolisti, but in that moment she found herself incapable of holding on to that anger and felt only gratitude toward everyone who had helped her get this far.

That cycle of emotions replayed itself several times before she shook herself free. She needed to do something to take her mind off everything that had happened over the last few weeks. She looked at the bell that she had set on the bookcase. It would be rude to disturb the monks so late at night and it wasn't as if she actually needed something.

Neither Joel nor the Abbot said that they couldn't leave their room. Those murals in the front hall were fascinating, and Sophie wished she could have examined them more closely. This place seemed safe enough, and exploring the monastery might help to clear her mind. She'd been with Eolisti every waking moment for almost two weeks. Perhaps she just needed some time to herself. Making up her mind, Sophie closed the book and set it on the chair as she rose. It wouldn't hurt to look around, just for a little while.

Quietly, she slipped on a pair of sandals, put her cloak around her shoulders, and crept to the door, pulling it open slowly. It must have been late, but the lanterns lining the hall were still lit. Were they kept that way all the time? She closed the door softly behind her and began to walk down the hall.

This must be where the initiates sleep, she thought,

looking at the doors on either side of the hall. That would explain how they would be able to hear if she rang the small bell.

When Sophie turned the first corner, she heard faint singing echoing in the hallway. Was there a service happening even in this storm? She couldn't imagine that anyone would have made the trip up the cliffside with the weather as it was. As she walked down the corridor, the singing gradually grew louder. When she reached the first intersection, she turned and tried to follow the sound, but ended up at another intersection and went left this time. She walked for a while, turning corners in the direction she thought the singing was coming from. Just as she began to fear that she might not be able to find her way back, it stopped.

Sophie paused, listening to see if whoever was singing would start again, but the monastery remained quiet. Frowning, she continued forward. It had been so close. Maybe if she kept going, she would still be able to find the source. Around the next corner, there was an open archway. Light flickered from inside, brighter than the light in the halls. Sophie walked through the arch, looking around at the room within.

It was almost like a miniature version of the entrance hall, but without the murals. Rows of benches wide enough to seat four or five people lined the aisle on both sides. A small altar stood at the back of the room with hundreds of candles burning on holders. Behind that stood another statue of the goddess Samar, her arms outstretched as if waiting to embrace those seeking her aid. A long shadow was cast behind the figure, climbing up the wall and towering over the room like a silent guardian.

Sophie almost didn't notice the man kneeling in front of

the altar, obscured by the front row of benches. Immediately, she could tell he wasn't a monk, or at least was different from the ones she'd seen. He wore a cloak, which she hadn't seen any other monks wearing. It was such a deep shade of blue that it looked almost black in the candlelight. As she drew up beside him, she could see his hands clasped in front of him, holding red-lacquered prayer beads. The hood of his cloak was pulled so low that all that was visible of his face was the tip of his nose, his mouth, and his chin. His skin was a golden bronze color, slightly darker than that of typical Omerans and Zo'rahni. He could have been from Alkhazai, though it was difficult to tell without being able to see his entire face.

He made no sign that he'd noticed her as she stepped up beside him.

She sensed something strange about him. It didn't feel like magic, which she perceived as a tingling sensation at the back of her neck. This felt, no *tasted*, vaguely of metal. However, as she turned her attention toward it more fully, the aura abated to the point that she wondered if she had imagined it.

Not wanting to be rude and openly stare at the man, Sophie tore her eyes off him to examine the statue of Samar. It was of excellent craftsmanship. As her eyes traveled down the statue, she noticed that unlike in the entrance hall, though also well kept, it was not quite as lovingly cleaned. Wax pooled at the bottoms of the candles, threatening to overflow onto the altar. There was dust in between Samar's marble toes and a few cobwebs in the corners of the ceiling. This room must have been built for the monks when they needed a quiet place to pray. A place where outsiders didn't typically venture.

"You don't belong here," the man said softly, making

Sophie jump. When she looked over at him, his head was slightly turned toward her, face still obscured by the hood. His voice was deep and smooth, like the rumble of thunder. His tone was not unfriendly, but neither was it warm.

"I'm not a monk if that's what you mean," she said, taking a deep breath to try to slow her racing heart. Sophie didn't know anything about this man, and she didn't know if he knew about her. It was best not to give him any information about herself. For all she knew, he might be a villager who couldn't get home before the storm. "Just a traveler passing through."

"A traveler," he repeated, turning back to face the statue, hands still held in prayer.

"Are you a monk?" Sophie asked him, though she was almost certain she already knew the answer.

"No."

She waited for him to say more, but the man remained silent. "Are you just passing through Bardov as well then?" she asked.

For the briefest second, Sophie thought she saw a hint of a smile. "You could say that." Again, she waited for him to go on but was met only with silence.

She shifted awkwardly. "Well, I'm sorry I bothered you," she said quickly, feeling distinctly uncomfortable. Turning to leave the way she'd come, Sophie bid a good evening to the man and walked back down the aisle. She paused at the archway and looked down the hall. Which way would take her back to the room? If she could only find the front hall, she thought she remembered the way back from there. Sophie looked over her shoulder at the man, still in the same position as before, and took a few steps toward him. Maybe she could ask him for directions...

"No, no," Sophie mumbled to herself, growling in frustration and heading back out the arched entry and into the corridor. He was busy praying, and it was her own fault for getting lost. She didn't want to bother him further. Sophie walked back down the hall and turned the corner in the direction she thought she'd come down.

After a few minutes, she turned another corner and came to a three-way intersection. She looked down both corridors, which looked exactly the same as all the others she had been through, and sighed. *Great*, she thought. She was definitely lost. If Eolisti found out about this, the Anai would never let her hear the end of it. She hadn't run into any monks wandering the halls from whom she could ask directions. They were probably sleeping or maybe having a late service. She had no idea what time it was. It couldn't have been that late, could it?

Deciding that standing there until morning wouldn't help, Sophie went down the hallway to the right. She thought about knocking on one of the doors to ask for help, but if the monks really were sleeping, that would be incredibly impolite. *Sorry, I was wandering corridors in the middle of the night. Can you show me back to my room?* They were already doing so much for her, she could at least be a courteous guest.

And *why* were they doing all this for her? Did Zephan have ties to these monks? How did he even know to contact the Anai? They didn't seem to like Zo'rahni wizards very much. Sophie hadn't considered it before when she'd been running from her master, but now that she wasn't spending every waking moment terrified she'd be caught, she couldn't help but wonder how Zephan, who was barely ranked in the wizard hierarchy, had orchestrated all this. Perhaps she would ask Tamrat when next they spoke. She hoped that Zephan had not gone in over his head to make this happen.

Sophie was so absorbed in her thoughts that she didn't notice that the corridor ended until she almost ran into the wall. She jumped back, nearly tripping over the hem of her dress. This was definitely not the way she'd come earlier. She sighed inwardly. Going out and exploring the monastery had been a terrible idea. Maybe she should just knock on one of the doors and hope they didn't take offense. Sophie whipped around to march back down the hall but stopped short. Standing in front of her was the man from the prayer room.

Shadows danced across the lower part of his face, making him seem much more ominous than when he'd been kneeling in front of the statue. He was at least a head taller than she was, and the hood of his cloak was still pulled so low that Sophie couldn't see his eyes. Under the cloak, he wore what appeared to be a half robe in a similar style as the monks, only dark red instead of green and tied at the waist with a gold sash, much like the one Tamrat wore. The sleeves were fitted closely, and his forearms were wrapped with cloth strips up to his elbows. Sophie had never seen anything quite like it. She took an involuntary step back, putting her back up against the wall. Had he followed her?

"Come," he said and turned to walk back the other way.

"Why?" Sophie stayed where she was. She didn't know what this man wanted, but it seemed foolish to just go off with him.

He paused when she didn't move and said, "I'll take you back to your room."

She felt the tension leave her shoulders. Relief colored her voice. "How...?" She shook her head. It must have been obvious that she was lost. He'd probably seen her wandering the halls aimlessly. "Thank you." Stepping away from the wall, Sophie followed after him.

Apparently, she had been more lost than she thought she was. The man took her down corridors that she didn't remember. She wasn't sure if this was the way she had come or if this was another way to get back. He didn't speak and Sophie didn't either. She was embarrassed that she had disturbed his prayers, and now he was showing her back to her room when she had been too timid to ask for directions.

After a few turns in what seemed like only a few minutes, she was standing in front of the plain wooden door at the end of the hall. Sophie sighed in relief as the man stepped aside to allow her to open the door. She turned back to him and smiled. "Thank you," she said again. "I probably would have been lost all night."

The stranger nodded and began walking the other way. Just as she was about to close the door behind her the man murmured, just loudly enough for her to hear, "You should be careful who you trust. Not everyone is what they seem."

CHAPTER

THIRTEEN

It was difficult for Sophie to fall asleep that night. She lay awake, staring at the ceiling for hours thinking about the mysterious man she had met and the ominous warning he'd delivered. When she finally did manage to sleep, her dreams were filled with images of blue-robed figures chasing after her, wearing cloaks with hoods pulled low.

Several sharp knocks startled her from her dreams, and she watched sleepily as Eolisti answered the door. The Anai talked softly with someone outside for a moment, then held the door open for a young man in brown robes, pushing a cart into the room.

Sophie yawned and forced herself to sit up. She felt more tired than she had when she'd lay down the previous night. Or had it been early this morning? Either way, she was sore and didn't feel rested at all. She briefly contemplated lying back down and sleeping for a few more hours, then caught the smell of freshly cooked food. Rubbing the sleep out of her eyes, she focused on the newcomer.

The man in the brown robe, so young he must have

been an initiate, took a tray off the cart and set it on the low table beside the lounge chairs, along with a pitcher of water and two glasses. The tray was full of delicious-smelling food. Rice, fried bread, fruit, eggs, and what looked like pork in little bowls and plates. Sophie's stomach rumbled just looking at the food. The initiate smiled at her and bowed his head briefly, then took a small bundle off the cart and set it on one of the chairs. He wished her a good morning that she barely registered and wheeled the cart back out the door.

Eolisti closed the door, then walked over to the chairs and picked up the bundle. "Oh, just our laundry." She set it aside and sat down in one of the chairs, grabbing a piece of fried bread and sniffing it. Sophie slid out of bed and stretched. The Anai watched her out of the corner of her eye. "Are you still mad at me?" she asked tentatively.

Sophie stared at the Anai, willing her brain into motion. With everything that happened with the stranger the night before and Sophie's nightmare-riddled sleep, she had almost forgotten that she had even been upset. The feeling of hurt felt distant now. She wasn't mad anymore, but she didn't think she could completely trust Eolisti, not yet anyway.

"No," she said. "Not really." Sophie sat down in the chair next to the Anai and took a small plate off the tray. Not sure where to start, she took some of everything. "What is this?" she asked, holding up the flakey fried bread.

"No idea, but it's good," Eolisti said, taking another bite. Then she went for the fruit. "The guy that brought this said that the Abbot would meet with us after the midday meal and that we should relax until then." She glanced at Sophie, a sly smile creeping across her face. "I think we should go explore."

At her words, Sophie almost choked on some rice. If Eolisti only knew about her adventure the previous night... "I don't know if that's a good idea," she said through a cough. "It's really easy to get lost here."

"Is it?" Eolisti asked, her eyebrows raised. "It seemed pretty straight forward last night. Just go all the way down the hall to that big room." She stuffed another piece of bread in her mouth. "We didn't really get a good look at the outside since it was so dark. I think there were more buildings. Do you think the storm has passed?"

Since there were no windows in their room, it was impossible to tell what the weather was like outside. Sophie shrugged. "I've never been in a snowstorm before. Maybe it has." She tried some of the meat, and tasted garlic and sesame oil. All the food was very well prepared.

"I guess we could look around," she hedged, feeling slightly guilty about going out alone the previous night. It wouldn't be fair if she told Eolisti she couldn't do the same. Besides, if Eolisti was with her, she probably wouldn't get lost this time. "I'd like to take a look at the grounds. Omeran architecture is supposed to be very different from Zo'rahn's. The buildings in the village didn't look like anything special, but this monastery is hundreds of years old."

The Anai rolled her eyes.

"What?" Sophie asked, quirking an eyebrow. "Different things don't interest you?"

"Of course they do!" Eolisti scoffed indignantly. "But I don't want to look at a bunch of old buildings. You can do that anywhere. I want to talk to some of the monks. It must be interesting living up here. You said before that a lot of foreigners came through here, right?"

"They used to back when this was a major trading

route. Some still do, but not as many as there once were." Sophie thought about the man she had seen last night. "Though I'm sure there will be some people here that are traveling from other countries. I think I've read somewhere that monasteries and churches house people, who couldn't afford to stay at inns, sometimes. Or, maybe some other people were caught in the storm."

Eolisti's eyes lit up, and she wolfed down a hard-boiled egg. "What are we waiting for then? Let's go explore!" She sprang up, still chewing, and pulled a fresh tunic and trousers out of the bundle of neatly folded laundry.

Sophie poured herself some water and drank, then decided to dress more warmly if they were going outside. She pulled a thicker dress out of the bundle and went to wash her face behind the folding screen while Eolisti dressed. After putting on clean clothes, she decided to tie a small pouch with a few coins in it onto her belt, just in case they decided to go down into the village. Once they were both ready, Eolisti set the tray outside the door and beckoned for Sophie to follow.

Unlike the previous night, the halls were bustling with activity. Initiates and monks walked the corridors, smiling and nodding to Sophie and Eolisti as they passed. Sophie didn't recognize any of the monks, but she nodded back to them all the same. When she'd heard that they were going to a monastery, Sophie had imagined a place where most of the monks would be training or in meditation, but Ta'Shela was livelier than she could have imagined. Both men and women were initiates or monks, with short-cropped hair for the men and simple braids and buns for the women. Quite a few of them looked foreign. Where most people from the eastern continent were typically darker of hair and skin, many of the monks were light-skinned with brown and blonde hair instead of black. Sophie wondered if it had been this way because Bardov was a trading route, or if people from foreign lands came here for other reasons.

Eolisti nudged her, breaking her out of her thoughts. She'd been staring at a pair of women who were looking uncomfortable. Sophie ducked her head and waved at them, her face growing warm. Eolisti seemed to know where she was going, striding confidently in the direction that Sophie assumed would take them back to where they'd first entered the building.

Turning down one more corridor, Sophie thought she recognized the door to the entrance hall that they'd come through the night before. As they approached, her nose filled with the heady smell of incense, and she heard the same low singing as she had the night before. The singing grew louder, and as they pushed the door open, the music poured out into the corridor.

It seemed that morning service was taking place. There were twelve monks next to the altar, singing a deep, melancholy song in a language that Sophie didn't understand and playing instruments that looked like lutes, except that instead of plucking the strings, the monks used bows. There appeared to be a few people from the village below sitting in the pews, listening to the music. The Abbot stood on the other side of the altar, eyes closed as if he was absorbing every note that echoed around the room. Sunlight poured into the large space, bringing out the beauty of the polished stone walls and floors. Cold air flooded the room, but the storm had passed.

Eolisti strode toward the altar after a curious glance at the singing monks. Although Sophie wanted to sit in the pews and watch the service, she followed the Anai down the aisle and out the front doors. Sophie took a deep breath.

The air was lighter and fresher on the mountain than it had been in Zo'rahn. Her cheeks stung in the cold, but it wasn't unpleasant. The lack of wind made the weather bearable even without her heavy cloak. Snow glittered on the ground, white and glistening in the sunlight. Furrows had been made on the main walkways to make it easier for the monks to work.

Men and women, mostly monks and initiates, strolled through the courtyard and into other buildings. Some carried baskets, others led goats to a building that Sophie assumed was a barn. Now that she could clearly see the structures that made up Ta'Shela, she saw how different they were from those in her homeland. The tall buildings were made of a light, sand-colored stone reaching several stories. The tops of the buildings were domed and painted with a vibrant blue that reminded Sophie of the ocean. There was a wall about six or seven feet tall on the cliffside that wrapped around the property and part of her wished it wasn't there. The view of the valley below would have been spectacular.

Near the wall by the front entrance was Joel bent over with a shovel, scooping up snow and tossing it into a pile. Eolisti waved, but he seemed too absorbed in work to notice them. The women picked their way through the furrows and across the courtyard.

"Hey!" Eolisti shouted cheerfully when they got closer to where he was. "What are you doing?" the Anai asked, looking around at the snow.

Sophie watched him work and looked around at the ground. Now that she was up close, she realized that he wasn't clearing the ground for walking but removing a few inches of snow to reveal the tops of plants in neat rows. She moved her foot and saw more plants crushed and hidden by the snow.

Joel looked up at them and smiled. He planted the shovel in the snow and leaned on it. "Morning. Sleep well?" Eolisti nodded and Sophie shrugged, remembering how tired she was. Joel chuckled. "The Abbot said you'll be here for a day or two. There'll be plenty of time to rest before you leave." He spread his arms wide. "Welcome to our garden." He gestured around at the snow. "There's not a lot growing right now, but we have a few vegetables that can survive the climate up here. I hope you like cabbage and turnips." Eolisti made a face. Sophie had to cover her smile. Joel grinned back at them and picked up his shovel again. "The snow was inconvenient. I'm surprised it came so early this year. I'll probably be out here most of the morning, but if you want to wait until after lunch, I can give you a tour."

Sophie looked around. There was still so much snow from the night before. Joel would be shoveling for hours. She fidgeted with the hem of her sleeve. They were out of Zo'rahn now, so it should be safe to use magic, but deep down, she was still afraid. Would they still be able to find her? "Would you like some help?" she asked hesitantly.

"Well, there are more shovels over there," Joel said, pointing to the barn. "But you don't need to help me. I've done this many times, and it's not the most fun project."

"Yeah," Eolisti said, eyeing Sophie. "That doesn't sound fun at all. I wanted to explore, not be roped into manual labor."

Sophie shot her a withering look. "I meant really fast help. Then he can give us that tour now instead of later."

A look of realization passed over Eolisti's features. "Oh. That would be much quicker." She tucked a strand of hair behind one of her pointed ears. "Well?" she asked. "Get to it. We haven't got all day."

Joel looked bemused as Sophie sighed in exasperation. "What are you...?" He trailed off as Sophie lifted a hand and concentrated on the air directly above the snowy garden. She expended some of her power, heating the air and at the same time, pressing it down into the snow until it began to melt. Steam rose from the melting snow, and she had to be careful not to roast the plants beneath. With a flick of her other wrist, she created a protective barrier for the vegetation even as the heat pressed down on it.

Within minutes, most of the snow had disappeared and the soggy earth below was exposed. Sophie released the spell, and the hot air dissipated. Joel just stared at the ground where the snow had just been. The hardy winter sprouts glistened with droplets of melted snow in the sunlight. After a few moments, he seemed to shake himself out of it and looked up at her. "I'm guessing you're a mage?"

She nodded, slightly embarrassed. Magic was so commonplace where she had grown up, it was hard to remember that not everyone was as familiar with it as she was. Even here, so close to Zo'rahn's borders, Joel had been shocked by the casual use of it. "Sorry," she mumbled. "I probably should have asked if that was all right first."

He let out a bark of a laugh so loud that it startled her. "You don't need to apologize! You've just saved me an entire morning of work. And don't look so upset." He winked at her. "It's not like I've never seen magic before. We have a few healers here, after all." Leaning the shovel against the stone wall, he pulled off the gloves he was wearing and shoved them into his pockets. "I guess I owe you ladies a tour. Shall we?"

Gesturing for them to follow, Joel began to walk away from the garden. Eolisti practically skipped after him. She seemed to be almost quivering with excitement. Sophie knew how much Eolisti wanted to explore Ta'Shela. She walked a little behind Eolisti, allowing her to ask Joel questions about the monastery, while Sophie looked around at the buildings. While there were definitely similarities in the designs, these structures had a liveliness to them that she'd never seen back home.

The monastery was bigger than Sophie assumed it would be. Even though it was a shadow of its former self, it was still an impressive display of what Bardov had once been. She counted at least fifteen smaller buildings that served various purposes, from water filtration to storage. They saw a few people on the grounds. Added to those she had seen inside, she guessed there were less than a hundred initiates and monks in all. She was beginning to wonder if most of the rooms she'd passed in the halls were empty. There seemed to be much more space than the current occupants could use or maintain. There were a few people like Joel out and about as well, dressed in normal clothing and probably employed by the monks.

"I came to Omer about twenty years ago from Morigael," Joel explained. "I lived in a small village that didn't have a lot to offer. I had some relatives down in Bardov, so I came here to work with them on their farm and ended up helping the monks after my uncle passed away. They have a few people who aren't in service to Samar that take care of things like trading and fetching pretty young women from the town." He grinned and winked at them. "So, I get to live here, and the monks pay me to handle whatever they might need. There's not a lot going on right now, so I just help out wherever I can."

"What was Morigael like?" Eolisti asked as they walked around the back of the main building. "How long did it take you to get here? Did you have to take a ship? Was it a big one?"

Joel chuckled. "You remind me of my sister, so curious about everything. Things are about the same in Morigael as they are here," he said, answering her first question. "There's more rain there, so it's much greener and it's to the north, so you get a lot of snow in the winter." He gestured around them. "Though being up in the mountains, you get a lot of snow, too, so there's not much of a difference to me. Oh, there's also a king. Which is different from Omer."

"Humans," Eolisti sighed. "A council is much more practical. What if the king is some sort of crazy person?"

"Zo'rahn has a council," Sophie said, giving her a pointed look. Eolisti rolled her eyes back.

"As does Omer. And Morigael, for that matter. The king in Morigael leads the council, but he doesn't control it." He scratched the back of his head. "That's the simplest explanation. It's actually a bit more complicated than that, and I'm not really one for politics." Joel glanced up at the sky. "The morning service should be over by now. It'll be time for lunch soon. There's not much more to see, so we should probably head back."

Sophie nodded. It hadn't felt like that long, but the sun was at a high point in the sky. They must've been out here for an hour or two. Ta'Shela was a very interesting place, but Bardov was so small that she was surprised it had been a major trading town at one point. Joel had said that they were only going to be here for a day or two. She wondered where they were heading next. Would they go further into Omer, or were they headed somewhere else?

Their tour ended near the small chapel Sophie had

stumbled upon the night before. Joel explained that it was said to be the original chapel that was built on the exact spot where Samar herself had sheltered travelers. These people became the first monks of Ta'Shela. As their little group passed back by the open archway to the chapel, a monk inside looked like she was standing to leave. Abruptly, Eolisti turned and walked into the small room. Moments later, Sophie heard the rapid-fire series of questions she'd come to expect from her excited Anai companion, and she smiled despite herself.

"You have to love her enthusiasm," Joel said with a grin.

Sophie smiled wryly back at Joel and shook her head.

With a sigh, Joel walked a few paces farther down the hall to where a long bench had been placed against the wall. He sat and gestured an invitation for Sophie to join him.

As she seated herself next to him, she noticed for the first time that the opposite wall of the hallway bore the faint traces of what she guessed had once been another mural. She tried to follow the sweeping curves and lines that she could make out, but her mind couldn't piece together the remnants into any distinguishable patterns. It was a shame that this ancient place was being swallowed by time, almost before her very eyes. On the other hand, she mused, some things *should* stay lost to time.

Joel cleared his throat, drawing her out of her dark and melancholy thoughts. "I don't mean to pry, but you seem..." Joel paused, struggling to find the right words. "You seem sadder than most of the people that the Anai escort to Ta'Shela." Seeing her slight frown at his words, he explained, "Most of the people are scared, but they are also happy—joyful even." He tilted his head as he studied her face for a few long moments before he added gently, "You seem haunted."

Joel's insights surprised her. As she thought about it, Sophie realized that she was sad about leaving home. She couldn't deny that there were things and people she missed. Zephan came to mind and she smiled wistfully. What was he doing right now? Was he safe?

"Yes, like that," Joel said as he gestured at her face, drawing her attention once again.

Sophie took a deep breath and let it out slowly as she collected herself. "Yes, I suppose I'm a little sad. It was the most difficult choice I've ever made—leaving—but I know it was the right choice."

Joel nodded and leaned back against the wall, studying the faint mural opposite them. "My sister and I were about your age when we left home. There wasn't really much for us to leave behind, but I can understand striking out into the unknown. When you don't know what lies ahead, there is a comfort in the familiarity of even the worst circumstances."

He was right. As sure as she was that she had done the right thing, part of her did still long to go back. As she thought of the home she missed, she realized that what she wished for was to return to the time before her hidden "talent" had emerged.

A crash that sounded like the toppling of a candelabra came from the ancient chapel. Startled by the sudden noise, Sophie leapt to her feet.

"Excuse me," said a deep voice right behind her, making her jump for a second time.

It was the man, the one she had met last night while exploring. He loomed behind her, dressed the same as he had been, with the hood of his cloak pulled down to his nose. How could he see like that?

Eolisti, who had just emerged from the chapel, looked him up and down, eyes narrowed. "Who are you?"

"The one the Abbot sent to find you," he said in a flat voice.

"I thought we were meeting after the midday meal," Eolisti said, sounding even more suspicious, "and you still haven't answered my question."

"Food will be brought for you," he said to Sophie, completely ignoring Eolisti. "The Abbot is waiting for you."

"It's okay," Sophie said quickly as Eolisti bristled. "Let's just go."

Eolisti glared at the man. "Fine." She wrapped her arm around Joel's and pulled him to his feet. He just looked at her, surprised. "But Joel is coming with us in case you try anything funny."

If that concerned the man at all, he gave no indication. He just turned around and walked toward the doors of the main building.

The Anai watched him walk away, eyes still narrowed. "Who the hell is that guy?"

Joel watched him as well. "I've seen him around here before, but I've only spoken to him once or twice. He doesn't seem to like other people." He looked back down at Sophie and smiled. "I'm sure he's a good man. Otherwise, the monks wouldn't let him stay here. Come on. The Abbot's expecting us."

FOURTEEN

The Abbot was waiting for them in a room just beyond the entrance hall. It was small and plainly furnished with a table large enough for six people to sit at. He sat at the far end of the table and stood as they entered. "Thank you for meeting with me." He smiled and gestured to the chairs. "Please, have a seat." The hooded man took a seat to the right of the Abbot and Joel on his other side. The Abbot glanced at Joel, frowning slightly but said nothing. Eolisti and Sophie took the seats the furthest from the stranger.

"We asked Joel to be here," Eolisti said, reading the unease on the Abbot's face. "That's not a problem, is it?"

He smiled, looking relieved. "Of course not, though it is best if we keep this conversation among ourselves. You've met Khalil," he said, nodding at the hooded man. "He helps us with cases that require the utmost discretion. As you already know, we work with the Anai to help people who need to get out of the area. Normally, just getting to Omer is enough, but some need to go much farther, and for that, we ask for Khalil's help—"

"So why do you wear a hood?" Eolisti interrupted, staring intently at Khalil. "Were you burned by acid or something?"

Khalil pointedly ignored her and spoke directly to Sophie. "We'll be traveling together for a while. There is still a long way to go until you're safe. Be careful who you trust," he said, repeating the sentiment from the night before, "no matter how far you think you are from your troubles."

Sophie looked down at her hands. She got the message. He was saying that she still wasn't out of her master's reach. Something about all this was still bothering her. She looked up at the Abbot, asking the question that had been on her mind since arriving at the monastery. "I appreciate all the help you've given me, but why are you doing this? Helping me could bring a lot of trouble here."

The Abbot shifted in his seat, propping his elbows on the table and steepling his fingers. "Have you heard of someone called the Raven?" When Sophie shook her head, he continued. "I didn't think so. Well, the Raven is a spy from another country who works to free slaves from places like Zo'rahn. The Raven sends people in need to us, with the help of the Anai, of course," he added, nodding to Eolisti. "And we help them integrate into a new life. To be perfectly honest, we're not sure who the Raven is. We don't even know if it's a man or a woman or who he—or she—works for, but Samar would never allow us to turn away those who need our assistance. We received a message from the Raven a few weeks ago that you needed help getting out of Zo'rahn. So, we've arranged for Khalil to take you to Morigael."

"To Morigael?" Sophie asked. Morigael was across the sea to the west. "Why so far?"

"Your situation is unique. You came from a Vizier's household. Someone like that is tough to outrun. Omer and Zo'rahn have a good relationship, and if he tries to take you out of this country by force, he could likely do so with little resistance from local authorities. As for the choice of Morigael, the Raven specifically requested us to arrange passage to that country for you. It doesn't politically have much to do with Omer or Zo'rahn, and distance will likely inhibit anyone coming after you. It would look very bad for your Vizier if his agents were caught in the western countries."

Eolisti glared at Khalil, her arms folded over her chest. It was clear that she didn't like him. "You expect her to go with this creepy guy by herself? What if he just takes her back to the wizards in Zo'rahn? How do you know we can trust him?"

Khalil's expression never changed at her questioning of his loyalties.

Tamrat cleared his throat. "Khalil has worked with us for years. The route that you'll take can be dangerous, but he has traveled it many times. We trust him to take Sophie to safety."

"Wait," Sophie interrupted, and she felt her voice get higher with panic. "I'm going alone?" She looked around at all of them, then stared at Eolisti, who wouldn't meet her eyes. She was still glaring at Khalil. "Where are you going?"

"Typically, the Vendarii will bring people here and then return to Elasariin," Joel said, speaking for the first time since being seated.

"Oh," Sophie said, a numb feeling overcoming her. "I didn't know that." She stared down at her hands again, feeling a knot forming in the pit of her stomach. Was Eolisti really going to leave her? She had been upset with Eolisti the previous night, but that didn't mean she wanted her to leave. It had never occurred to her that the Anai would be going back home, she thought Eolisti would be with her until she settled in a new place. If she took the time to think about it, it made sense, though. Her people would need her back in Elasariin to help with the next person this Raven sent to them. She felt so stupid. Eolisti had never told her that she would leave her here, but maybe she thought Sophie should have already known?

"Khalil is highly skilled," Tamrat said in a reassuring tone. "He'll be able to protect you in Eolisti's place."

"No," Eolisti said, transferring her glare to Tamrat. "I'm going, too. It's my responsibility to get her to safety and I'm going to make sure that happens. I may not know exactly where we're going, but I do know something of what we might face if those wizards catch up with us. My people have been at odds with the Zo'rahni wizards for years. I think I'm better equipped to handle them than this guy." She gestured dismissively at Khalil. "If this is as dangerous as you're saying it is, are you sure that he will be able to handle this by himself?" She sat up a little straighter and looked around, daring anyone to argue with her. "They call us Vendarii for a reason."

Khalil's mouth pressed into a tight line, and Sophie held her breath. Eventually, he nodded.

To the surprise of everyone, Joel broke the silence. "Forgive me for speaking out of turn, Abbot, but given the circumstances would it not be better for the young woman —" he glanced at Sophie and corrected himself. "For Sophie to have all the protection we can offer her, including the continued service of the Vendarii," he said nodding toward Eolisti, "if she is willing?"

Eolisti beamed at Joel, clearly pleased to have found an ally in her cause. In anticipation of her victory, the Anai crossed her arms and glared at Khalil with a remarkable combination of menace and smugness.

Sophie shifted uncomfortably, sensing the crackle of tension once again in the room like a palpable thing.

Tamrat looked first from Eolisti to Khalil, then from Khalil to Sophie. "Very well," he said after a moment. "We will prepare for three instead of two." He shifted in his seat again. "The plan is for you to leave tomorrow at dawn, so please relax for the rest of the day. I shall send Shaman Vyraeli an update. I'm sure the Anaiian High Council will want to know why their Vendarii will not be returning on time."

Eolisti opened her mouth to say more, but there was a soft knock at the door. "Ah, that must be the food," the Abbot said. "Enter."

The same young man who had brought food to Sophie and Eolisti's room that morning opened the door. He pushed a cart, this time filled with large bowls of rice, fish, and that same fried bread from breakfast. He smiled at everyone and set the food on the table along with a pitcher of water, cups, and clean plates with flatware for each of them. After bowing to the Abbot, who thanked him, he left and shut the door behind him.

"Finally!" Eolisti reached over and grabbed a plate, beginning to spoon food onto it.

"Where exactly are we going in Morigael?" Sophie asked, following Eolisti's lead and taking a plate off the pile.

"Only Khalil has that information," the Abbot said. "We feel that it's necessary to keep your destination secret in case anyone here is questioned. Suffice it to say that you will begin your journey by going through Omer."

Sophie filled her plate as she pictured a map of the area.

There were two ways to get to Morigael from where they were. They would have to travel down the mountains, and then they could either head west to the coast or north through Omer to Elizash, where the two continents touched. Both routes would take weeks, if not months, to travel. Sophie was already sick of traveling. How would she feel in a few months? Would she arrive in Morigael only to be told she was going elsewhere? "Is Morigael the final destination?"

"I'm sorry," Khalil said softly, "but I can't tell you that in present company."

"And what's that supposed to mean?" Eolisti growled.

"It means what was said," he replied without any heat in his voice. "None of the monks know where exactly I will be leading you. *You*," he turned his head toward Eolisti, "will find out where we are headed only when I deem it necessary."

Eolisti flushed, her cheeks turning pink, as she stared daggers at Khalil. She opened her mouth, no doubt with an angry retort on her tongue, but Sophie touched her arm. "It's all right, Eolisti," she said as the Anai turned to glare at Sophie instead. "It's wise to have the information limited for now." She glanced at Khalil and tried to make herself sound more confident than she felt. "But we *will* find out where exactly we are going once we leave here."

Khalil made no indication that he'd heard her. Tamrat filled a plate and handed it to him, then filled one for himself. Only Joel made no movement toward the food. He looked extremely uncomfortable.

"As I was saying before," the Abbot began after taking a few bites. "We will have your horses and supplies ready to depart at dawn. If there is anything specific you need, make sure to let one of the initiates know today so that we can ensure it is included with your supplies."

"Why do we need to leave so soon?" Eolisti asked with a mouth full of fish and rice. "We just got here." She looked over at Joel. "I thought we would be here for a couple of days?"

The Abbot answered before Joel could speak. "It's best if you stay on the move. Ta'Shela is a sanctuary of sorts, but we don't have the skill or manpower to defend it if someone with magic came to take you from us. I'm afraid that you won't be safe until you are far from here." He looked down at his plate and sighed. His food was barely touched, but he pushed the bowl away. "Sophie, I wish there was more that we could do for you, but this monastery isn't what it once was."

Sophie held up a hand to stop the Abbot. "Please, you and the monks have already done so much for me. I couldn't ask anything more of you." She bowed her head to him. "Thank you for your hospitality." She glanced over at Eolisti. The Anai frowned but said nothing. Sophie thought she knew how the Anai felt. They were both tired of traveling and had thought that this would be the end of it, but in actuality, there was still so much farther to go. It was a little disheartening. "We'll be ready to depart at dawn."

"Excellent," the Abbot said, little enthusiasm in his tone, and pushed out his chair and stood. "I have a few things to attend to. Please enjoy your meal." He walked around the table and bowed to them before opening the door and leaving.

Joel cleared his throat and stood. "I have some duties to attend to as well. If you need anything, just let me know." He grinned at the girls. "I'll be about the grounds, shoveling more snow probably." He waved to them as he followed the Abbot out the door.

They were left alone in the small meeting room with Khalil. He ate his food in silence. Sophie and Eolisti glanced at each other, and Sophie could tell the Anai was thinking the same thing. There was something very odd about this man.

Sophie picked at her food for a few moments, then put down her spoon. She wasn't hungry anymore. All the uncertainty and doubt she felt was nauseating.

Khalil stood, making her look up. He bowed his head to her and, without a word, left the room, closing the door softly behind him. Sophie sat in silence for a moment while she gathered her thoughts, listening to Eolisti eat her food with such ferocity that Sophie was amazed she didn't choke on it.

"I don't trust him," Eolisti said when she was finished, setting her plate down with unnecessary force. She glared down at it as if it had insulted her.

"I'm not sure I trust him either," Sophie admitted, watching the other woman warily. "There's something you should know." She took a deep breath. "I actually met Khalil last night." She told Eolisti of her excursion the night before, how she had gotten lost and how Khalil delivered the warning after taking her back to their room.

By the time she finished, Eolisti looked crestfallen. "You went out exploring by yourself last night? Without me?"

Sophie tried to hold back a smile. Eolisti sounded so offended. "Is that all you took away from that? That you were left out?"

Eolisti scowled. "No, but it's not safe for you to go out and explore by yourself. Even here, there are weirdos." She glanced pointedly at Khalil's empty chair. "I don't think we should go with him alone. He might be dangerous. I mean, I could take him, but what do you think about Joel coming with us?"

A little surprised at the question, Sophie just shrugged. "Can he come with us? Doesn't he have work here?"

"Don't you remember what he said earlier? There isn't that much work to do here right now. He could come with us for a few weeks and then he can come back here and do whatever for the monks again. I'm sure he'd like to travel. It seems so boring here."

Sophie raised an eyebrow. "You do realize that Morigael is across the Silver Sea? It will take at least a few weeks to get there if we take a boat and longer if we go by land. We'd have to go all the way up to Elizash. He might be gone for months."

Eolisti waved her hand like she was batting away a fly. "That doesn't matter. They have plenty of people here to help out. Besides, the Abbot did say that if we need anything, we should just ask for it. I think that we need Joel to come with us. He's already shown that he's on our side, and that will give us the advantage in case Khalil tries anything."

"Do you think he'd try something?" Sophie asked, tapping a finger to her bottom lip in thought. "He does seem suspicious, but the monks trust him. Doesn't that mean that your mother does too?"

The Anai grimaced. She obviously hadn't considered the possibility that Vyraeli knew of Khalil. "She and the Council probably don't know exactly what goes on after a Vendarii leaves Ta'Shela. They just come home and report to the Council. I'm sure my mother wouldn't approve of him," she huffed. "I just want to make sure that you get to Morigael safely. We need someone to watch our backs.

Also"—her lips split into a grin—"it'll be much more fun to travel across the ocean than just going back home. I'll be the most well-traveled Vendarii ever!"

Sophie rolled her eyes but smiled anyway. She had to admit to herself that she was both relieved and happy that Eolisti wanted to come with them. Khalil made her nervous. She didn't know if Joel would be able to come along as well, but she thought it would be good if he could. He was kind and helpful, and he did say he was from Morigael, so he would probably know the route they were taking. "Morigael does sound interesting," she admitted. "I've always been curious about it. My mother was from Morigael. Maybe I have some family there, though I really wouldn't know where to look." She leaned back in her chair and sighed. "I wonder where we're going. Maybe Agrigentum. That's the capital. Have you heard of it?"

"Nope," Eolisti said disinterestedly and pushed back from the table. "I'm going to go find Joel and ask him if he wants to come with us," she said as she stood. "I'll let you know what he says. You should go talk to the Abbot. Tell him you want Joel to come with us. He'll probably listen to you. To be honest, I don't think he likes me very much. He didn't seem to like the idea of me coming along."

Sophie stood and followed Eolisti into the hall. "I don't think it's that he doesn't like you, just that he's not used to your... boldness. Being the Abbot, the other monks probably just do what he tells them to."

"Well, I'm not going to do what he tells me to. Now, where did he go?" Eolisti looked down the hallway. "I'll meet up with you later, okay? Don't forget to talk to Tamrat!"

Before Sophie could say anything, Eolisti bolted off down the corridor and around a corner. Sophie stared after her. Last night, she had thought that her journey was over and that she could start building a new life. Now, she wondered when all this would end. Would she ever truly be safe?

With that unsettling thought, Sophie went to go find the Abbot.

SOPHIE SEEMED like such a nice girl. It was a shame, really. He had expected her to be like all the other lost souls who came to Ta'Shela. Hollow and beaten down by their circumstances. When he'd been informed that she might pass through here, he thought it would have been a simple job like the others. Report on their location and when they would be leaving the monastery. But now he felt a little guilty. Handing over those slaves had been like returning stolen property. Sophie was different. She wasn't a slave. Technically, she was a free woman, only beholden to her family by tradition. It didn't sit quite right with him, but it really wasn't his decision to make.

He rarely had to get his hands dirty. All he had to do was send a message, and occasionally guide someone in the wrong direction, and the wizards took care of the rest. He passed through the archway to a prayer room that the monks rarely used these days and made sure that he was alone before pulling a small emerald out of his pocket. If they were leaving at dawn, he needed to send a message right away. If all went as planned, the wizards could be at Ta'Shela by nightfall.

FIFTEEN

A loud banging at the door almost caused Sophie to fall out of bed. It felt like she had only been asleep for a few minutes. It couldn't be dawn already.

Eolisti sprang out of bed as Sophie was still struggling to sit up, and reached for her sword, pulling it from the sheath. She looked odd creeping toward the door in nothing but a long tunic. It would have been comical if they weren't so tense. The banging repeated. "Who's there?" Eolisti demanded, holding up her sword, ready to strike.

"It is I," said the Abbot's muffled voice through the door. "Please, we must speak immediately." He sounded strained. Eolisti let out a relieved breath and pulled the door open for the Abbot. He looked disheveled and tired, as if he had been woken up and gotten dressed quickly, and Sophie noticed he was missing his sash. There was another younger initiate with him that was out of breath, and she realized it was the same young man that had brought their meals the day before.

Tamrat surveyed the two women, Sophie sitting up in bed and Eolisti next to the door, sword in hand. He swallowed and nodded to Eolisti, then strode into the room with the young initiate following closely behind. "I apologize for waking you so late, but there has been a change of plans. You need to leave. Now."

"Hold on," Eolisti said, still holding her sword. "It can't be dawn already."

"No, it's just after midnight," the initiate said, visibly withering as Eolisti turned her gaze on him.

The Abbot gave the boy a stern look. "Yes, we had originally planned for you to leave at dawn, but you need to leave now." He looked directly at Sophie. "Riders arrived in the village not long ago. One of our runners informed us that they are asking around about a young woman with red hair."

Sophie felt the bottom drop out of her stomach. She untangled herself from the sheets and stood. "Are they coming here?" she asked, her voice shaking.

"It's only a matter of time before they come up to Ta'Shela. At least an hour to climb the cliffside. We're hoping you'll be long gone by then." He glanced over his shoulder. "Khalil and Joel will be waiting by the stables. They should have everything prepared by the time you arrive. I urge you to make haste. We'd rather not have a confrontation with the Zo'rahni wizards if we can avoid it." He bowed his head quickly and left, taking the young man with him.

Sophie and Eolisti gathered their things and dressed quickly.

"How did they follow us?" Eolisti asked as she pulled on her trousers and looked at Sophie sharply. "Did they track you by what you did yesterday?"

"It's possible," Sophie said, thinking furiously. "But that wasn't a particularly powerful spell, and Joel had said that there are healers here. My magic shouldn't have been discernible from theirs from afar. And Tamrat said they just arrived in Bardov. They would have already been traveling the pass days before I used any magic."

Eolisti was silent for a time as they dressed. "You don't think someone told them we were here, do you?"

Sophie placed her cloak around her shoulders and picked up her bag. "I don't think one of the monks would do that."

"Not a monk," Eolisti said darkly.

Sophie didn't say anything. She knew what Eolisti was thinking, but she just couldn't bring herself to believe that the monks would place their trust in someone who would betray them. "Let's go. We don't have time to discuss this right now. We can figure out what happened later." Eolisti looked like she wanted to say more but just nodded.

People hurried down the halls. As they passed, men and women looked at them with wide eyes and whispered among themselves. Sophie's nerves only increased as they approached the entrance hall. What if they were already here? Who had the Vizier sent after her? She couldn't go back, but she also couldn't let the people here be hurt because of her.

"Hey," Eolisti said to get her attention, placing a hand on Sophie's shoulder. "Calm down. You look like you're about five seconds away from throwing up." She smiled at her. "We'll be fine."

Sophie tried to meet her eyes but couldn't. "It's not me I'm worried about."

The Anai glanced at the monks hurrying past them. "They'll be fine, too. Just worry about getting out of here."

The entrance hall looked much as it had the first night they had come to Ta'Shela. The murals were bathed in soft candlelight and the floor had been cleaned since the earlier service. Only two initiates were present, sitting together in the first row of pews whispering to each other. They looked up as the women entered and stood, bowing to them. Eolisti and Sophie hurried past them with only a brief nod and headed out the front doors.

The air in the courtyard was still and cold. Moonlight reflected on the fallen snow, giving the grounds of Ta'Shela an unearthly glow. Torches were lit by the stables and Sophie could see figures standing by the doors. As they made their way over, Sophie could see it was Khalil, Joel, and the Abbot, with four saddled horses, the two that Sophie and Eolisti had ridden in on, plus a sleek midnight black stallion and a bulkier brown mare.

"I've sent Sahl ahead of you with your supply horse to light the way," he said to Khalil. "Sahl will be going with you for the time being. We feel that under the circumstances, it would be best to have one of our own there to help." He smiled at Sophie. Khalil's mouth turned down a little, but he nodded curtly.

"Great," Eolisti said flatly. "Can we get going now? I thought we were in a hurry." She took the reins of her horse from Joel and mounted. Joel held his hand out for Sophie and helped her up onto her mare, then climbed onto his horse.

Khalil handed the Abbot a small package and bowed to him, then swung onto the black stallion. "Follow me. Don't light any torches. We don't want to be seen." He wheeled his horse about and trotted toward the side of the cliff opposite from where the path down to Bardov began.

Sophie mouthed, "Thank you," to the Abbot, who smiled and bowed to her in return, then dug her heels into the sides of her mount. The mare jumped forward to follow Khalil.

He led them behind the buildings, to where the mountainside resumed its steep slope upward into the night. There was a small path that led off the cliff that cradled Ta'Shela, and curved around to a patch of barren trees growing out of the rock. The trail was so well hidden that it looked like just another part of the rocks until their horses were stepping off the side of the cliff. Sophie almost yelled a warning at Khalil, but suddenly the horse's foot connected with a rock that seemed to materialize from nowhere. The trees in front of them disappeared into the mist, and the entrance to a yawning cave appeared in their place.

"What the hell is happening," Eolisti blurted apprehensively from behind her. She pulled on the reins and her horse shuffled nervously. "Did you see that? This cave definitely wasn't here before."

Sophie reached out to the rock with her senses. She could feel the pulsing of an enchantment placed there. There must have been runes carved somewhere on the rocks, invisible in the darkness. The magic was subtle enough to make anyone looking think it was just rock there, only changing the scenery slightly to conceal the path and cave. It hadn't been strong enough for her to sense before, so she doubted anyone would be able to find it unless they knew exactly what they were looking for. "There's magic concealing the cave. It's old." Maybe the monks put it here for supplies when the monastery was being built, or an escape path, in case they were ever under siege.

"I never knew this was here," Joel's voice drifted up to her, sounding amazed. "I've worked here for years, and they've never mentioned this."

Khalil's horse nickered as he pulled it up to the cave

entrance. The entrance wasn't completely black. Lights flickered somewhere in the darkness, beyond what they could see. "We don't have time for this," he growled and pulled his horse to the side. "Joel, you go first. Then, the Anai and Sophie. I'll guard our backs and extinguish the lights as we pass them."

Joel followed Khalil's orders without hesitation, spurring his horse forward into the mouth of the cave, which Sophie realized was large enough to allow both horse and rider to pass through. She and Eolisti glanced at each other. If Khalil was going to betray them, this would be the perfect opportunity. Eolisti gave her a look that told her to be careful and flicked her reins. Her horse trotted into the cave after Joel.

Sophie watched Eolisti's form melt into the darkness, then glanced at Khalil, waiting on the ledge like a silent sentinel. She took a deep breath and puffed out her cheeks. The idea of having Khalil riding behind her was not something she was happy about, but she was out of time and options. The people looking for her in the village would be on their way up the cliff by now, and they could reach Ta'Shela any minute.

Letting her breath out in a rush, she urged her horse forward and into the darkness of the mountain.

CHAPTER

SIXTEEN

The cave was not as dark as Sophie had expected it to be. Dim light flickered around the corners ahead of them, casting long shadows. If it were possible, the air inside the cave was even colder than it had been on the cliffside. The walls were damp and cut with such irregularity that the formation could only have been natural. Sophie shivered and pulled the edges of her cloak closer around her. This place unsettled her. She couldn't quite put her finger on it, but she could sense an unpleasant aura that seeped out of the walls along their path. Khalil's presence at her back didn't give her any comfort. He was like a specter looming over her shoulder.

They rounded the corner to find a lamp with a glowing candle inside, hanging from a sconce that had been nailed into the rock. "Follow the lamps," Khalil instructed from the rear of the group, his voice echoing off the cave walls. "They'll light our path through the mountain. Do not deviate. I don't know where the other ways might lead us." He let his ominous words hang in the air.

Joel chuckled nervously. "All right, so we just follow the lights then. That's easy. It's a tunnel, right? So only one way to go." He passed the lamp, moving deeper into the mountain.

Sophie passed the lamp as well, and a few seconds later, it went out, plunging them into darkness again. Startled, she turned around in her saddle to see the faint outline of Khalil, pulling his hand back from the lamp. Even though Sophie knew that they needed to hide their trail as best as they could, it was alarming for the light to suddenly disappear.

The next lamp was a long way ahead of them. The light it cast was just bright enough to let them see where they were going, but made every crack and crevice in the stone appear miles deep. Even if they couldn't see the next light, once Khalil put out the previous lamp, a dim flickering glow guided their way to the next one. The cave widened and narrowed as they went, at times, forcing them to dismount and walk a short distance before remounting and riding on. Twice the trail forked, and they continued down whichever way there was light. Sophie could tell they were descending given the way the ground sloped, but it was hard to determine their rate of descent.

They were all tense, all except for Khalil, it seemed. Sophie could feel him behind her. It was like having an itch between her shoulders that she wasn't allowed to scratch.

Time seemed to melt into the darkness. How long had they been riding through the mountain? Minutes, hours? She kept thinking she heard something behind them and had to resist turning around in her saddle. Voices? Or the wind echoing through the cave? No one spoke as the horses trudged along. The others must have also been feeling some of the effects of the oppressive atmosphere inside the mountain. They all seemed almost fearful to break the silence, as if by talking, they would announce their presence to whatever else lived in the cavernous depths.

Sophie wondered if the monks were all right. The people looking for her would know she had been there since she'd used magic in the garden. Would they be able to recognize that it was she who cast the spell? Who had the Vizier sent?

An overwhelming sense of guilt threatened to crush her in the near blackness. The monks had been kind enough to shelter her and provide her with a way to escape. And now that they were in trouble, she'd just left them to their fate. What else could she have done? She couldn't fight ranked Zo'rahni wizards. Sure, she'd trained in combative magic, but she had no practical experience. She'd been useless when Eolisti fought the bandits, only stopping an arrow once the battle was all but over. All she could do was run away while others were hurt in her place.

A creaking noise made her jump and she turned around in the saddle, forgetting for a moment that Khalil's horse was directly behind hers. Khalil was replacing the lamp on the sconce. He must have lifted it off to extinguish it. He turned his head toward her, face entirely obscured by shadows, as if there was only a black void under the hood of his cloak like a *Soulless*.

Sophie whipped back around as her heart threatened to burst from her chest. She rubbed her forehead with her free hand and took a deep breath to calm herself. The darkness and silence were playing tricks with her mind. She didn't know how much more of this she could take.

As she passed the next lamp, the flame sputtered,

making the shadows flutter across the stone. Eolisti jumped and glared at the lamp over her shoulder. It was hard for Sophie not to smile. Eolisti was always so confident and seeing her jump made Sophie feel like she wasn't the only one who was afraid.

After what felt like days of riding, Sophie's eyes stung, and her shoulders ached. They hadn't gotten much sleep before the Abbot had roused them, and now that the initial danger seemed more distant, she was becoming exhausted. Sophie started ignoring the sounds she thought she heard in the cave as her weariness became all-encompassing. She closed her eyes, trusting her horse to follow Eolisti's as they walked. *Just for a minute*, she thought to herself.

Sophie didn't remember falling asleep but was jerked awake when she almost slid off her horse. She gasped as she caught herself and clung to her mare's neck while trying to regain her bearings.

"Are you all right?" Eolisti asked over her shoulder.

"Yeah. Just dozed off, I guess," Sophie said shakily as she sat up again. The air quality felt different than it had when they first entered the cave. It was heavier and didn't feel as cold. "Does it feel different here? Warmer?"

Khalil spoke from behind her, making her jump again. "We should stop and rest. There's still a long way to go."

Damn this cave, Sophie thought darkly as she glared at the tunnel ahead of them. At that moment, all she wanted was to be outside where she could see more than ten feet in front of her. The area they were in was wide enough to allow all of them to dismount and sit against one wall, while the horses congregated together and ate out of the feed bags that Khalil produced. He handed each of them a small roll of bread, a piece of hard cheese, and some salted meat that Sophie suspected was goat. Khalil sat near Sophie on the ground, but maintained a bit of distance between himself and the rest of the travelers. They ate in silence under one of the lamps.

Sophie glanced at Khalil occasionally, wondering why he wore his hood so low still. How was he able to see where he was going? She could see that Joel already had bags under his eyes, and Eolisti laid her head back on the rocks and closed her eyes, her goat meat lying in front of her untouched. They were all exhausted, except for maybe Khalil, who showed no sign of fatigue.

"You should sleep," Khalil said as if reading her mind. She looked over at him and his hood was turned toward her, the candlelight flickering over his nose and chin. "There's a little time. I don't think anyone has followed us into the cave yet."

"How do you know?" Eolisti's accusing voice came from Sophie's opposite side.

Khalil didn't answer her and turned his head to face the wall in front of him.

Joel cleared his throat. "Both of you should sleep. I had a few hours before we left, so I'm fine to keep going." He smiled at Sophie and Eolisti. "I'll keep watch with Khalil."

It wasn't nearly as cold anymore, so Sophie took her cloak off and balled it up as a pillow. She lay on the ground and closed her eyes after a wary glance at Khalil, who was still sitting in the same position. She wasn't very comfortable, but it was the best she could do.

The next thing she knew, she was being shaken awake by Joel. As she sat up, he handed her a tin cup filled with water and smiled apologetically. "Khalil thinks we should go. We can't afford to spend any more time here."

Sophie nodded and took the water from Joel. It was cool on her parched throat and helped her wake up. She glanced over at Eolisti, who was already climbing onto her horse. Khalil was giving his black stallion some water from a small bowl. Sophie got to her feet and brushed off her clothes. She picked up her cloak and shook it out before putting it back on. Joel helped her up into her saddle, then mounted his own horse.

They continued in the same fashion as before. Joel led the group, followed by Eolisti and Sophie, with Khalil bringing up the rear and extinguishing candles as they went. However, there was now a noticeable difference in the group. Sophie felt less tense than she had before, and, though she was still scared of what was behind them, she tried to focus on what was ahead instead. Where would this cave lead? Would they come out at the bottom of the mountain in Omer? That would mean that they would be inside this passage for days. Sophie thought she would forget what sunlight looked like before she got out of this cave.

After a while, the air grew even warmer, so warm that Sophie considered asking to stop so that she could change into something cooler. But there would be plenty of time for that once they were out of the mountain. She felt a warm breeze on her face and, a moment later, noticed that the glow ahead was not flickering and was much too bright to be from a single candle. She could see all around with increasing clarity as they went forward. With a start, Sophie realized that there must be daylight ahead. There were no more lamps on the rocks that she could see, so they must be nearing the exit. Had they been inside the mountain long enough for the sun to rise?

"Hey, is that sunlight?" Eolisti asked, excitement lacing

her voice. "Does that mean we can finally get out of this cave?"

They went around a bend and the tunnel suddenly opened up to a large chamber. Stalactites hung from the ceiling and small pathways shot back into the mountain. Dark shapes huddled around the base of the stalactites, undisturbed by their presence. Light coming from a large opening in the rock face to their left looked like there was just enough room for their horses to squeeze past.

As they passed through, they realized they were exiting the mouth of the cave. Sophie was temporarily blinded by the brightness outside. After being in the dark for so long, it took her eyes a couple of minutes to adjust to the daylight. Eventually, she realized she was looking down on a rocky valley. The stone had turned from a dark gray on top of the mountain, to a sun-bleached yellow. The ground ahead of them was hard and compact, like a dry riverbed. Walls of jagged rock rose from both sides, creating a gorge that water may have flowed through long ago. Their horses stood on a ledge that extended past the cave entrance and snaked along the side of the mountain until it connected with the dry riverbed. The trail created by the compact earth descended between the rocks and down into the gorge. It seemed they were not entirely out of the mountains, but looking back up at the peaks above them, Sophie guessed that they were well over halfway down. Going through the mountain had been much faster than the route Sophie and Eolisti had taken to get up to Bardov.

The air was hot and dry, much drier than that of Zo'rahn. Sophie unfastened her cloak and folded it in front of her. That explained why the temperature inside the mountain had changed as they descended. It was much warmer here than Sophie was used to. There weren't many plants growing in the area and the ones that did make their way between the rocks were scraggly and barren. Sophie shielded her eyes and looked up to the sky. The sunlight felt good on her skin. From what she could see beyond the rocks, the sun was low on the horizon, bathing them in gold, and casting long shadows from the walls of the gorge. They had been inside the mountain for an entire day.

"Where are we?" Eolisti asked, looking over the ledge and down into the gorge. Sophie frowned. She had obviously never seen anything like this before either. In retrospect, she wondered if she should have suspected sooner that Eolisti's self-proclaimed credentials as a Vendarii were a little exaggerated.

"Omer," Khalil answered. "But we're very close to the border with Alkhazai. We'll be skirting the desert, so it's important not to waste too much time. Joel," he said, turning his head toward the older man. "Follow the path down between the cliffs for now. It'll open up before nightfall, and you should be able to see our first waypoint. It will look like a pile of white rocks."

Joel nodded and urged his horse toward the ledge leading down to the gorge. The rest of them followed in the same order as they had traveled for the past day.

Eolisti fanned her face with her hand. "Why is it so hot here? It was snowing up in Bardov."

"Omer is mostly arid," Sophie answered automatically, remembering her studies about the areas surrounding Zo'rahn. "Northern Omer is a bit cooler, but being so far to the south, the climate is very similar to Alkhazai's, which is entirely desert. Bardov was so cold because of its elevation, being near the top of a mountain."

The Anai groaned. "Great. So basically, it's going to be like this the entire time we're in this stupid country?"

"Basically. Though"—Sophie glanced back at Khalil—"how long we're in Omer depends on which route we take to get across the sea."

Khalil made no indication that he had heard her hinted question about where they were going. He remained silent after giving Joel the instructions to descend from the ledge and follow the path.

Once they were down into the old riverbed, Sophie looked back up at the cave. The rock face in front of the cave entrance completely hid it from view. If someone was looking for it, they would have to climb up to the ledge to know anything was even there. The ground was so hard that they left no tracks in the dirt that she could see. It was almost as if they had never been there, which was probably the point of taking this route. Apart from being a quicker way down the mountain, the terrain must make it difficult to track anyone moving through it. Sophie wondered how long the monks at Ta'Shela had been smuggling slaves out of the area to have such an established escape route.

Again, she was struck with a pang of guilt for having led danger to the door of the peaceful monks. If anyone in Zo'rahn did know of their smuggling operation, they probably didn't care enough about an escaped slave here or there to do anything about it. Someone like her though...

As they rode, the walls on either side of the gorge gradually lowered until they could see over them and toward the horizon. To their right, rocky mountains with dry scrubland continued as far as the eye could see. To the left, the land flowed down into the desert Khalil had mentioned earlier. She could see sand dunes in the distance, like hills in a valley. The dunes dissolved into a haze in the setting sun.

"Isn't that one of the monks?" Eolisti asked, drawing

Sophie's attention ahead of them. "It's that kid from last night. And it looks like he has our other horse."

Under a short leafless tree far ahead of them, Sophie could barely make out a figure with a larger shape that could be a horse next to him. If Eolisti hadn't pointed the figure out, Sophie would have thought it was just another rock. When she looked more closely, she could also see there was a pile of snow-white rocks near where the young man was waiting, presumably the waypoint Khalil had mentioned.

"That must be Sahl," Joel said, shielding his eyes from the sun with his hand and squinting into the distance. "He's the acolyte that brought us lunch yesterday."

So, the initiate that they had seen around the monastery had been the runner that lit the lamps through the cave. He couldn't have been that far ahead of them this whole time. It seemed odd that they would send just one young initiate. He'd looked no more than fourteen or fifteen. The Abbot must have been confident that the cave was safe for him to pass through.

Sahl seemed to have spotted them as well, waving to indicate where he was. Joel waved back and prodded his horse into a trot.

The young man was dressed in light, breathable breeches and a tunic with a linen cloth wrapped around his shoulders to protect his skin from the sun. Sophie would have never recognized him as a monk in training if she hadn't already known him. His clothes were in shades of browns and tans so that he almost blended in with his surroundings. No wonder she hadn't noticed him before. She doubted that anyone but Eolisti could have picked him out against the background.

Sophie felt sweat beading at the nape of her neck as she

and Eolisti trailed after Joel across the rocks. Hopefully, they would get another chance to eat and rest soon. It was good to be out of the cave, but with mountains on one side and an endless desert on the other, she had the feeling that what lay before them would be more difficult than anything they had already been through.

CHAPTER

SEVENTEEN

Traveling in the desert was like nothing Sophie had ever experienced before. The days were oppressively hot. Khalil provided them with shawls, similar to what Sahl had been wearing when they'd first seen him, to protect their head and shoulders from the sun. Even with her lightest dress on, Sophie still found it difficult to think straight in the heat. It felt like she was boiling from the inside. They would stop to rest around midday, finding a shaded area to stretch out in and give the horses a break. Usually, this was behind a large rock or at the base of a hill on which one of the white stone waypoints stood, but if they couldn't find shelter, Khalil and Joel would set up a small canopy that they could rest under. They would have food and water, then after a few hours when it cooled off, they would pack up and ride until dusk.

Night in the desert was the complete opposite of the day. Once the sun set, the air rapidly grew cold. Sophie found that she often needed to put on extra layers at night to sleep comfortably. When they stopped to make camp, Khalil would start a small fire to cook over and keep insects away while Sahl set up cots for them to sleep on. Once they had eaten and were resting on the rocks they placed around the fire, Joel would tell them stories that he'd heard from other travelers while living at Ta'Shela. Sophie, Eolisti, and Sahl would listen intently while Khalil sat a little ways away from the rest of them, always with the same disapproving expression on what little she could see of his face.

It wasn't that he was disinterested in what they were doing exactly, but he seemed to be consciously trying to distance himself from the group. Sophie had tried to strike up a conversation with him on occasion but was met with moody silences or short replies. She felt terrible for having suspected him while they were at the monastery, but Khalil refusing to talk to anyone else wasn't helping at all.

"Just let him brood," Eolisti advised loudly enough for Khalil to hear her when Sophie had told her of his attitude. "If he wants to be the outcast, that's fine. We don't really need him."

The Anai still didn't seem to think much of Khalil. Sophie knew that Khalil's quietness and refusal to answer her questions had solidified in Eolisti's mind that he was an enemy. Sophie thought his presence was a little disconcerting, especially since she still hadn't caught a glimpse of his entire face, but it was hard to justify mistrusting him when he was helping her get away from her family. She wondered if Khalil would ever open up to them.

Sahl turned out to be a smart and confident young man. He'd volunteered back at the monastery to light their way through the cavern and accompany them on their journey. He was older than Sophie had initially guessed and was actually a year older than she was. Sahl was small for his age and was able to squeeze onto the horse carrying their supplies without much difficulty. Eolisti seemed to find him interesting, and Sahl liked to talk, so the two of them chatted most of the day while they rode, with Sophie and Joel joining in occasionally and Khalil only speaking to give them orders.

After almost a week of riding from waypoint to waypoint, the mountains to their right finally started to recede, giving way to dry plains filled with short, scrubby bushes and trees. They never quite entered the sandy desert of Alkhazai, but it was always within sight, a reminder of the barren wasteland that lay to the south.

"This place doesn't get much rain, does it?" Sophie asked, speaking mostly to herself as she looked down at the dried grass crunching underneath her horse's hooves. She was thirsty and tempted to try to pull some moisture out of the plants with magic, but she didn't think it would work. For one, they were too dry. Khalil gave them water to drink throughout the day, but she sweated it right back out again.

It was probably also not a good idea to use magic out here, in the middle of nowhere, but that thought had been secondary. Sophie missed her magic. It was like a part of her that she couldn't let out, and the power built up and buzzed under her skin. It had been a few weeks since she had been able to use spells freely. Sophie hadn't thought that it would take this long for her to get away from her old life. Magic was like breathing. She wanted to use her power and she was afraid that if she wasn't able to use it soon, it might start spilling out accidentally.

"No. It mostly just rains in the winter," Khalil said, surprising Sophie with an actual response. Today, he rode almost beside her, just a few paces behind so that his head was in line with her mare's tail. "But it rains more here than over there." He indicated the rising and falling dunes of sand far in the distance.

"That doesn't really matter to us, I guess, since we'll be out of here soon." She glanced at Khalil. "Hopefully." It was hard to keep the dryness out of her voice.

The right side of his mouth twitched. If Sophie didn't know better, she would have thought that he was trying not to smile. "Do you know why we are going this way?" he asked. "I'm sure you've figured it out."

Sophie had been thinking about it for a while. Ahead of her, Eolisti was talking animatedly to Sahl, so she doubted they could hear Khalil. "We're heading toward the coast of southern Omer to take a ship across the Silver Sea. If we were going to go north to Elizash, we should have already changed course by now. The lack of roads and towns suggests that no one lives around here, probably due to the inhospitable weather, so there's less of a chance that we'll be seen. Judging by the fact that we haven't seen anyone the entire time we've been traveling, there doesn't seem to be much traffic between Alkhazai and Omer. I'm guessing any travel between the countries would be done by ships since it's faster and safer than moving on foot through the desert. The hard ground also makes it more difficult to track, so anyone following us would have to be an expert at tracking in this kind of terrain."

Khalil frowned. "Yes, but there is one more reason."

His horse trotted up a few paces so that they were almost shoulder to shoulder. Sophie turned to look at him, but Khalil still faced forward. "Now that you are out of Zo'rahn, we need to be even more careful."

"What do you mean?"

"While working within Zo'rahn, the wizards are closely scrutinized by the other rulers of the country. Those in power usually look for weaknesses in those that they share that power with and exploit them. Being unable to retrieve one of their own would look very bad for them so they would not be able to exert their full power for fear of this mishap becoming widely known. But now that you are out of the country, I expect that they will be able to use more resources with less fear of discovery."

Sophie swallowed. She suddenly felt cold despite the glaring sun. What Khalil was saying made sense. In fact, when she thought about it for a few moments, it seemed obvious. Why hadn't she thought of it before?

"You're not using your magic since you know that an area can retain a trace of that power for a few days before it dissipates." Khalil continued when she didn't say anything. "That's good, but if they do manage to catch up to us, I need you to be ready to act."

"Ready to act?"

"If they use magic against us, none of us will be able to fight that. You must not hesitate. Do you understand?"

It took her a moment to answer. It felt as though her thoughts were going a million miles an hour. The fact that they were even having this conversation when Khalil had been silent previously, meant that he felt it was vital for her to understand the situation. He usually took the first watch as they slept, and he must have seen something that convinced him that facing magic was a real possibility. If she had to, would she be able to go up against a ranked wizard of Zo'rahn? She knew the theory of offensive magic. She'd even practiced it diligently back at the estate, but she'd never used it in practical application. She'd never had to fight for her life or freedom against another spellcaster.

Finally, she nodded, though she felt as if she was going to be sick. "Yes."

This time he smiled. It was lopsided, but definitely there for just a moment. Khalil pulled on the reins and his horse slowed, allowing Sophie to get a few paces ahead of him again. She continued to stare at him over her shoulder, her mouth slightly open, but he fell into silence once again.

He didn't say anything else until right before they normally would have stopped for food and rest.

"Hide!" His voice came from behind them and cut through Eolisti's and Sahl's conversation. Sahl had been telling Eolisti a story of the time that he had hidden one of the monk's sashes on the roof of the barn back at the monastery when Khalil had interrupted them. He looked a little crestfallen, but Khalil ignored it. "Now!"

Heart pounding, Sophie quickly led her horse behind a large boulder to one side of their path. She slipped down from the saddle and crouched, gently pulling the reins so that the mare would pull her head down as well. She could see Eolisti close by, peeking out from behind a tangle of branches, her horse somewhat visible but still mostly hidden.

Sophie risked a glance and poked the top of her head out from behind the rock. The shawl would hide her hair and make it harder for her to be seen. Hopefully.

Khalil was crouched low to the ground, slowly creeping back up the hill they had just come over. His stallion was standing next to a thick bush close to where Sophie was hidden, the shabby branches tall and thick enough to hide the horse. The horse waited patiently while Khalil crested the hill and vanished out of sight.

Minutes went by without him reappearing. Sophie could hear her own heartbeat in her ears. Was there something waiting for them on the other side of the hill that had gotten Khalil? She remembered their conversation earlier and her mouth went dry. She had to be ready to act if there were wizards. But what could she do? She had never attacked anyone before.

After what felt like a lifetime, a shape moved at the top of the hill. Khalil snaked through the rocks and trees until he arrived back where his horse was hidden. He patted him gently on the nose then motioned for everyone to follow him. Sophie came out from behind the boulder, coaxing her horse along as she trailed after Khalil, acutely aware of the crunching of dry grass and rocks beneath her feet. They slowly made their way farther down into the valley with Khalil in the lead, all of them tense and looking around at anything that moved. Eolisti tried to speak, and Joel shushed her. Sophie thought that would have enraged the Anai, but the other woman just nodded and continued without speaking.

Once they were far from the hill, Khalil led them over to a decaying tree with dry, cracked roots. The barren branches provided little shelter from the sun, but there didn't seem to be any other options around. When they were all gathered by the tree, Khalil finally spoke.

"We are being followed," he said calmly.

Sophie's stomach sank. "Who is it?"

"I don't know," he said, pulling out a water skin and drinking deeply from it.

"I couldn't see anyone when we were on that hill. There's been no sign of anyone following us." Eolisti sounded slightly uncertain, but her eyes dared anyone to contradict her.

"We'll rest here for a little while, then we'll need to continue on so that we can put as much distance between us as possible," he continued as if Eolisti hadn't spoken.

Eolisti narrowed her eyes at Khalil, and Sophie could tell that she wanted to argue. If Eolisti hadn't seen anyone following them, then she doubted that Khalil could have. But if Khalil was lying to them, what was the real reason that they needed to take an alternate path?

"I don't like this," Eolisti muttered to Sophie as she sat down next to her in the scant shade the dead trunk provided. "There isn't anyone following us."

Sophie was about to agree with Eolisti when Sahl sat down on her other side. "The Abbot trusts Khalil and he's worked for Ta'Shela before," he said as he took a drink from his own waterskin and wiped the sweat off his brow with his sleeve. "You should trust him, too. It's not like he's going to lead you into a trap or something." He grinned, but the smile faded at the look on their faces. "Look," he said as he leaned back to rest on his elbows, "Khalil's kind of distant and cold, but he's actually not a bad guy. He just doesn't like to talk very much."

She watched Khalil and Joel talking a few paces away from them. Khalil pointed to the south and Joel said something, but Sophie was too far away to hear. "Have you ever seen his face?" Sophie asked, the question popping into her mind. "Why does he cover it?"

"Uh, no, I haven't," Sahl said, sounding suddenly uncomfortable. "I've only been at the monastery for two years, but I heard some of the monks talking about him. Something happened to him. He came to the monastery and trained there for a while, but they didn't say what." He laughed nervously. "Once they discovered me listening, they seemed to think it was none of my business and had me go scrub pots."

"Sounds like something my mom would have me do." Eolisti took a sip from her waterskin. "I wonder what he's hiding."

"Well, the monks seem to think he has a good reason

for hiding whatever happened to him. They tend to be good judges of character."

Eolisti scoffed but didn't say anything else. Sophie did agree with her, no matter what the monks thought. It would be easier to trust Khalil if he were a little more open with them. The conversation they had earlier was a step in the right direction. She knew where they were going now, but being able to see his face when she talked to him would have made her feel more at ease.

Sophie was struck by the realization that, despite the stories that Sahl and Joel had been telling as they traveled, she had not given any thought to the monks since they'd first emerged from the long path through the mountain cave. When she thought of the monastery, all she could picture was Ta'Shela as it had been when Joel had given them the tour. She was ashamed to realize that the concern for the welfare of its inhabitants had faded over the last few days, as though the travel had somehow made them less important. No, they were still important, but she realized that her distance probably put them in less danger. She hoped that was true.

Sophie was about to lay back and rest for a moment when she felt it, a tingling that went through her entire body and made the hairs on the back of her neck stand on end. She got to her feet, breathing shallowly. She stared around wildly, looking for the source that she'd felt.

"What's wrong?" Eolisti's voice seemed distant. Khalil and Joel had noticed her abrupt distress and were making their way back to the tree. *They won't make it in time,* she thought as she reached out with her senses to the feeling of building power. It was strong, much too strong to attempt to negate before it hit them.

Then she spotted it. A wall of sand and wind

approaching them at rapid speed from the south, much faster than a natural storm would move. It engulfed the hill they had descended from earlier and would be on them within seconds. Eolisti and Sahl saw it as well and got to their feet on either side of her. "What is that?" the Anai asked, staring at the oncoming sandstorm.

"Magic," Sophie breathed, eyes wide as the storm engulfed them.

EIGHTEEN

The wind howled in Sophie's ears. She could barely see five feet in front of her. Every attempted breath made her choke. Her lungs burned and she gasped for air, which made her choke even more. The shawl that she'd been wearing whipped about her face. She grabbed a handful of the cloth and covered her mouth with it, gratefully breathing in sand free air.

Next to her, Eolisti must have had the same idea. She tied the shawl about her nose and mouth, squinting against the wind and sand battering them. "Are you alright?" she shouted, but the howling wind nearly drowned out her voice. Sophie nodded, looking around frantically. The others were gone. Even Sahl, who'd been standing right next to her, had disappeared. The winds were strong, but they shouldn't have been able to blow him away.

Eolisti grabbed her arm and pulled her in the direction where the horses had been before the storm hit, shielding her eyes with her other hand. She let herself be pulled along by the Anai. She could still feel the swell of energy pulsing behind the storm, but the wind and debris pelting her made it hard to concentrate.

Sophie tripped over a rock and nearly fell, but Eolisti steadied her. They stumbled forward together, nearly blind, until they found the Anai's horse, standing with its back to the oncoming gale. Eolisti let go of Sophie's hand and rushed to the horse, immediately going for her scabbard and shield.

A hand touched Sophie's shoulder and she jumped, turning quickly to find herself face to face with Khalil. He, too, had tied a cloth around his nose and mouth, making his already obscured face look featureless and unsettling. "Are you hurt?!" he yelled over the wind. She shook her head. "We need to find shelter! Stay close!" He took her hand in much the same way Eolisti had and started pulling her away.

Eolisti's hand caught Khalil's wrist and, with one smooth movement, broke his grip. "Don't touch her!" she shouted and pushed back on his arm, making him stumble.

He caught his balance in an instant and spun around to face the Anai. Sophie couldn't see his expression, but she could tell by his body language that he was furious. Eolisti tilted her chin up at him, her hand firmly on the hilt of her sword as the wind whipped strands of her hair around her face. Khalil clenched his fists and the two looked moments away from attacking each other.

"Stop it!" Sophie stepped between them, one hand on each of their chests to keep them apart. Even if she didn't fully trust Khalil, this was no time to get into a fight. "We need to find the others, and I think there's more to this storm—"

The feeling of something slick and oily slid across Sophie's skin, making her shiver. The energy was foul and nauseating. Sophie grabbed both Khalil and Eolisti's shirts, pulling them down as something passed just over their heads.

The howling in her ears seemed to quiet as she stared over her shoulder at the thing that had leaped over them. The wind calmed as the figure rose to its feet, the sand seeming to change course and swirl around them in a circle. Its cloak and robes were black and tattered, seeming to float around it in the wind. Skeletal hands covered with rotting skin poked out from beneath its sleeves and under the hood, its face was wrapped in shadows. A wicked-looking jagged blade in one hand, the other pointing a finger directly at Sophie.

Come, croaked a raspy voice in her head, like the sound of leaves scraping across stone. It was all she could do not to scream. She recognized it, felt the dark energy emanating from it. The creature was a Soulless, a monster made from necromantic energy, death magic, that haunted nightmares.

The sandstorm cast the clearing in a hazy, twilight-like darkness. Khalil held his arm out in front of Sophie and gently pushed her behind him. He reached into his cloak and drew out a sword that was a little smaller than Eolisti's. The blade was thinner at the base and widened near the tip, making it curve slightly back toward the hilt. The Soulless was closest to him, and he tried to block Sophie from its view.

Eolisti crouched low as she drew her sword and shouted, "What the hell is that thing?!"

The creature's rattling breath sent shivers up Sophie's spine. "It's called a Soulless!" she yelled over the wind, trying to keep her voice steady as it drew another rattling breath. "It's the reanimating of a human corpse with magic!" Its very existence was wrong. She'd heard stories about these creatures. Most children had. They were used to warn children not to go outside alone at night and to encourage them to stay close to their parents. Sophie had learned what they really were while she studied in Zo'rahn. "The practice is illegal in most countries since the casting usually involves ritual sacrifice."

"Illegal?! It's trying to kill us! I don't think that matters to whoever is controlling it! How do we stop it?" Eolisti asked desperately, not taking her eyes off the creature. "Can we just cut off its head or something?!"

Sophie racked her brain for anything she had read about how to destroy a Soulless. "Fire!" she called over to the Anai, remembering a passage about how they hated light. "Or you can remove the source of power from its body, usually a gem embedded in their flesh or runes carved into a bone!" Her stomach lurched at the thought of cutting up the Soulless until they could find the spell's focus. "Otherwise, overwhelming force can break the enchantment if it takes enough damage."

"Can you use your magic to overwhelm it?" Khalil asked over his shoulder, still facing the Soulless with his back to her. He sounded much calmer than she felt.

"Maybe," she replied, not feeling very confident. "I've never actually seen one before. I'm not sure what it's capable of."

The Soulless moved forward, it's sword arm outstretched. It seemed to sense that she was not going to come peacefully. One more time, its rasping voice echoed in her head. *Come...*

Sophie covered her ears with her hands. "No!" she screamed. "I'm not going back!"

Eolisti leaned close to Sophie and pulled one of her

hands away from her ear. "I'll distract it," she said just loudly enough for Sophie to hear. "Then, you can use your magic on it."

"What if I can't?" Sophie gasped, her eyes wide. "What if I can't do anything?"

"You can." Eolisti smiled and winked at her, turning away to face the Soulless again.

Without warning, the Soulless darted at them, it's cloak billowing as it charged. Khalil raised his sword just in time to parry the blow, but the strength of the monster's advance knocked his arm aside. Its weapon changed direction in a flash, and the Soulless drove the hilt of the sword toward Khalil's face. He tried to block the strike but missed it by an inch. The weapon connected with Khalil's cheek and sent him stumbling to the ground with a grunt of pain.

The Soulless loomed over Sophie. A long boney finger reached for her and it felt like time slowed down. She could see the rotting tendons clinging to each joint. Her only instinct was to scream, but when she opened her mouth, her voice was gone. She wanted to run or jump away or do something other than just stand there, but her legs wouldn't move. *This is it*, she thought, *this is the end of my journey*.

A silver blade swung into her vision and time snapped back to normal speed. Eolisti's sword came down on its outstretched arm, knocking it away from Sophie. The Anai twirled and stabbed the sword into the monster's abdomen, then pushed with all her might. It let out a hoarse sound and staggered back. Eolisti tore her sword out of the Soulless and jumped out of reach.

The Soulless turned to Eolisti and raised its blade, seemingly unfazed by what the Anai had done to it. There was no blood that Sophie could see, and the folds of black fabric hid any visible damage. The thing pressed Eolisti, driving her back a few steps. She blocked and parried its attacks, steel ringing on steel. On the other side of Sophie, Khalil was rising to his feet.

"A little help would be nice!" Eolisti shouted as the Soulless swung at her again, and she barely dodged out of the way. She whipped her blade at its leg, causing it to stumble.

Khalil picked up his sword and dashed at its back, bringing the curved blade down right between its shoulder blades. It whirled around to face him. Without skipping a beat, Eolisti attacked while its back was to her.

They fought the Soulless in tandem. Sophie had seen Eolisti fight before, but Khalil was able to match her step for step. They worked in concert, and it was almost like a dance they both knew by heart. Eolisti would strike first and pivot away. Then as it stumbled, Khalil would step in and slash at the Soulless while it was focused on the Anai. The two dodged and wove around its blade as the black cloth flapped and billowed around them, but the creature wasn't slowing down.

Eolisti and Khalil were.

Their dance was becoming a little less graceful, a little less coordinated the longer they fought. Their attacks were starting to miss more often and when they dodged, the counterstrikes seemed closer and closer to meeting flesh. They couldn't keep it up for much longer.

I have to do something, Sophie thought to herself as she watched the two grow tired. She remembered Khalil's words. "*I need you to be ready to act.*" But she wasn't ready. What could she do against a monster like that?

Eolisti flicked her blade out, but the Soulless side-stepped it and turned to bring an elbow smashing into

Khalil's side. It lashed out a booted foot and swept his legs out from under him, sending him crashing to the ground. Then it twisted around, its jagged blade slicing across Eolisti's thigh. She cried out in pain and fell to one knee. Eolisti stared up at the Soulless. For the first time since Sophie had known her, Eolisti looked afraid.

No, Sophie thought, her insides burning as she watched the Soulless raise its sword to finish the Anai. In an instant, her mind was still, and power flickered at her fingertips. She raised her hand and concentrated as the jagged blade reached its apex. The Soulless's cloak burst into flames.

It flung its arms out and dropped the sword, its rattling breath trying in vain to scream. Eolisti seemed to shake off her fear in time and rolled out of the way, eyes wide. Sophie stepped toward the creature as she poured more power into the spell, her fear driven away by the need to help her companions. The flames grew hotter and brighter, stinging her eyes from the brilliant light, but she didn't blink, instead, pushing out more and more magic until the fire was white-hot, and she could feel the heat threatening to burn her skin from where she stood.

The flailing abruptly stopped. The Soulless collapsed to the ground, a burning mass of ash. Bone crackled and burst in the heat. The cold, slithering magic dissolved and the winds around them began to calm. As quickly as it came, the storm died. Sunlight peeked through the descending dust.

Within moments, everything was covered in a thick layer of sand. The pile of ash that was once the Soulless still burned, but its flames were only a dull flicker now that Sophie wasn't pouring any power into it. She approached it cautiously. There was something in the heap that she couldn't quite see, a bump hidden among the embers. With a flick of her wrist, a strong breeze blew the top layer of ash away, revealing a bleached-white bone. A femur by the look of it. The long bone was untouched by the fire, save for a crack down the middle, splitting the bone in two. As she had guessed, runes were carved into the bone, swirling patterns that made her nauseous to look upon. The crack marred the symbols. She leaned in closer. There was something wrapped around it. A fine red thread almost like...

Her stomach turned over, and she jumped back. Hair. Her hair. Wrapped around the bone. As she watched, the hair caught fire and sizzled away into nothing while the femur remained unaffected.

"Sophie," Eolisti said, sounding as if it wasn't the first time she had called her name. Sophie looked over at the Anai, who was on her feet again. She, too, was covered with sand, so much so that she looked like she had been painted with it and left to dry. Eolisti held a piece of cloth to her leg and limped toward her. "Are you all right?" she asked, pulling away the shawl that she had tied over her nose and mouth.

"Yeah..." Sophie glanced back at the bone. It was just now starting to blacken. Any trace of her hair had burned up with the still glowing embers. "Just a little shaken, I guess."

Eolisti let out a laugh then winced. She swayed dangerously, and Sophie ran the few steps between them before she could fall. "Dammit," Eolisti growled. "It didn't hit an artery, but it hurts a lot."

Khalil was suddenly on Eolisti's other side. She glared at him but didn't protest as he took one of her arms and helped Sophie lower her to the ground. Sophie pressed a hand to Eolisti's, still pressing the cloth to her wound, and reached out with her senses again. "It's not deep," she told them. Eolisti glanced at her, eyebrows furrowed and teeth clenched in pain. "I know some healing," she reassured her, "enough to heal this."

She looked over at Khalil. With his back to the sun, the shadows pooled beneath his hood and reminded her of the monster they had just fought. It took her a moment to find her voice again. "Do you have water?"

He nodded and reached into his cloak, pulling out a waterskin, which he handed to her.

"Okay, Eolisti, I need you to move your hand. I need to rinse off the wound before I heal it. You don't want any more sand getting in there."

Eolisti grimaced but pulled her hands and the bloody cloth away, allowing Sophie to pour water onto the gash. The Anai sucked in air through her teeth and grunted, but otherwise stayed still. When she was satisfied that it was as clean as it was going to get, Sophie handed the waterskin back to Khalil, then held her hands a few inches above the wound, concentrating. The magic she used on the Soulless had tired her, especially as she had been channeling raw magic with no focus to ease the strain, but since she'd been storing all of her unused power for weeks, she still had some to give. Sophie drew in a deep breath, feeling the life swirling in the air around them. From her companions, from the hardy plants and animals living in the desert, and from herself. Sophie siphoned off some of that energy and focused it into the droplets of water that still clung to Eolisti's skin. Then she touched the skin right above the wound, releasing her will into the Anai's body.

Through her power, she could feel the blood vessels repair themselves and tissue knit itself back together. Sophie gave Eolisti's body the energy it needed, but the Anai's body knew how to repair itself. She was just speeding things up. The tricky part was making sure nothing went wrong, picking out flaws in the healing process and correcting them, otherwise it could create even more problems. Still, Eolisti's wound closed without issue as far as Sophie could tell, and all that was left was a fine line of pink skin.

The whole process had only taken moments.

"Wow," Eolisti said, staring at her leg. "It doesn't even hurt anymore. That's a useful trick."

"You might be a little tired," Sophie said, fighting off a bout of dizziness. She had used quite a bit of energy in the past few minutes and was beginning to feel the drain on her own body. "But you should be able to stand and walk around on it. It might be a little tender for a day or so."

"We should find Joel and Sahl," Khalil said, standing. "And make sure the horses haven't run off.

Sophie helped Eolisti to her feet and gazed around, scanning the landscape. She spotted movement near some bushes about forty feet away from where they were. "Joel?! Sahl?!" She listened, hoping they could respond.

"Help!" Joel's voice called back, frantic and high pitched. Sophie's heart leaped into her throat.

Before she knew it, she was running with Eolisti and Khalil, her faintness forgotten.

Joel was kneeling on the ground next to Sahl, both hands covered in bloody sand caked up to his elbows. He was putting pressure on a wound in Sahl's side, but the blood had already soaked through the initiate's clothing, staining the sand and dust a dark, muddy brown. Joel said Sahl's name over and over, tears streaming off his face and falling onto his hands, but Sahl was already so pale.

"What happened?" Khalil asked when he reached them.

It took Joel a second to answer and when he tried to

speak, his voice cracked. "I reached Sahl a few seconds after the storm hit. He was on his knees. I think the force of the winds turned him around and he stumbled away from the group." Sophie knelt down in the dirt across from Joel while he spoke. His eyes met hers, red and brimming with tears. "I was helping him to his feet when we heard something moving around and that thing came at us from out of the sand. We were too disoriented to get out of the way and—" He choked, and it took him a moment to catch his breath. "It stabbed the kid and disappeared back into the sandstorm."

"Joel," Eolisti said gently, staring down at Sahl's wound. "I don't think..." Her voice trailed away.

Sophie took a deep breath as her hands hovered over Sahl's shirt. She tried to clear her mind.

"What are you doing?" Joel asked, the desperation plain in his voice.

"I'm going to try to heal his wound," she said, fighting down the fear and doubt that surged within her. She was already exhausted from the fire and healing Eolisti's wound, but she had some strength left. She didn't know if she was skilled enough to heal him, but she had to try. She focused her energy and reached out a hand, but she couldn't sense any life coming from him. When she looked at his face, his eyes half-closed, she barely managed to choke back a sob. His eyes were glassy and unseeing under the lids. No air entered or left his lips and his chest was still. Hot tears began to stain her cheeks as she turned away from him, shaking her head. They were too late. Sahl was already gone.

No amount of magic could bring a soul back from the dead.

CHAPTER
NINETEEN

Rajani watched from the crest of the hill as the giant cloud of dust and sand settled in the distance. The wind whipped the edges of his cloak. He'd placed himself right where they had been earlier that day, on the crest of a large hill. He could see the broken stems of trampled grass all around him.

The enchantment must have been broken. He smiled a little to himself. He hadn't really expected it to work. From what he had heard of his target, she was strong, and, with enough coaxing, she would have had to use her magic. No, the point of the Soulless had been more of a statement. *I'm coming for you now.*

He doubted they had made it out of the sandstorm unscathed. Soulless were good at killing, and the spell had lasted much longer than he'd anticipated. The girl must still be nervous about fighting. Good, she should be.

It hadn't been all that hard to track her once the package from the Vizier had arrived. He'd been enjoying himself in Alkhazai when the message came a few nights ago. Find the girl and return her to the Vizier. Payment upfront as usual and a few strands of her hair for good measure. He'd left that night and journeyed across the desert. He didn't know or care why the Vizier would want the little half-breed returned. So long as he was paid, he did what he was told.

The man known as the Spider was tired. Conjuring up a sandstorm and binding it to his newly created Soulless had been no easy task, but before he rested, he should report to the Vizier that he'd found her and that she seemed to be heading toward Nobarum, the closest port city. They were probably trying to get her onto a ship then. Rajani opened the flap of the satchel that hung off his shoulder and pulled out a slender stone tablet with a wax face that gleamed in the afternoon sun. He held the tablet in one hand while he fished in his pocket with the other, eventually pulling out a sparkling emerald the size of a quail egg. The emerald fit perfectly into the socket at the top of the tablet. It snapped in with a soft clicking sound, and Rajani scoured the satchel for the stylus that matched the tablet.

Once he finally found it, at the very bottom of his bag of course, he looked back at the tablet and was surprised to see words carved into the wax.

We will await you in Nobarum. Go to the dry dock and ask for passage to the homeland. Wait for the warrior to be away from the girl. My agent will act at that time.

The message must have been sent to him between the last time he checked the tablet and now. He didn't keep the gem socketed, in case his satchel was compromised. Without the gem, the tablet was useless. He normally checked it at night, so that meant that the message had come either very late the previous night or sometime this morning.

So, the Vizier had an agent who was with the girl? If

they were traveling with her, his Soulless might have just killed them. Oops. How ever would he sleep at night?

No matter, the message didn't change anything. If the Vizier's agent was dead, he'd just have to make his own opening. He preferred working alone anyway.

Rajani pressed his thumb to the socketed gem and held it there. Gradually the carving in the wax faded until the surface was smooth and shiny again. Then he gripped the stylus and began to carve a message of his own into the wax.

CHAPTER

TWENTY

They buried Sahl's body at the base of the petrified tree. Death was something that Eolisti was familiar with. Even the Anai in Elasariin died, but Sahl's death was different. The way that he'd died was not neat or tidy, but violent and bloody. Eolisti wasn't sure how she felt. She and Sahl had talked a lot and she liked him, but she didn't really know him that well. What bothered her more was that instead of the young initiate, it could have been her bleeding out into the sand, the one buried in the dirt. It had almost been her.

Joel had promised that when they got to a town, he would write to the monks so that they could extract Sahl from the desert and give him a proper burial at Ta'Shela. Khalil seemed satisfied with this, but Sophie looked more miserable than ever, no doubt blaming herself for the initiate's death. Her eyes were red and swollen from crying, and she wouldn't meet anyone else's. After praying to Samar and Azorah, the goddess of fate, to prepare Sahl's soul for the afterlife, they rested and ate. No one talked, not even Joel.

They moved on as soon as they had finished eating and changed out of their sandy, bloody clothes. Khalil wanted to get away from the area where the Soulless had attacked them, in case more weren't far behind. They left the remains of that monster right where it fell. Eolisti wanted to poke at it, maybe take the blackened bone back to Elasariin as a trophy. Sophie came out of her daze long enough to say that it was safer to leave it there, and that the enchanter might be able to track it if they took the bone with them.

Sophie had saved her life twice that day. Once when the Soulless had first appeared and again when she had stumbled to the ground. Eolisti hadn't heard the Soulless when it came up behind them as they argued in the sandstorm. And when she'd been kneeling on the ground in front of it, she truly thought it was going to be her end.

She'd seen Sophie do little tricks with magic, but only a few times. She claimed that using magic would lead the people after them right to her. Eolisti had started to believe that Sophie wasn't very powerful, and that tracking nonsense was just an excuse, but seeing her use her power on that creature...

It was terrifying.

Eolisti had never seen anything like it before. Timid, scared little Sophie had reduced a monster—a monster that Eolisti herself couldn't beat—to ashes in a matter of seconds. It was so unfair. Her mother had always told her that Zo'rahni wizards were dangerous, and now she finally understood why.

Eolisti should have been enjoying herself. She was beautiful, talented, and was finally somewhere far away from home where her mother couldn't watch her. People should have been staring at her in amazement everywhere they went, but so far, they had only been out in the middle of nowhere with no one interesting to talk to. She'd wanted to see Sophie safely to her destination and she didn't trust Khalil, but all this rough, boring travel was getting a little ridiculous. At least traveling up the mountain had been dangerous and exciting.

Well, the Soulless had definitely been dangerous. There was also the tiny matter that she was going to be in a lot of trouble when she went home, which she wanted to put off as long as possible. The image of her mother's furious face made her shiver.

She knew she should have been grateful to Sophie, but she wasn't. She was angry. Angry at herself mostly, for not being stronger. For needing help from the person that she was supposed to be protecting. Eolisti knew that death was always a possibility, but it never really struck her as something that would actually happen. At least not to her. All her life, she had trained to become a Vendarii, but how could she protect anyone if she couldn't even protect herself?

They traveled for hours in silence, Eolisti stewing in her thoughts. All around them were the same barren trees, scrubby yellow grass, and desert dunes far in the distance to their left. She was so tired of being hot and thirsty. She wanted a bath. She wanted not to have sand in her boots. They had been traveling in this stupid desert for over a week. When were they going to get back to some sort of civilization?

As the sun was beginning to set, Khalil stopped their procession and told them to rest for a few hours. Sophie had slumped forward in her saddle and almost fell off her horse, but Khalil caught her arm and steadied her. Clearly, she'd overexerted herself. Eolisti had jumped off her horse and almost punched Khalil, but Sophie waved her off. Fine. If Sophie didn't want her help, then she wouldn't get it. If she wanted to let that hooded jerk deceive her, then Eolisti would let her do what she wanted. Why should she care?

Eolisti took another swallow of water from the waterskin and glared at Khalil. Night had already fallen, and they were sitting around the campfire Joel had built. Khalil was seated apart from the rest of them as usual. He'd finished his food and appeared to be resting against a rock, his head slightly tilted back. That damned hood still covered half of his face.

Eolisti had the sudden urge to jerk it off his head. Sure, he could fight, but what was the worst he could do to her? If he tried to kill her, she had Sophie and Joel as back up. The three of them could take him.

Sophie sat beside her, staring down at her small bowl of soup and rice, eyes unfocused. Eolisti forced herself not to roll her eyes, then leaned over and nudged Sophie's shoulder with her own. "Hey, are you going to eat that food or just stare at it?"

The mage gave her a weak smile and just stirred the soup with her spoon. Eolisti did roll her eyes then. She couldn't help it. How could someone be so dangerous and yet so melancholy at the same time? "Eat," she ordered and nudged Sophie again. "You're no good to me starved." That got Sophie to actually take a few bites. She didn't like having to goad her into eating, but Eolisti would take what she could get. What happened wasn't Sophie's fault, but she knew that was all the human would be thinking about for the next few days.

It wasn't like Sophie's brooding was her problem, but she thought she understood how the other woman felt to a small degree. Eolisti clenched her fists hard enough to feel her nails cut into her palms. She knew it was irrational to think that if she had been better, she could have defeated the Soulless by herself, but she kept playing that fight over and over in her head, highlighting where she had failed to sense its attacks or where she could have been quicker.

Ugh, if she kept thinking about this, she would turn into Sophie, sulking around and blaming herself endlessly. Eolisti stood and stretched. "I'm going to get some sleep." She smiled at Joel and threw another glare in Khalil's direction for good measure.

She'd helped Joel set up two canvas tents earlier, and Eolisti stomped over to the one that she had designated for herself and Sophie. She was surprised when she opened the flap and found that Sophie had followed right behind her. With a look over her shoulder, she raised an eyebrow. "Finished already?"

"Yes. I'm not hungry. I just want some sleep," she said, staring at the ground in front of her. Eolisti nodded and moved aside to hold the flap open for her. She could tell that Sophie was lying. She'd just wanted to get away from Khalil and Joel. And who could blame her? Khalil was almost as bad as the Soulless. How did a little weasel like that win over the monks at Ta'Shela?

As Sophie passed her and retreated into the tent, Eolisti remembered the last thing Sahl had said to them.

The monks seem to think he has a good reason for hiding whatever happened to him. They tend to be good judges of character.

~

As TIRED AS SHE WAS, Sophie couldn't sleep. She lay awake, staring up at the tent canopy, the canvas swaying back and forth on a gentle breeze. Eolisti was breathing steadily in the cot next to hers. The Anai had lain awake for a while as well, but eventually, she'd succumbed to her fatigue. Healing magic took energy from both the healer and the patient, so Sophie wasn't surprised that the other woman was so soundly asleep. She was exhausted herself, but every time she closed her eyes, all she could see was Sahl's still and bloody form lying on the ground in front of her. She kept replaying the scene in her mind. Was there something else she could have done to save Sahl? After the Soulless was dead, she could have acted more quickly, but even so, she'd never dealt with a mortal wound before. Could she have even healed it? She should have sensed the storm long before it was on them. She could have grabbed both Eolisti's and Sahl's hands so they wouldn't have been separated when the storm blew over them. She could have done something, anything more than what she had.

Sophie turned over for what felt like the hundredth time. It was her fault that Sahl was dead. He would have never left Ta'Shela if she hadn't been there. Surely, there were people that he cared about back at the monastery, waiting for him to return. Did he have a family? She'd never thought to ask.

Who else had been hurt because of her? Had Zephan convinced the Vizier that he didn't know anything about her disappearance? Or had their master figured out that he had helped her? Was Zephan all right? And the Anai? Did the Vizier's agents follow her into the forest? Were the monks at Ta'Shela all right? She felt sick thinking about all the people who had helped her, all the people she'd put in danger for her own sake. Was there another way she could have done this? Should she never have left Zo'rahn in this mad quest for freedom?

Then there were the people who were still helping her. Eolisti, Joel, and Khalil. They were still in danger, no matter how skilled or competent they may be. She didn't know what she would do if something happened to Eolisti or Joel. Sophie would never be able to forgive herself if they were killed because of her. She couldn't let that happen.

Sophie sat up. She needed to clear her head. There was no way she was going to be able to sleep. Quietly, she slid out of her blankets and pulled her shoes on. Eolisti stirred and Sophie froze, but the Anai only mumbled softly and turned over. Tiptoeing toward the tent opening, she pushed the flap aside and slipped outside.

The cool night air made her shiver. It was almost unbelievable that the days could be so hot, but the nights were so cold. It was exceptionally dark that night. Clouds covered the moons and stars for the first time since they had emerged from the cave passage from Ta'Shela. The dull reddish glow of the fire lit the immediate area just enough for Sophie to see where she was going. She rubbed her arms with her palms for warmth and walked toward the fire.

Khalil sat in the same spot he had been in earlier, with his head slightly tilted back and resting on a rock. His arms were folded across his chest and his legs stretched out in front of him, one crossed over the other at the ankles. The hood of his cloak was still pulled low over his face. If she didn't know better, she would say he was asleep.

His head turned slightly in her direction as she sat down on one of the other rocks and made herself comfortable. "Is everything all right?" he asked, his low voice breaking the otherwise still night.

Sophie had been expecting the question, so it didn't startle her. "Yes, I'm fine. I just can't sleep." She sighed. "I thought maybe the cold air would help me think."

He didn't respond to that, but she could feel his awareness across the fire. The flame had been reduced to small flickers that crawled among the embers that glowed red hot in the center. With a sickening jolt, she was reminded of the Soulless's cracking flesh and bones and turned away from the fire, suppressing an urge to retch.

Even though Sophie knew she had done the right thing by destroying the monster, using her magic to destroy felt wrong. She had been taught that magic was the essence of life itself and that power came from that energy. Granted, a Soulless wasn't really alive, but she had wiped away its very existence. It felt like something was broken inside her. It reminded her of what had happened before she ran away.

Sophie heard movement as she was trying to steady her breathing. When she turned back to the fire, Khalil was looming over her, blocking it from view. He held out one calloused hand toward her. "Let's go for a walk," he said softly.

Looking up at him, his features were so deep in shadow that she could barely tell he was human. He looked more like the Soulless than ever. The thought sent a shiver down her spine, but after a moment's hesitation, she took his hand and let him pull her to her feet. Maybe a walk would be good.

They didn't go far from the camp, just far enough that they wouldn't wake Eolisti and Joel. Khalil helped her navigate between the rocks and brush. She tripped more than a few times and ended up holding on to his arm for support. How was he able to see where he was going? She could barely see anything at all.

Eventually, they found an area clear of dead prickly grass and bushes and they sat a few feet apart. Aeris had finally peeked out from behind the clouds, and the desert was washed once again in its bluish glow.

She watched Khalil. He faced out toward the landscape. The mountains that they had traveled from gleamed in the distance, their peaks still touched with snow.

Why did he wear that hood so low? He must have known that it would make it more difficult for people to trust him. He couldn't have been that much older than she was. There were no lines around his mouth or any wrinkles that she could see. She sometimes caught a glimpse of shaggy black hair. Perhaps he did have some sort of deformity that he wished to hide. If it was something like that, it didn't reach his nose. Sophie opened her mouth to ask him why he wore his hood like that when Khalil spoke.

"That creature today. I think I know who sent it."

Sophie just stared at him, shocked. That was the very last thing that she had expected Khalil to say. "What do you mean? How do you know?"

He continued facing forward. "I've heard rumors about a man who uses the Soulless to hunt his victims. He works for the Viziers, and he usually only operates outside of Zo'rahn. They say he was banished from the country, if such rumors can be believed."

His words brought to mind a story that Sophie had heard a long time ago.

"Wait," she said, holding her hands up. "I think I've heard this before." She tapped her chin with one finger until the memory came back to her. She recalled sitting in her father's lap for a long time and listening as he told her the story. Sophie cleared her throat and spoke in a dramatic voice, imitating what she remembered of her father. "Back in ancient times, there was a powerful wizard that over-threw the mundane ruler of Zo'rahn and established the magical hierarchy. That wizard had eight sons. Seven of them would go on to be the first Viziers, but the eighth was so cruel that he experimented on the citizens, turning them into corpses that walked the night. When the other wizards, his brothers, found out about his dabbling, he was banished for his crimes against the people. Wracked with longing to be accepted back into his father's embrace, he now haunts mages that dare to betray their responsibilities and heritage. He is so powerful that he can control the Soulless like puppets and takes his revenge on traitors to the magical families, lest they end up like him." Sophie laughed nervously when she finished the story. "That's just a myth. It's a story to scare children."

Khalil smiled. "Yes, most of that is a myth. But there is a man who does work as a mercenary for the Viziers and knows how to create Soulless, like the one we saw today. I've never met him, but I have encountered his creatures before. Only last time, I wasn't so lucky and the person I was trying to protect was killed."

A long silence stretched out between them. Sophie looked down at her hands, suddenly embarrassed for laughing at the story. It must have been really hard for Khalil to tell her that.

"I'm sorry," she said finally. "That's terrible."

Khalil sighed. "It happened a long time ago, and he wasn't able to fight them. You can. Don't feel guilty about ending a life when you must, and don't feel guilty about losing a comrade. There wasn't any more you could have done. It took me a long time to accept that man's death wasn't my fault. You shouldn't make the same mistake."

"But," she began, feeling her eyes begin to water. Now was not the time to cry. "He wouldn't have been in danger if it wasn't for me. How can I not feel guilty?"

"He chose to come with us. Sahl knew the risks. You didn't kill him, so why are you blaming yourself?"

She turned away from Khalil and gazed back toward the camp. Sophie could barely see the glow of the fire from here. She took a deep breath and closed her eyes.

"I know... I know I couldn't have healed him, even if I'd gotten to him in time. I just don't want anyone else to get hurt because of me." She looked back at him. His face was turned toward her, the moonlight reflecting off his cloak and making it appear to glow. "Why are you helping me, Khalil? You don't know me. Isn't there anyone waiting for you to come back?"

As soon as it left her lips, she knew it was the wrong question. Khalil's mouth pressed into a thin line as it did right before he started ignoring Eolisti. He got to his feet suddenly, his shoulders tense.

"Nobody is waiting for me. It's time to go." He didn't offer to help her up, he just walked past her and back toward the tents.

Sophie scrambled to her feet and trailed after him, picking her way through the brush much more slowly without Khalil's help. Her skirt kept catching on branches, and she stumbled over rocks she couldn't see. By the time she found her way back to the tents, she was panting and thoroughly annoyed. What was wrong with him? One minute he was comforting and the next, he was back to his old self. She didn't think her question had been that far out of line. She just wanted to know him a little better. He was the one who wanted to go off and talk in the first place.

Sophie sat next to the fire and crossed her arms over her chest as Joel stumbled out of his tent, having just been woken up by Khalil. He yawned and rubbed at his eyes, which still looked a little swollen. He saw her and blinked. "Are you all right?" he asked. "You look upset."

"I'm fine," she said tersely, glowering at Khalil as he poked his head into the other tent.

Joel looked like he was about to say more but was distracted when Khalil took a few quick steps back. Eolisti stormed out. She wasn't wearing any shoes and looked like she had just rolled out of her cot. Her face was flushed, and her brow furrowed. Both hands were balled into fists, and she looked ready to take a swing at Khalil.

"Where do you get off telling us to move in the middle of the night?! We're all tired from fighting that Soulless that *you* let find us and *you* couldn't handle!" She glared at him, her arms shaking with barely suppressed rage. "Why don't you ever show us your face? Are you just pretending to help us so that you can betray us to those wizards when we have our backs turned?" Her voice grew louder and angrier with each accusing question. "How do they keep finding us? Are you sending them messages, telling them where we are?!"

Sophie stood, having a feeling that the altercation was only going to escalate. Eolisti was worked into a rage and wasn't going to back down. She did have a point. Sophie knew that the Soulless had found them using the hair that had been woven around the enchantment, but there had also been those men that had arrived in Bardov only a day after them. How had they known they were there?

"You weren't trying very hard when we were fighting the Soulless! You were going to let it kill me!" Eolisti shouted and lunged at Khalil, reaching out her hand to snatch his hood from his head. His hands blurred as he caught her wrists and took another step back. The Anai didn't back down and pressed forward, straining to reach for his hood.

Khalil held her wrists as they struggled, trying to keep her hands away from his face while Eolisti kept pushing him back.

Sophie felt her temper flare. It was clear that he was not trying to hurt the Anai, but she didn't like how he was grabbing her. Joel seemed frozen where he stood, transfixed by what was happening. The two locked in struggle passed where Sophie was standing, and Eolisti's elbow bumped her arm as Khalil attempted to push her back.

Without giving herself a chance to think, Sophie reached over and pulled Khalil's hood back.

CHAPTER

TWENTY-ONE

Khalil wasn't disfigured. His bronzed skin was smooth and unmarred by flaws or wrinkles. As Sophie had guessed, his hair was dark and shaggy, a mess of locks pushed back from his face. He must have been in his early twenties, and the square jaw and sharp features could have almost been considered handsome, if it wasn't for his eyes.

The pupils and irises were clouded over with a milky white film, a tinge of a golden color shining around the edges. They were disturbingly mesmerizing, as if there were a breeze within them, making the colors undulate and swirl. It was difficult to tell what color his eyes actually were in the near darkness, but one thing was unmistakable. Khalil was blind.

He released Eolisti's wrists and took another step away from her, brushing off his clothes. Eolisti had stopped fighting back and her arms fell to her sides. She stared at him, slack-jawed with morbid fascination. Sophie found it difficult to look away, too. It was partially because of shock at what she had done, partially confusion at what she was seeing.

Khalil stared at Eolisti with his unseeing eyes until the Anai shifted uncomfortably. She cleared her throat and glanced at Sophie, almost looking embarrassed. "I'll pack up," she mumbled and turned away from Khalil, striding quickly back into the tent.

He turned his gaze on Sophie, and she took an involuntary step back. Khalil closed his eyes and flipped his hood back up over his head, pulling it low again.

A burning feeling crept up Sophie's neck toward her face. Sahl had said that Khalil had a good reason for hiding his face, and now she could see why. His blindness was unsettling and would probably bring unwanted attention that would do nothing to help those he was guiding to safety. Even though he did seem to be able to function perfectly, if those working against him knew he was blind, surely, they would try to take advantage of that.

Khalil stood next to the same rock that Sophie had found him leaning against earlier that night. Joel hurried away, presumably to pack up, leaving her alone with Khalil. Sophie fidgeted with the hem of her sleeve. She felt incredibly guilty. Yes, she had been curious about what was under his hood, and not knowing had made her almost as suspicious as Eolisti of his intentions, but she should have respected his privacy and given him the chance to tell them in his own time, if at all.

Mustering her courage, Sophie approached Khalil. He gave no indication that he heard her aside from a slight shifting of his hood. "Khalil," she said softly so the others wouldn't hear her, "I'm sorry for doing that. I shouldn't have pulled your hood off. You have every right to be upset with me..." She trailed off, watching his face.

He didn't say anything. Sophie stayed where she was, watching him in awkward silence. She didn't blame him for being angry. She turned to go help Eolisti pack everything up when she heard him murmur, "It's good that you're not so trusting anymore."

She looked back to see one corner of Khalil's mouth tilt up in a smirk.

"I need to know something," he began, then paused as though he was trying to choose his words carefully. "Usually, I don't ask for any additional information than what the monks tell me, but I need to know how far these wizards will go. I need to know why you left Zo'rahn."

Sophie stared at him, stunned. She'd told no one besides Zephan about what had happened, and no one had asked. She wasn't sure if she should tell Khalil. She'd only known him for a little more than a week. *But*, a little voice in her head whispered, *the monks had faith in him. Maybe you should, too.*

What if he didn't like what he heard? She wouldn't blame him if he decided that he wanted to just leave her here to fend for herself. Would he tell the others? Would they abandon her too?

"Sophie, I can't help you if I don't know what's going on. I will do my best even without the information, but,"—he smirked—"I'll be going in blind."

Sophie almost laughed at his choice of words. After all, his smirk told her his pun was intended. But she still thought it would be in poor taste. Now that she knew the reason he covered his face, it didn't seem so odd to look at him and see the hood pulled over his eyes. She still wasn't sure she trusted him, but he was right. He had a right to know what he was getting into. Sophie inhaled deeply and puffed out her cheeks as she exhaled. If she was going to tell him everything, she should start from the beginning. "Do you know much about Zo'rahn?"

One corner of Khalil's mouth quirked in thought. "Just the basics, really. Information that could be found anywhere. The country's major exports are magical materials and products, the class system puts those with magical abilities above everyone else, and it's ruled by a council of seven Viziers. The climate is fairly mild, warm, but nothing like Alkhazai or Omer."

She smiled to herself. Khalil's description was very basic knowledge. "Yes, magic is at the very core of life in Zo'rahn. The upper class is made up entirely of wizards and their families, even if some of their relatives can't use magic. Only about five percent of the population is born with the ability, which is more than double that of other nations due to the selective breeding that the magical families practice."

Khalil's mouth compressed into a thin line, but he didn't speak.

"Inter-family breeding had been shown to produce highly undesired and unstable personality traits, especially in those that can use magic, so the ruling families started branching out to the greater population a few centuries ago. Now the practice has been in use for so long that it's part of the laws and customs of Zo'rahn. Magical ability can be unpredictable and manifest itself even in those in the merchant and lower classes. It's rarer, but with a population as big as Zo'rahn's, it happens often enough. All children are tested when they reach twelve or thirteen for magical aptitude, since their abilities begin to manifest in various ways once they reach adolescence. If they show any talent whatsoever, they are taken and adopted by one of the ruling families or their relations. Their birth families gain wealth and respect in their community, which for many is a great honor, but the connections between the birth family and the child are severed."

"That happened to you," he guessed, and his voice sounded wary.

"Yes," she said, remembering a warm summer night almost eleven years ago and a man coming to her home wearing black robes.

"Only, I was seven." The memories were blurry and had faded over time, but she still remembered the fear in her mother's voice, even if she could barely remember her face. "My mother was a foreigner and my father was a wealthy merchant. They moved to my grandfather's estate after I was born. I started showing signs earlier than most children, and I was exceptionally strong for someone so young." Sophie smiled bitterly, watching as Eolisti and Joel broke down the tents.

"My mother tried to escape with me, but we were caught, and I was taken away." Sophie sighed before continuing. She'd never found out what happened to her mother after that night. "As you said before, there is a council of seven ruling wizards, called Viziers, who each oversee a province in Zo'rahn. They and their families are the ruling class. Mayors and governors in the provinces are also typically relations of the Vizier, though distantly and at a lower social standing than those in the Vizier's immediate household. I was adopted by the Vizier of the province my parents lived in. His name is..."

Sophie trailed off, afraid to say it, as though if she said his name out loud, he would hear it and know where she was. She knew that was silly, but it was difficult to shake the feeling. Khalil had a right to know. There was no one else here. No one to overhear in the middle of nowhere.

"Lau'ren. Vizier Lau'ren Tashiir," she said, glancing around, but the night was still and silent. Nothing that her eyes could detect moved in the gray and black moonlit landscape.

Sophie took a few slow, deep breaths to regain her composure, and Khalil waited patiently for her to continue.

"Most children who are adopted into the magical families are treated very well since they're trained as Zo'rahni wizards and eventually marry into the family, but I was different." Sophie sighed. "Zo'rahni people are highly distrustful of foreigners, and I'm what they call a 'half-breed,' someone with one parent not from Zo'rahn. It probably wouldn't have been so bad if I looked a little more Zo'rahni, but I take after my mother. The red hair is definitely not native to the East." She stared down at her hands. "Most of the children wouldn't talk to me, even the ones who were also adopted. So, all I had was my training and very few friends.

"About a year ago, the Vizier took notice of me. I'm not sure of the reason, but I assume it was because I was considered powerful for my age. He took me on as one of his personal apprentices, and I started assisting him with his work along with others." She felt her face heat up, and she moved on quickly.

"The real trouble started a few months ago. There were these artifacts that had just been lying around his workshop." She shivered as she recalled those memories. It felt dangerous to talk about those *things*. "They're ancient." She rubbed her suddenly sweaty palms on her skirt. "Evil. They take everything good about magic and twist it.

"Magic is the essence of life. It's used to create and destroy depending on the user's will, but it's always in balance. Magic comes from not only inside us but from every living thing around us." She straightened and looked around.

"Take a stream for example. There is an abundance of life there. Fish, plants, insects, even the motion of the water. Then there are the animals that rely on the stream for food, for water. The trees depend on it to hydrate their roots. Magic draws power from life, the energy of nature and every living thing. We shape the magic within ourselves, mixing our personal power with the energy we draw until it's what we want it to be. Usually, we can't take anything but small bits of that power outside of ourselves by force. A wizard can dangerously drain their own life essence with a spell, but not another's. Ritual sacrifice is an exception."

Khalil frowned a bit at that, but still didn't say anything as Sophie collected her thoughts.

"These artifacts are different. They can drain the energy from a living thing against its will, and they don't stop until there is nothing left to take." Sophie grimaced.

"For years, the Vizier didn't know what these artifacts did. He couldn't activate them. For all he knew, it was just a bunch of junk collecting dust in the corner of his lab, but then I came along. My touch activated the artifacts and I—" Her voice broke. She didn't want to continue.

Sophie took a shaky breath and forced herself to go on. "I don't know how, but when another apprentice touched me..." Sophie swallowed down the lump in her throat.

"I drained the magic out of her until she... she died. I didn't know what was happening, but by the time my master reached us, she was gone." Sophie gazed out at the moonlit desert, eyes unfocused. Her mind replayed what had happened in dizzying detail. The look on the young woman's face lying on the ground.

"After everything calmed down, the Vizier was over-joyed. He didn't care about what happened to his other apprentice, a member of his family. He finally knew what these artifacts did. He had me test more of them. I don't know why, but only I could activate them. I didn't want to, but I didn't have a choice. Eventually, I figured out what these artifacts were designed to do."

She looked up at Khalil intently, though she knew he couldn't see her frustration or fear. "They're weapons. Weapons, unlike anything I've ever read about before. They allow the user to drain as much life energy as they want and add it to their own power. They allow the wizard using them to harness that power. They kill everything around them and grant their user the ability to reshape the world, to alter reality if they desire it." Sophie hid her face in her hands. She felt like she was going to be sick.

"The worst part is, it felt good when I used it. Really good. I wanted more, to take from everyone there, to drain them of all their power. What kind of monster wants that? To kill everyone around them? I'm no better than the Vizier. No, I'm far worse than he's ever been." Her eyes stung with unshed tears while her stomach roiled. The memories made her nauseous. She was disgusted with herself.

"Worst of all, instead of stopping myself or trying to destroy them, I just ran. I wasn't brave enough to do anything, so I ran," she finished, choking out the last few words.

Sophie tried to breathe deeply, slowly, over and over, trying to find calm. She finally gathered herself enough to drop her hands and look at Khalil again, but he remained silent. She rubbed her palms on her arms again, trying to fight off a different kind of cold that had settled over her. Her legs shook. She wanted to turn around and run from him, but she forced herself to stay where she was. His mouth was pressed into a thin line, and his hands were fisted at his side.

"You asked me why I'm doing this," he said through clenched teeth, then took a deep breath. When he continued, he sounded calmer. "I was a lot like you once, a long time ago. I had a skill that was being used—no, abused—by someone I cared about to hurt people, but unlike you, I chose to stay, to revel in it, and it almost consumed me. After I lost my sight, it was either leave or let myself be killed by those who had abused my abilities. A woman who works for the same people as your Raven found me and helped me escape. She told me I could either live my life in guilt and fear, or I could use my skills to help others." He took a step toward her.

"You chose to leave your life behind, knowing it would be difficult and knowing you would be pursued. You chose to do what you felt was right, even though inaction would have been easier and safer. Most wouldn't make that choice."

He placed a hand on her shoulder. She looked up into his hood, imagining she could still see those swirling clouds over his eyes. Khalil was about a head taller than she was. "That doesn't sound like the actions of a monster to me," he said gently.

Sophie looked away from him as tears ran down her cheeks. The nauseous feeling from earlier remained, but now she also felt a sense of relief, the comfort of a kindred spirit. She rubbed her eyes and wiped at her cheeks with her sleeves. "I doubt that I'm the only person in the world who can use those things—" she sniffed—"but if I am, he'll never stop hunting me."

"Let me worry about that." He squeezed her shoulder

lightly, then released her. "Come on," he said, turning toward where Eolisti and Joel were waiting for them. "If we push, we should be able to reach Nobarum just after sunrise. Hopefully, the ship will be ready to set sail when we get there."

TWENTY-TWO

There was no ship waiting for them in Nobarum when they arrived. Khalil explained that they were supposed to have arrived the night before, but the incident with the Soulless had delayed them so much that the ship Khalil previously arranged passage on had left without them. So, he took Sophie, Eolisti, and Joel to an inn near the docks. He told the women to stay in their room while he and Joel went to make other arrangements.

Eolisti complained half-heartedly about being confined but promptly fell asleep after lying down. Sophie sat by the window, looking down at the narrow streets and the passing carts and people starting their day. Although the people she could see from her perch were more diverse than even those in Bardov had been, Sophie still kept her head covered, in case anyone happened to look up at her. She could have disguised herself as she had back in Tanzar, but Khalil had warned her not to use magic again until they were well on their way out to sea. This wasn't a big city compared to the Zo'rahni capital, and it was highly likely that those after her were still on the lookout for traces of magic.

She hadn't slept at all the night before and found herself nodding off at the windowsill, awoken only when her arm slipped, nearly hitting her head on the wooden frame. After that, Sophie forced herself to go lie down. She had to push a couple of Eolisti's limbs out of the way, but the Anai just rolled over. The bed wasn't much better than the cots they had been sleeping on in the desert, and the musty-smelling hay mattress poked at her through her clothes.

It seemed like she had barely closed her eyes when Eolisti called her name. Sophie briefly contemplated feigning sleep. Instead, she slowly opened one eye to look at the Anai, who was sitting up next to her with pillows propped behind her back. "What?" she murmured sleepily.

"I'm going to go downstairs and get some food. Want to come?"

Sophie blinked her eyes open and yawned. "Khalil told us to stay here," she mumbled.

Eolisti scowled. "If he thinks he can keep me here all day, he's a bigger fool than I thought." She crossed her arms, looking surly. "I just want to go downstairs and get a drink, maybe have some breakfast. We were traveling all night. He can't possibly expect us not to eat anything all day."

Sophie sighed and pushed herself up. Apparently, she wasn't going to get any sleep. Eolisti did have a point. They hadn't had a chance to rest after packing up their camp and heading to Nobarum. Judging by the sun coming through the window, it was close to midday. Sophie shook her head a little to wake herself up, then tucked her feet under her and sat back on her heels. "We don't know how long he'll be gone. He could be back soon."

The Anai raised an eyebrow. "Can you honestly tell me that you're not hungry at all? Come on, it won't hurt to go downstairs," she pleaded. "We'll still be in the building."

Almost as if on cue, Sophie's stomach growled loudly. She was more tired than hungry, but it didn't seem like Eolisti would let her go back to sleep. "All right," she said grudgingly, then glanced at the door as if Khalil would burst through it at any moment. "Let's just make it quick."

The women climbed out of bed. Eolisti rummaged in one of her travel pouches looking for some coins while Sophie grabbed the key to the room off of the table and cautiously opened the door. Sounds washed over her, floating up from the first floor. The muttering, chattering, and raucous laughing of many voices filled the hall where rows of doors to other rooms lined the wall.

"Wow," Eolisti said as she stuck her head out the doorway and looked around. "There must be a lot of people downstairs."

Sophie couldn't help but notice that she sounded excited about the prospect of going into a room full of people. Sophie, on the other hand, was starting to have misgivings about agreeing to accompany Eolisti. "Maybe we should just stay here," she said nervously. "There could be people down there who are looking for us."

"Don't be such a coward," Eolisti snorted and pushed Sophie out into the hallway. Sophie stumbled into the opposite wall. Eolisti closed the door. "It'll be fine. I'll be with you."

"But you're not even wearing your sword," Sophie protested.

Eolisti rolled her eyes. "Calm down. We're not going

outside." She smirked. "Besides, I think I saw a rapier mounted over the fireplace. If we have to fight, I'll just pull that down."

Somehow, the prospect of Eolisti pulling down a weapon that may or may not be mounted to a wall was of little comfort to Sophie. Reluctantly, she locked the door, and the pair made their way down the stairs.

The tavern was indeed crowded. Men and a few women filled the bar and tables. Most of them wore clothes that were dirty and stained, but they seemed genuinely happy to be there. Sophie wrinkled her nose. The air stank of sweat, ale, and something slightly fishy. A ship must have just come in from a long voyage at sea. A few of the men leered at her and waved for her to join them. She quickly looked away, feeling anxious. She should have put her cloak on before coming down. Why hadn't she thought of that?

There was only one table left that had any room for them to sit. An Anai was already seated there, reading a book. He had the same build and angular features as the people that Sophie had seen at Elasariin, but unlike the Anai she had seen before, he had long, honey-blond hair that was tucked behind his delicately pointed ears and pale, almost luminescent skin. He was dressed modestly, but his clothes were much finer and cleaner than those of the men surrounding him. He was obviously not one of the sailors that had come ashore.

It was clear that he wanted nothing to do with what was going on around him, and the rest of the crowd gave him a wide berth. None of the others talked to him or even looked in his direction. Sophie didn't know how he could read with all this noise, but he seemed engrossed in what he was doing. It wasn't hard to guess that the Anai wanted to be left alone, but when she glanced at Eolisti, her friend had zeroed in on the lone Anai and was grinning in a way that Sophie knew meant trouble.

Noticing that Sophie was looking at her, Eolisti winked and strode confidently over to the bar. Sophie trailed after her, weaving and dodging through the crowd as a couple of sailors cackled and whistled at her. They were inebriated and probably harmless, but she still made sure not to get too close to any of the men. When they reached the bar, Eolisti asked the bartender, a large man with a scraggly, gray beard, for two ales and some bread. The man reached below the bar and passed her two tankards and grunted that he would bring over the food. Eolisti nodded and shoved one of the mugs into Sophie's hands.

"Follow me," she said to Sophie and sauntered over to the table with the lone Anai, plopping herself down in an empty chair. The Anai looked up at them, first at Eolisti then at Sophie, his expression blank. Sophie squirmed under his gaze, but Eolisti seemed not to be bothered by it at all. She raised her glass as Sophie sat next to her, and loudly proclaimed, "There's nothing like a cold, fresh ale," and took a sip from the tankard. She immediately pulled the drink away from her mouth and made a face of utter revulsion. "THAT is nothing like a fresh ale."

The corners of the blond man's mouth tilted up in a smile, and one of his perfectly shaped eyebrows arched. Looking down at her cup, Sophie raised the ale to her lips. She almost gagged. The drink was watery and bitter, nothing pleasant about it at all. Sophie was tempted to spit it back into the tankard, but the other Anai was watching her now, so she swallowed it instead, unable to keep herself from frowning down at the ale.

Eolisti laughed at her, then looked back at the Anai. "You don't mind if we sit here, right? There isn't room at any of the other tables. And, uh"—she glanced around at the sailors still reveling around them—"we'd prefer quieter company."

The blond Anai stared at Eolisti, his eyes a startling shade of blue, and gave her a ghost of a smile. "Not at all," he said, his voice rich and silvery. Eolisti stared back at him, evidently fascinated. Sophie had learned by now that Eolisti liked interesting people, and this Anai was definitely interesting. She could tell Eolisti was almost vibrating, ready to launch into hundreds of questions but also trying to appear calm and collected. She thought it best not to distract her. Eolisti had been uncharacteristically quiet, apart from the confrontation with Khalil the night before. It was good to see that she was starting to return to normal.

"You don't look like you're from around here," Eolisti said casually. She picked up the ale like she would take another sip, then seemed to remember how bad it was and put it back down.

"I am not," he replied curtly and looked back down at his book.

"Where are you from then?" she asked, undeterred by his tone.

"Across the sea," he answered without looking up.

Eolisti seemed to think about that for a moment. "Nemethy, then?"

"Yes." He turned a page in his book and continued reading.

Her eyes lit up, excited at the prospect of hearing about the Anaiian court of the west. Sophie hid her smile behind her tankard. Eolisti was practically quivering in her seat. "What's it like there?"

He shrugged, still not looking up. "It's fine, I suppose."

His response made Eolisti narrow her eyes. The Anai

was giving them short replies, trying to discourage further conversation, and she did not look very happy about it. The Anai clearly didn't want to talk but was too polite to flat-out ignore her. Sophie almost felt sorry for him. Eolisti's smile started to crack, but she continued to stare at him intently, as if pitting her will against his.

"What are you reading?" she asked, trying to sound interested.

"Just some research." The Anai turned another page, which made Eolisti frown in earnest. He definitely was not interested in conversation.

A tap on Sophie's shoulder made her jump in her seat. She looked up to see Khalil looming over her, the hood of his cloak pulled characteristically low, his mouth pursed into that thin line again. "I thought you both were going to wait upstairs until I returned. I don't think it's a good idea for you to be down here."

Sophie felt a flush rising up her neck, but before she could say anything, Eolisti intervened. "Did you really expect us to just wait up there all day? It's not like we need food and water or anything," she said sarcastically.

In response, he reached a hand into his cloak and took out a cloth bundle. He pulled out the remaining chair at the table and sat, then proceeded to unwrap three fried balls of dough the size of his palm, rolled in small seeds. He plucked one up and handed it to Sophie. She examined the ball and took a tentative bite after glancing at Khalil. The dough was lightly spiced and savory, filled with a paste that tasted heavily of cumin and turmeric. She took another, bigger bite. To her empty stomach, it tasted like heaven.

"It's a curry bun. They are very popular here," he said as Sophie took her third bite of the pastry.

"Let me have one of those." Eolisti reached over the

table to snatch one up. Khalil's fingers twitched, and Sophie had the feeling he wanted to pull the buns out of her reach, but he remained still. "Mmm... that's pretty good. Did you only get three?"

The blond Anai eyed the last dough ball.

"Yes." He wrapped up the bun with the cloth and put it back in his cloak. Khalil's head turned toward Sophie's tankard of ale. "I wouldn't drink that if I were you."

Eolisti snorted. "Yeah, we figured that out on our own, thanks."

Khalil turned back to Sophie. "We should speak privately." She assumed he wanted to talk about what they were going to do next. Since they had missed their ship, he must have another plan.

"I'll be right back," she said to Eolisti, who waved an acknowledgment without looking away from the blond Anai.

Sophie shook her head and allowed Khalil to help her up and lead her over to the stairwell they had come down earlier. This corner of the room was mostly empty. The sailors were sitting around the bar and at tables. While many of them glanced at her and Khalil as they passed, the men must have sensed that Khalil was not someone to be trifled with since they didn't whistle or leer at her. They stood off to one side of the stairs, and Khalil leaned down so that he didn't need to shout to be heard. She turned her head away from him, slightly embarrassed by how close he was. "We'll be leaving tomorrow afternoon. The ship just docked in the harbor a few hours ago, and they'll be unloading their cargo today and tomorrow morning. After that, they'll be setting sail for Tanalin."

She glanced back at him, surprised. "How did you find a ship so fast?"

"There are a few captains I know who are willing to help the monks. When I'm delayed, one of their ships is usually available."

It made sense that Khalil would need to have a backup plan in place in case something happened during his journey, and, given the nature of what he did, Sophie doubted that things often went smoothly.

"I'd like you to stay in the room so we don't attract unwanted attention," he continued. "I've already had to dodge a few men who were trying to tail me. I'm not sure who they were, but I'd rather not take the chance of them seeing you."

Her heart leaped into her throat. Someone was trying to follow Khalil? Back to her? She glanced back around at the sailors. Could one of those men be hiding in the crowd? Sophie took a shaky breath. "Yes. I'll stay in the room."

"I'm sorry it has to be this way," he said sympathetically. "Once we get to Tanalin, you'll have a little more freedom." Tanalin was the country south of Morigael. Khalil squeezed her shoulder and held out his arm to escort her back toward the table.

They made their way across the room, and Sophie sat in the chair she had occupied earlier. Khalil remained standing next to her. Eolisti was still trying to engage the blond Anai in conversation, but she didn't seem to be having much success. The book was closed at least, but he maintained his bored expression. Sophie leaned over to Eolisti and whispered into her ear, "Khalil was able to get us on another ship that departs tomorrow." She glanced at the other Anai, who didn't seem to be listening. "I think it's time to go back upstairs."

"Mmm... I don't think so," Eolisti said loudly enough for everyone at the table to hear.

"We need to prepare to leave. You both should stay out of sight until tomorrow," Khalil said firmly, causing the Anai man to glance at him.

"I don't want to. You don't need to have me locked up in a room. Besides"—she gestured at the Anai—"we're having a good time here."

Khalil looked like he wanted to say more, but he must have noticed that the chatter around them had grown softer. Some of the sailors were looking at them and muttering among themselves. Making a scene here would be a bad idea. "Fine," he said. "Just come up after you are done." Khalil turned on his heel without another word and marched toward the stairs. He stopped at the base and waited.

Sophie glanced at Eolisti, who was still glaring furiously at Khalil. She was sure her Vendarii could take care of herself, but it would be just like Eolisti to do something reckless just to spite their guide. Sophie thought about asking her to be careful, but settled on a quick, "I'll see you soon," and rushed over to where Khalil was waiting for her. He stepped aside and allowed her to pass, then followed a few steps behind. Sophie took one last look at the tavern and hurried up the stairs.

TWENTY-THREE

Eolisti watched Sophie and Khalil leave, glaring at the latter as he ascended the staircase. *He can't tell me what to do. I'm not going to be imprisoned in that room all day.* She understood why Sophie needed to be hidden, out of sight, but there was absolutely no reason for Eolisti to be locked away in some tiny room. She could take care of herself. She didn't need to be treated like a child.

The handsome Anai was watching her with those intense blue eyes as she turned her glare to the disgusting ale. "There has to be a better place to get a drink than this," she said, mostly to herself.

The Anai's lips curled up in a genuine smile. Eolisti was convinced that she'd never seen someone so attractive in her entire life. "I know somewhere we can go," he said in that alluring voice of his. He reached into his jacket pocket and pulled out a gold coin. "Allow me to get the tab." He smiled a radiant smile at her. "My name is Elindiir, by the way."

"I'm Eolisti," she said, feeling her stomach jump when

he grinned at her. Elindiir... That was such a pleasant-sounding name.

Elindiir set the coin on the table and stood up, straightening his clothes. "Shall we?"

Eolisti hesitated. Khalil never explicitly said she had to stay there. He'd only told her to come up when she was done. He wouldn't like it, but if he didn't want her to leave, he should have been more specific. She stood and grinned at Elindiir, following him through the crowd and out of the inn.

The streets were busier than when her group had ridden into town. Men and women had set up stalls on either side of the road and were shouting what wares they had as carts rolled past. Men carried crates and boxes into and out of buildings, delivering goods that had come by sea. Ragged-looking little boys and girls ran in either direction, holding bundles and waving sticks at each other, and the slight smell of fish and salt of the sea permeated the air. The inn was only a few streets away from the docks. She assumed that Khalil wanted to be close so that when their ship was ready, they could leave right away, but Eolisti could really do without the smell. She imagined it was going to be even worse on the ship.

The two Anai headed to the left, Elindiir in the lead. He took Eolisti up a few streets, getting further and further away from the docks. The buildings gradually became nicer and more well-kept, with fewer vendors trying to sell things to them. Elindiir eventually turned into a narrow alley with three-story buildings on either side. Looking around, some part of her realizing that she was following a perfect stranger to some unknown location, Eolisti briefly wished that she had retrieved her sword before she'd left but followed the other Anai anyway.

Halfway down the alley, there was a plain black door set below street level, with steps leading down to it and a guard rail to keep the unobservant from falling in. Elindiir descended the stairs and knocked on the door three times while Eolisti waited a few steps up, just out of arm's reach. The blond Anai was pretty and all, but Eolisti wasn't stupid. She knew this could go wrong if Elindiir was only pretending to be kind to her and was actually leading her into a trap. Eolisti was determined not to let that happen. If it did, she'd never hear the end of it from that hooded jerk.

The lock clicked and a tall, muscular man opened the door. He had black hair, dark skin, and his ears came to a point in the telltale way of an Anai. Eolisti frowned. Wait, that wasn't quite right. His ears were pointed, but they were smaller than an Anai's and more rounded. His face wasn't angular, and his body was a bit too stocky. Eolisti had never met a Sul-Anai before, half Anai and half human, but she guessed this man was just that.

He took one look at Elindiir and nodded, then looked at Eolisti and scowled. Elindiir held up a placating hand. "She's with me, Corym."

Corym the Sul-Anai glanced at Elindiir and nodded, then took a step back from the door so they could pass. A man of few words. Elindiir looked back at her with one eyebrow raised and a smirk dancing at the corners of his mouth, then walked through the door.

Well, it was too late to turn back now. Eolisti sized up Corym. He looked strong but slow, and she pegged him as a brawler, not a real fighter. Confident that she could take him, she strode in after Elindiir.

They walked down a few more flights of stone stairs, lit only by a few torches in their brackets. That small part of her that warned this might be a bad idea tried to surface again. Where was he taking her?

Elindiir stopped in front of another unmarked black door that gleamed in the torchlight. He looked over his shoulder at Eolisti and winked one of those glistening blue eyes. Eolisti felt her heart leap. He really was the most handsome man she'd ever laid eyes on. With a loud creak that echoed off the stone, he pulled the heavy door open.

Eolisti shielded her eyes as a burst of sunlight temporarily blinded her. When she was able to see again, she stared in amazement at the room beyond the black door. It was much bigger than the tavern they had come from. It could have fit the inn where they were staying twice over with room to spare. The walls here were made of stone, but it looked like the area had been carved out of the rock rather than placed stone by stone like the buildings that lined the streets above. The sunlight came from four large crystals that were attached to the middle of the ceiling by gold fittings. It gave the place the illusion of being outside on a pleasantly sunny day instead of being underground. Eolisti couldn't believe a place like this was under the streets of *Nobarum*, of all cities. Being this close to the sea, how was this not underwater?

People milled about or sat at tables situated around the room, laughing and drinking. There were two bars on either side of the space, and each had a sizable number of patrons sitting at them. Eolisti scrutinized the crowd. They were loud, but everyone seemed to be enjoying themselves, and the best part of all was that none of them were human. There were Anai like her and Elindiir drinking a dark violet liquid out of crystal glasses, and short, stout creatures drinking a frothy substance out of large tankards. Eolisti suspected they were Dal Korra, but she couldn't be sure since she'd never actually seen one. All she knew was that no human looked like that.

There were a Dal Korra and a Sul-Anai, like Corym, sitting at a table near the middle of the room. Their right elbows were on the table, their hands clasped together, each trying to force the other's arm down to the side. Bystanders cheered and placed shot glasses filled with an amber drink on the table in front of both men. The competitors took the shots with their left hands and continued struggling against each other while the spectators whooped and hollered. In the back corner, there was a group of people, mostly Anai, two of whom had skin as dark as the Abbot's, throwing daggers at a target while sipping from their glasses and chatting among themselves. They threw dirty glances at the table with the Dal Korra and the Sul-Anai after a particularly loud roar, but just shook their heads and kept drinking.

Eolisti was almost shaking in anticipation. This was the most exciting place she had ever been!

A tap on her shoulder brought her out of her reverie. Elindiir grinned at her, obviously taking pleasure at the look of amazement on her face. He gestured toward the bar, and she nodded eagerly. She wanted to try all of it.

"What kind of *better* drink would you like?" he asked as they made their way through the room and up to one of the bars. "They serve a lot of unique concoctions here that humans usually don't consume."

Eolisti shrugged, not wanting to let her ignorance of Anaiian beverages show. "What would you recommend?"

Elindiir casually leaned against the bar, smirking at her. "That's a dangerous question," he mused, his eyes smoldering. "You know, you shouldn't let strangers lead you down dark alleys or pick your drinks."

In response, Eolisti leaned against the bar as casually as she could and tossed her hair over her shoulder. She grinned at the other Anai. "What can I say? I like to live dangerously."

TWENTY-FOUR

A hot breeze blew through the Spider's hair as he approached the port town, making the black strands whip around his face. The sun was setting in the west, the buildings casting long shadows as he approached. Women were herding their children inside while men packed up the stalls lining the streets. Dirt and rocks crunched under his feet as he passed, but no one gave him a second glance as they went about their business.

The little group he was following should have arrived earlier that day. The girl and her companions had gotten farther ahead of him than he would have liked, but after expending so much energy on the storm and the Soulless, he'd chosen to take a full night to rest. He found where they'd buried the body of a young man. After digging it up, Rajani decided that the boy couldn't have been the Vizier's informant. If he had, there would have been a gem much like his own on the boy, but there had been nothing when he searched the body. The others could have taken the gem, but there were still money and other items in the corpse's pockets, so it was likely that no one had searched him before they laid him to rest.

That meant that the Vizier's agent was still alive. There had been a message waiting for him on the tablet that very morning from the Vizier, saying that his storm had delayed them enough that they had missed their ship. The informant must have reported back to the Vizier once they reached Nobarum. Rajani was reasonably sure he knew the identity of the "warrior" the Vizier had referenced. But there were two others with the girl.

He'd found the ashes of his Soulless not far from where the body had been buried. The girl had used her power to utterly destroy it. Rajani was surprised. He hadn't thought she was capable of such a feat, but he'd sensed the flare of her power during the storm. He'd have to be careful once they finally met. He doubted she would be able to best him, but he would still need to be on his guard.

Rajani turned down a deserted alleyway and used a little of his power to aid him in climbing up the stone wall to the roof. From that vantage point, he surveyed the harbor. He didn't think that they'd been able to set sail on such short notice. There were a few ships in the docks that could be candidates to take the girl across the Silver Sea. Men moved around on the docks, loading and unloading cargo in the remaining minutes of daylight. The sea reflected the light of the sun, glowing orange and red as if on fire.

He pulled the emerald out of his pocket and the tablet out of his satchel. After the unexpected message a few days ago, Rajani had taken to checking the tablet every time he rested. He snapped the jewel in place and waited. Sure enough, as he watched the wax shifted.

The message was only one word:

Tomorrow.

~

HE ROLLED the green emerald in his palm a few times then stowed it back in his pocket. After sending the message to the Vizier an hour ago, he'd just sat in his room, holding the gem, thinking. This didn't feel right.

As much as he tried to remain cold and distant to Sophie, he couldn't help but feel sorry for her. She had been through so much, and now that he knew her better, he really did want her to make it onto the boat and to escape the Vizier. He knew helping the Vizier had never been honorable, but this felt different from the other times. What he was doing made him sick to his stomach.

He wished he'd never found out what happened to her in Zo'rahn. It just made it harder. I have to do this, he told himself. It's all for her.

TWENTY-FIVE

It was the middle of the night when Sophie was awakened by a stumbling Eolisti returning from wherever it was that she'd gone for the rest of the day. Sophie sleepily tried to ask where she'd been and tell her that Khalil was furious, but the Anai just waved her off, either unwilling or unable to answer her questions. The Anai smelled heavily of alcohol and, after kicking off her boots, collapsed onto the bed.

Concerned, Sophie checked Eolisti's pulse and her breathing, but she seemed to just have passed out. She must have gone to another tavern with that other Anai. She knew Eolisti would be in for a rough time in the morning.

After heading back upstairs, Sophie had spent most of the day in the room, either talking with Khalil and Joel or catching up on the sleep she'd missed the night before. She'd sent Eolisti's clothes off to be laundered along with her own. They'd realized that Eolisti was missing in the late afternoon, and Sophie had been worried. Even so, she found that she couldn't be mad at Eolisti for running off.

Sophie knew how bored she had been in the desert, and the loss of Sahl had hit the Anai particularly hard.

When morning came, it was much as Sophie had predicted. Eolisti was very quiet, tiptoeing around the room and wincing at even the slightest sound. Sophie asked her how she was feeling, but the Anai just laid her head down on the room's small table with a groan. Sophie shook her head and smiled to herself as she slipped out of bed and dressed. At least Eolisti had a good time the night before.

She sat at the table across from Eolisti, being careful to make as little noise as possible. Sophie couldn't help but feel excited. Today, she would be leaving her old life behind her. She knew deep down that there would always be the threat of her adopted family finding her, but even the Vizier wasn't powerful enough to influence governments halfway across the world. Everything they had been through had led to this. Once they left the harbor, she would feel a lot safer.

She felt giddy thinking of the possibilities. She would be able to use her magic again as she liked. Perhaps she could even attend one of the mages' colleges she had read about. The money that Zephan had given her should be enough to cover the cost of tuition. At least, she hoped that it would be.

Sophie had to admit that she was also a little sad. To her, departing on the ship meant the last part of her journey. It would take weeks to get across the sea, but after that, what would happen to her friends? Joel had made it clear that he would be going back to Ta'Shela from here and would not be accompanying them to the western continent. She'd have to say goodbye to him today. And what would Eolisti do once they reached the opposite shore? Would she continue with them to Morigael or return to her home?

There was a knock at the door, bringing Sophie out of her thoughts. Eolisti, still face down at the table, groaned and covered her ears with her hands. Sophie stifled a laugh and padded over to the door. Khalil and Joel waited on the other side, the latter looking rather tired. She stepped back to let them into the room.

Joel glanced at Eolisti and frowned but didn't say anything about the state she was in. Khalil leaned against the wall, his arms folded over this chest. He could probably smell the lingering alcohol coming from the Anai. "There are a few supplies we need to get before leaving," he said softly.

"I thought the ship wasn't departing until this afternoon," Sophie said in surprise. Had the time frame moved up?

"Yes, but I'd rather have everything ready before then."

"Why are you telling us then?" Eolisti said, her voice slightly muffled from her position. "Just go get it."

Khalil pressed his lips together disapprovingly. "I don't want to leave Sophie here by herself all day," he said shortly, "and you're in no condition to safeguard her, *Vendarii*. So she will be coming with me."

Eolisti's head snapped up so fast that Sophie worried she might have whiplash. The Anai stared daggers at the hooded man. "I'm in better condition than you are to *watch* her back," she said through gritted teeth.

He ignored the jab. "I need you to take the extra food to the docks. Liam, the bartender downstairs, has an extra cart that you can use. The ship is a caravel called the *Westwind*. Ask for Capitan Alvar, and he'll get you situated. You can meet us back here once you're done with that."

Sophie had the strange suspicion that Khalil could have just paid the proprietor to deliver their supplies to the ship and that the only reason he hadn't was to give Eolisti something to do.

Eolisti scoffed, obviously irritated to be ordered around by Khalil. "I should go with you. After all, Joel will be busy making sure you don't walk into a wall or something," she said defiantly.

Khalil's hands curled into fists and Eolisti glared at him. Sophie cringed at Eolisti's words. She had gone a step too far. The air was so thick with tension that Sophie felt like shrinking into a corner.

Before things got out of hand, Joel intervened. He cleared his voice loudly, making Eolisti wince and look at him. "The sooner you all are away from here, the safer you will be. Getting the food to the ship while we're fetching everything else would save us a lot of time."

Eolisti turned her glare on Joel, but it was somewhat ruined by her pouting bottom lip. "But I can't trust this guy with Sophie's safety," she gestured at Khalil. "I'm her Vendarii. What if he does something fishy and I'm not around?"

Joel knelt down so that they were eye to eye and patted Eolisti's hand comfortingly. "Don't worry, I'll be with them. I won't let anything happen to either of them."

Eolisti let out a long sigh. "Fine," she said with a huff and turned her head away from Joel. "I'll take the food over to the boat, I guess." She stood slowly and rounded up her boots.

"We're going to get you some different clothes," Khalil said, speaking to Sophie. "It will help you blend in once we reach Tanalin."

"What about you and Eolisti?" Sophie's eyes roved over his clothes. They weren't exactly what she'd seen the average person wearing.

"I already have what I need, and the Anai will stand out regardless," he said, guessing what she was thinking. "Anai aren't as uncommon over there as they are here, and from my experience, their clothing style doesn't differ much between the courts." He hesitated before continuing. "I don't know exactly what you look like, but from how you've been described to me, you should be able to blend in fairly well. We'll also pick up some dye for your hair in case we end up needing it."

Sophie's hands instinctively went to her head, thinking of her disastrous dye job years ago. She remembered the bottle of strong-smelling dye in their supplies, but was hesitant to let Khalil know they already had some. The longer she could hold off, the better.

Eolisti, having finally located her boots and donned them, slipped out of the room with another glare at the man.

Joel scratched his chin in thought. "I think I know a place where we can find that. I know a tailor who has a place not too far from here. Or at least, he used to. It's not in the best part of town, and it's been a while since I've been here, so I can't make any promises, but at least it's a place to start."

Sophie slipped on her sandals while the men talked about the area where the tailor was located. She wrapped the shawl around her head and neck, then followed Khalil and Joel out the door.

The tavern downstairs was empty, save for the same burly barkeeper that had been there the day before, drying a glass with a clean white cloth. It was too early in the morning for any of the sailors to be awake, much less looking for a drink. There was no sign of Eolisti. She must have already talked to the man behind the counter and left.

He looked up from his busy work as the three of them came downstairs, and nodded at them as they headed toward the door.

The sun was shining brightly upon the little port town and was almost blinding to Sophie, who had stayed inside since she had arrived. A cool ocean breeze ruffled the shawl about her head, and she took a deep breath, savoring the smell of the sea. Tanzar, Zo'rahn's capital and where she lived most of her life, was also a port city.

It was nowhere near as hot here as it had been in the desert, thanks to the cool breeze coming in off the ocean. The cobbled streets were beginning to fill with people, mostly families setting up stalls on both sides of the road or eating breakfast under the shade of an awning. It was like walking down to the docks with Zephan when they didn't have lessons. Sophie was hit with a wave of sadness. Nobarum was much smaller than Tanzar. The residents' clothing was different and their demeanor more cheerful, but altogether it reminded her of the place she had left behind.

Despite everything, Zo'rahn had been her home. Now she didn't know what was going to happen. Yes, she was going to Morigael, but would she remain there or be moved somewhere else? She glanced at the back of Khalil's head. His hood was up like always, and the dark fabric fluttered in the breeze. Surely, he knew something of where she would end up.

She shook her head. There would be plenty of time to figure that out later. Right now, she needed to concentrate on getting onto the ship and out to sea. She could ask Khalil what he knew once they had set sail.

Sophie and Khalil followed Joel through the streets to the west, bringing them closer to the docks, and she spotted a few dockworkers heading the same direction, probably to report in and start moving cargo for any ships that had come in during the night.

As they continued, the number of people gradually thinned until they were by themselves on the street. The structures around them had changed from townhouses and shops to warehouses and empty dwellings.

"It should be just a little further," Joel said to them over his shoulder as he turned a corner into a narrow, deserted street. The buildings here were obviously less cared-for than the ones they'd seen a few streets over. They were very close to the docks now. Sophie could see the top of a ship's mast over the roofs of the buildings on her right. It looked as if the salty sea air had warped the wood on the outside walls and several of the windows had spiderweb cracks or were missing chunks of glass. The area looked abandoned.

Why would there be a tailor down here? Did they work mostly for the dockworkers and sailors? Sophie looked at the two-story buildings surrounding them, but none of them had signs posted. This seemed like an area that had once been used as storage for ships coming in and out of the docks but was now abandoned. She opened her mouth to ask Joel if he was sure this was the right way when he turned to a door on his left and reached for the handle.

"This is it," he said confidently, making Sophie bite back her question. The building didn't look like much, more like a warehouse than a store. It had two stories like the other buildings and had a few windows on the second floor, but none on the first. She thought it was an odd place to run a business, but perhaps they just didn't advertise what they did. Joel held the door open as Khalil walked in first, with Sophie following close behind.

When they entered, the first floor was large and mostly

dark, the only light coming from windows high above, near the ceiling. There was a walkway that ran around the perimeter where the second floor should have been. Paint peeled and flaked from the walls. Crates and boxes were piled high all around them, hiding much of what lay beyond. The building smelled musty, and the floor was covered with a fine layer of dust and dirt in which she could make out footprints as she and Khalil walked farther inside. The floor creaked, and Sophie wondered if the wood was stable. Khalil seemed tense, creeping forward and stopping in the middle of the room, tilting his head to one side. It looked as though this place hadn't been occupied in years.

Sophie glanced back at Joel, who looked utterly perplexed, and said, "Are you sure this is the right place? I don't think there's anything here."

Joel gazed around, brows knit together. "It was here before," he said, all the earlier confidence gone from his voice. "I guess it must have moved." He glanced nervously around at the dark shapes of crates stacked high, clearly uncomfortable. Sophie couldn't blame him, the room that they were standing in seemed menacing even to her. "Let's go elsewhere..." He turned back around to leave and stopped dead in his tracks.

Two brawny dock workers with dark hair and scraggly beards stood shoulder to shoulder in the doorway, blocking their exit. They were dressed in similar clothing and looked about the same age, but the man on the left had an angry red scar over one eye. A creak in the rafters above them made Sophie look up just as Khalil grabbed her arm and jerked her toward him. Something came crashing down right where she'd been standing. She felt the air rush by her as whatever fell missed her by mere inches.

Once the dust cleared, there was only a pile of rotting

wood that could have once been a small crate. Sophie didn't think that the blow would have seriously injured her, but it would have hurt a lot.

Khalil kept his tight hold on her as she looked around wildly, seeing shapes moving in the dimness of the warehouse. She'd hoped that it was just her eyes playing tricks on her when two more men emerged out of the shadows, flanking them on either side. They looked much like the men guarding the door except that these two had clubs in hand. Joel backed up to where Sophie and Khalil stood, scanning the crates and pulling a short sword out of his cloak.

"Well," came a rough, low voice from the dimness above them. "That didn't go quite as expected."

Khalil pushed Sophie behind him, much like he had when they'd faced the Soulless.

A new shape moved into a beam of light overhead, revealing a middle-aged man with bronze skin and short, black hair. He wore a neatly pointed beard, and the shadows of the warehouse made his face look gaunt and severe. Could this be the man that Khalil had told her about? The one who summoned the Soulless to attack them?

The man above stepped out of the light and moved along the shadowed rafters. "You can't protect her from me."

TWENTY-SIX

The men who'd appeared from the shadows advanced, their steps making the floorboards creak. Khalil didn't react to the earlier taunt, maintaining his stance as he pulled out his curved sword and faced the men slowly closing in on them.

He was much calmer than Sophie was. She stared at the man crouched low in the rafters, shaking. She reached out with her senses and could feel magic radiating off him, energy that he had gathered in preparation for this ambush. The dark man dropped from the rafters and onto the tallest stack of crates in one fluid, graceful motion. He stood up straight and crossed his arms, surveying them as a wide grin spread across his face.

"Foolish little Samarans," he said, looking directly at Khalil. "Do you think it's a secret that your order helps escaped slaves? Do you think it's a secret that more important fugitives seek to hide themselves with your help? Do you think it's a secret that there are larger powers outside of our continent helping you?"

Khalil didn't answer.

"So predictable." The thug chuckled, and it sent chills up Sophie's spine. "Did you really think it would be so easy to escape from the Spider? There are few—if any—who can keep secrets from me." He tilted his head slightly, and his menacing demeanor shifted to one of quiet curiosity as he surveyed Khalil.

"I was very impressed by your survival skills. Traveling through the desert is no mean feat, much less while trying to elude someone with my prowess." He shifted his weight from side to side. Sophie felt the slight pulling of magic, the Spider was using it to keep his balance on the crates. "Not all of my contracts are for hunting and killing. Some of them are very similar to what you are doing now. I would hate to see talent such as yours squandered over such a trivial matter. We could make a very profitable team. All you have to do is give me the girl. I'll even pay you for your trouble."

He watched Khalil intently from his position on the crates, but Khalil said nothing. Sophie shuffled nervously behind him. The silence was like the calm before the storm, the tension almost palpable. Everyone watched Khalil, waiting for his answer. He wasn't really considering the other man's offer, was he?

"Khalil," she said tentatively, reaching out to touch his arm.

Khalil held up a hand to still her. She pulled her own back as Khalil's hood tilted up to where the other man stood above them. "No," he said through teeth clenched so hard the word was barely more than a hiss, then held his sword out in front of him in a defensive position. "You won't have any of us."

The Spider assessed Khalil for a moment before sighing. "Pity," he said, sounding genuinely disappointed, then looked at his men. "I need the girl alive. Kill the others."

At his words, the two men in front of the door approached Joel while the others closed in on Khalil.

"Are you ready?" Khalil asked softly, his head turned so that Sophie could see his nose and mouth over his shoulder.

Sophie remembered the conversation they had had in the desert. Had it only been a couple of days ago?

"Yes," she whispered. She could see his lips curve into a smile. Sophie took a few steps back to give him some space and took a deep breath, clearing her mind. Her hands shook, but she clasped them together to still them. She was afraid, but she couldn't let her fear get in the way, not when they were this close. She wouldn't go back willingly, and she would *not* let anyone else die for her.

The man closest to Khalil lunged at him, sword aimed at his chest, but Khalil dodged nimbly, sidestepping the swing and bringing his own blade down. The thug jumped back, narrowly avoiding the cut and swinging his sword again. Khalil parried the blow. Steel rang against steel as he turned aside a second attack. The other man rammed his shoulder into Khalil's chest while he was distracted, causing him to stumble back, and took the opportunity to thrust his blade at Khalil's midsection.

Khalil turned with the blade and it cut through empty air. He grabbed the man's arm and pulled him forward, bringing a knee up into his abdomen. With a hiss of expelled breath, the man fell onto his side, clutching his stomach and retching.

The second man rushed Khalil. Sophie almost

screamed, but Kahlil fell back to the ground to avoid the swing, driving his foot up and into the man's groin, and using the momentum to flip him over his head. The man crashed to the ground in a heap, moaning in pain.

Khalil's movements were smooth, with an almost cat-like grace, each step and swing executed as if he had done it a thousand times. Every blow used with the perfect amount of energy so as not to be wasteful. Sophie kept her guard up, but at the same time, watched him in awe. How had he mastered fighting like this without sight?

One of the men Joel was desperately trying to fend off gave a short cry of anger and disengaged from his fight in an attempt to grab Sophie, but Khalil blocked his path, deflecting his initial swing and slamming the hilt of his sword into the side of his face. Sophie winced as the man lurched sideways, spitting blood.

Sophie felt the flare of power right before a line of white-hot fire flashed at Khalil's face from where the Spider was perched, but Sophie extended her will, diverting the magic before it could touch him. The man didn't seem surprised at her counter and immediately followed up with a burst of force designed to knock her off balance, but she deflected it into a pile of crates beside her. The containers erupted from the strength of the blow, raining splinters down on them.

He grinned at her, white teeth gleaming in the darkness. He looked as if he was thoroughly enjoying himself.

"So, the little girl *does* know a couple of tricks." He flicked his wrist at her, and Sophie felt a surge of energy. She barely blocked it in time, directing it upwards, causing it to blow a hole in the ceiling. The Spider raised a hand, and she felt an immense pressure attempting to push her backward. Sophie held up her own hands, pitting her abilities against his. It was more vicious than anything she had faced before. At that moment, with their power touching, she got a sense of the man who called himself the *Spider*. His anger and his conviction welled up inside her mind and threatened to overwhelm her.

With great effort, Sophie pushed away his awareness and felt the pressure lessen. She lifted her arms and directed the energy over her shoulder, smashing another stack of crates behind her to pieces. The Spider stared at her, his grin gone. There was no way she could take him on by herself. He was too strong.

Panting, she stepped back and felt her foot sink into the floor. Startled, she fell to one knee and looked down. Shadows had wrapped around her leg, cold and greasy where they touched her skin. The tentacle-like patch of inky blackness began to pull her backward. Sophie slid a few inches toward the shadows before she was able to grab one of the loose floorboards, her fingers digging between the planks. She couldn't hold on for long.

The air popped and crackled around her fingertips as she gathered energy to her free hand and reached down to the writhing blackness. Sweat dripped into her eyes as she concentrated. She had to be very careful since the thing was slowly coiling itself around her. Otherwise, she would burn herself. Fire burst to life in her outstretched hand, the flame growing bigger and brighter the more energy she poured into it. She felt the heat on her skin. A few degrees hotter, and it would sear her flesh, even from a distance. Since the thing was made from shadow, it couldn't be set on fire like the Soulless, but the flame had the effect Sophie had hoped for. It writhed and retreated from the light, loosening its grip on her.

Khalil parried another blow and kicked the remaining man attacking him in the chest, causing him to stumble back. In the momentary reprieve, Khalil leaned down to grab Sophie's arm, pulling her the rest of the way out of the shadow's grip.

She looked up at Khalil, as the man who had stumbled regained his footing and rushed back at him. Without any time to think, she threw the fire in her hand at the man's face, causing him to pitch backward with a scream of surprise and pain. Khalil let go of her and spun, sword flashing. The attacker crumpled to the ground, groaning.

Sophie felt another surge of power from the Spider and pushed Khalil aside as a lance of green energy flew past them. She wove her hands in and out over her chest, weaving magic into a shielding spell as another flash of green light ricocheted off her newly formed barrier. She concentrated on curving the buffer of solid air and energy around them. "Stay behind me!" she shouted to Khalil as another strike came for them, flashed against the shield spell, and rebounded into a wall.

"Foolish mageling," the Spider snarled, his calm facade cracking. "You cannot defy me forever! It was a mistake to run from the privileges your master gave you! You had everything and threw it away!" His eyes shone with a fury unlike Sophie had ever seen before. His words rang with a hatred that was so personal it stunned her.

"If your master did not require you back alive, I could have killed you in the desert. You don't deserve all you have been given! Instead, you selfishly run from those who value you, and in the midst of it all, you coldly throw anyone who helps you in my path." He took a few deep breaths, and when he spoke again, his voice calm and steady. He grinned vindictively at her. "Perhaps you are more Zo'rahni than I thought. Crushing those less valuable beneath you."

The air grew dense and crackled around Sophie at his words. Fear and anger threatened to overwhelm her, and she let the shield spell flicker and dissolve as she faced him. "No," she said, her words barely a whisper. "I'm not like that."

The Spider openly laughed, the sound hollow and grating. "How many corpses will you step over to get what you want?"

"No!" she screamed, and magic flared to life, barreling away from her with the speed and power of an avalanche. The sudden force knocked everyone back off their feet and sent the Spider toppling over the edge of the crates he stood on.

Sophie stood in the middle of the room alone, her chest heaving. Everything around her was destroyed. Broken and splintered wood lay in heaps as a fine cloud of dust settled over them. Nothing moved. Sophie sank to her knees, her mind reeling from the uncontrolled burst of magic.

Some of the debris shifted, and Joel got to his feet coughing. He looked a little worse for wear and dirty, but uninjured. He looked around frantically and stumbled over to her, grabbing her arm. He pulled her to her feet and toward the door. "Come on, let's get out of here."

"But Khalil..." She looked back, her eyes searching through the rubble but unable to find their companion. Had he been hurt in the blast? Was he buried somewhere in here?

Joel seemed to sense what she was thinking. "He'll be fine. Come on." He dragged her out the door and into the daylight.

The sunlight temporarily blinded her, but Joel

continued to pull her along, and she was eventually able to run with him. The street was deserted as it had been when they entered the building. Sophie still felt disoriented from what had happened inside the warehouse. Spots floated at the edge of her vision and her legs felt weak. She didn't know where they were running to, but even through the haze in her mind, she could tell that this wasn't the way they had come. They were running closer to the docks.

They turned a corner into an alleyway, and Joel released her arm, gasping for breath and leaning back against the wall.

"Can you check to see if anyone is following us?" he asked, wiping his forehead with the back of his hand.

Sophie nodded and slowly stuck her head around the corner. There was still no one on the streets. She could see the warehouse in the distance, but the building remained silent and still. If Khalil wasn't wounded, he should have been able to get out by now. "I don't see anyone. Should we go back for Khalil?"

Just as she was about to turn back to Joel, an arm grabbed her from behind. Sophie gasped, but before she could cry out, a cloth was placed over her nose and mouth. She struggled, trying to push the fabric away from her mouth, but the hands kept it firmly in place. There was some sort of substance lacing the cloth, something that smelled slightly sweet and left a bitter taste in her mouth. Her body started to tingle as she breathed in the fumes and fought harder, trying to pull his hand away from her mouth.

Her eyes filled with tears as she struggled, Joel's face coming into view. Joel. Why was he doing this? Hot tears ran down her cheeks and soaked the cloth.

Sophie scratched at his hand and tried to turn her head

away, but it was no use. She began to feel weak, and her vision started going black around the edges. She felt tired. So tired. Sleep sounded really lovely. Why had she been panicking before? Sophie closed her eyes and leaned back into the arms wrapped around her.

A voice floated to her out of the darkness, whispering softly in her ear. "I'm so, so sorry…"

CHAPTER
TWENTY-SEVEN

Joel sat in the empty room back at the inn. They had all agreed to meet there once they had finished their errands that morning. It had been a couple of hours since the altercation, and he knew he should have gotten out of town immediately, but he couldn't bring himself to leave. Guilt wracked his conscience, and he felt like he was going to be sick.

The way Sophie had looked at him as she lost consciousness... She had trusted him. They had *all* trusted him. They'd been his friends, and he'd betrayed them. Especially Sophie. For what? Protection? Money?

In all the years he had been passing information to his faceless employer, he had never before been asked to do anything more than observe and report the comings and goings at Ta'Shela. He wished he hadn't met the girls in Bardov that stormy afternoon. He wished they hadn't insisted he join them in their flight from the monastery. He wished he could have just continued existing in blissful ignorance of the real impact of his actions.

Everything he'd done had been for Lana, but what

would she think if she knew how he provided for her? She would be disgusted with him. She would have rather died than be supported by such despicable work.

He'd been a much younger man when he'd made his bargain. Money and medicine in exchange for harmless information. When they first came to Omer, they needed help. He and his sister had nothing, and Lana was sick. His uncle couldn't help her, so the deal he'd struck with the Vizier had seemed like a gift from the gods themselves.

Now, he and Lana were both much older. Her sickness had subsided over the years. She had no idea how he obtained the supplies they needed, and she'd never asked. She trusted him implicitly, much as Sophie had. He could no longer lie to himself about what he'd been doing to people, good people who trusted him. What kind of person was he, working for someone who was everything he and Lana had crossed the ocean to escape?

He didn't know how he'd gone through with delivering Sophie to that mercenary. His gut had been screaming at him that what he was doing was wrong, but after over-hearing her conversation with Khalil, he rationalized that her home in Zo'rahn couldn't possibly have been as bad as she'd made it sound. Perhaps she had been imagining the dire consequences she feared if she'd stayed there in the safety and luxury that her family offered. He knew that people tended to blame themselves for the deaths of others close to them, and he'd convinced himself that she was doing the same. How could sweet little Sophie have killed another apprentice, even by accident? The Vizier was prob-ably sick with worry over one of his favored relatives.

Those delusions melted like ice in the hot afternoon sun when he'd met the Spider, after the confrontation in the abandoned warehouse. A part of him had known the man was a sadistic bastard from their few moments of interaction earlier, but when he saw the other man fasten that cruel implement around Sophie's ankle…

Even unconscious, Sophie made a face of pain as the Spider whispered an incantation. "No, you're hurting her," Joel said in protest, but all the other man did was sneer and toss him a small bag of coins. Anger overtook him, and he threw the bag at the man's feet. As he had pushed forward to try to help Sophie, the Spider knocked him back with what he could only guess had been a spell, which had left his head spinning.

Through blurred vision, he recalled the sinister man crouching in front of him saying, "Run along home like a good dog."

Joel had struggled to get to his feet and ended up watching helplessly as the Spider carried Sophie away. He *had* to go after her. He *had* to make things right.

There was a click from the doorknob that drew him out of the memory. The door swung open slowly to reveal Eolisti, back from delivering the supplies to the ship. Her hair was windblown, and she appeared to be a little disgruntled, but otherwise seemed to have recovered from her hangover. The Anai noticed Joel sitting on the bed, then looked around the room. She frowned when she realized he was the only one there.

He stood and took a step toward her. He would need to tell her everything that happened if they were going to do something about it, if she'd even let him help make it right. Eolisti, who reminded him so much of Lana. Would she be able to forgive him? Would *anyone* be able to forgive him?

"Where are Sophie and the hooded jerk?" Eolisti asked, nudging the door shut behind her with her boot.

Just as it closed, the door crashed open again so hard

that Eolisti had to jump back to avoid being struck. Khalil stormed in, rushing past Eolisti.

Before Joel could do anything, Khalil's fist connected with his jaw and sent him tumbling to the floor, his vision a burst of stars. He was still reeling from the blow when he was lifted by his shirt. Khalil swung him and slammed him against a wall so hard that the furniture in the room shook. The snarl of fury on Khalil's face would have made any man cower.

"What did you do with her?" he said, his voice so low that it chilled Joel's blood more thoroughly than if he had screamed the words.

In his action, Khalil's hood had fallen back, and Joel couldn't help but stare into Khalil's unsettling eyes.

Eolisti grabbed the arm that was pinning Joel against the wall. "What is wrong with you?!" She pulled at him to get him off Joel, but Khalil still held him with surprising strength.

"What did you do with her?" he repeated, ignoring Eolisti entirely.

Joel looked away from his eyes, a fresh wave of shame welling in his chest. "I gave her to the Spider," he said in a whisper.

Eolisti had pulled her arm back to hit Khalil, but at Joel's words, she dropped it and stared at him, perplexed. "Who? You did *what*?"

Joel closed his eyes, letting the pain and confusion in her voice wash over him. It made him sick to think that he'd betrayed these people that trusted and cared about him. Worse, he had condemned a young woman who was just trying to live a better life.

"I've been reporting on our movements to the Vizier since Ta'Shela," he sighed.

"I've actually been working with the Vizier for years." Joel proceeded to tell them everything. He told them of the circumstances that had brought him and his sister to Omer, how after their uncle passed, they were orphans under the care of Samar's disciples, how his sister was sick and none of the monks could treat her, and how, when she had taken a turn for the worse, he'd received an offer he couldn't refuse if he wanted to save her life.

"So, he has me spy on the monks and report to him when runaway slaves or persons of interest pass through Bardov. Usually, nothing happens to anyone. At least not that I've known of." He looked away from them. "I've betrayed a lot of people, but this... I can't live like this anymore. I only want to help get her back," he pleaded, looking up again first at Khalil, then Eolisti.

The other two were silent. The pressure on his chest lightened, and Joel was able to stand on his own. Khalil still held his shirt, but the unbridled fury that had been there before was gone. "How can we trust you?" he said, his voice still hard. "How do we know you're not leading us into another trap?"

Joel looked back at them, imploring them to see that he was sincere. "I know it's difficult to believe after what I've done, but I don't want to live like this anymore. You've got to believe me. I care about what happens to Sophie. I need to atone for what I've done, and this is the only way I can do that."

Letting go of his shirt, Khalil turned away from him. Joel let himself slide down the wall until he sat on the floor. Eolisti just stared at him with tears shining in her eyes. He looked down at the floor, unable to face her. Of course they wouldn't believe him. Why would they after all he'd done? He almost wished Khalil had hit him again. He deserved it.

"It's all right," Eolisti's voice cut through his thoughts, making him look up at her. She'd moved closer to stand over him, looking down at him, the sunlight behind her creating a bronze halo around her hair. Her lips curved up in the ghost of a smile. "You really do want to help. I can tell." She held out a hand to him. Joel blinked at it, then took it, letting himself be pulled to his feet.

"Eolisti—" Khalil began.

The Anai cut him off. "Do you have a better idea of how to find her? Some plan that will get her back in time to get on the ship and get out of here?"

She waited for an answer and Khalil remained silent.

"Yeah, I didn't think so," Eolisti said harshly. "He wants to help. He wants to reverse some of the damage he's done." She paused for a few moments before continuing in a softer tone. "I used to cause a lot of trouble in Elasariin, so I understand what it's like to try to do the right thing, only to have no one believe your intentions."

She looked back at Joel, green eyes blazing. "But if you're lying to us, I'll kill you myself."

Joel felt a chill go down his spine and nodded his understanding. She could and would make good on that promise.

"Now then," Eolisti said as if she hadn't just vowed to carry out an execution, "where is this 'Spider'?"

TWENTY-EIGHT

The sun sat in the eastern sky. Even though it was still morning, the air was already hot and damp, another typical summer's day in Zo'rahn. Sophie hurried down the open-air corridor that led from the apprentice quarters to the second largest building on the estate.

She stepped quickly through the archway, pushing aside a thin silk curtain that kept out insects. Inside was an antechamber that she hurried through to another archway and into the main hall of the building. Marble stairs led up to the second floor, the kind that were wide at the bottom and narrower near the top. There was a set of double doors at the top of the staircase, leading into the Vizier's private rooms.

Servants nodded at her as she passed, and Sophie smiled back, in too much of a rush to do anything else. She wasn't exactly late, but she had overslept. The Vizier had summoned her the night before to go over a few calculations, and they had been up much later than she was used to. She felt her cheeks heating up and shook her head vigorously. There was no time to think about that now.

There were two doors, one on either side of the staircase. Sophie trotted over to the one on the left and paused for a few moments to catch her breath. It wouldn't look good if it was obvious she'd been rushing to get here on time. After her heart rate slowed to an acceptable level, she pushed the door open slowly.

The Vizier's library was an enormous room, and the walls were lined with floor-to-ceiling bookshelves. Tables were scattered throughout the room, and magically lit lamps floated tranquilly above them. To either side of the large chamber, passages led off to smaller adjacent rooms filled with more tables and books. Through one open door, Sophie could see a young wizard focused intently on a small silver cube spinning lazily in his hand, illuminating the room in a soft green hue. There were five others in the main room of the library with her, working on various projects or doing research. All of them were at least a few years her senior. She scanned the faces and sighed with relief. There was one fellow apprentice in particular that resented the fact that Sophie had been given apprenticeship three years early, but, thankfully, she was nowhere to be seen.

At the far end of the room, opposite where she had entered, stood two ornately carved double doors. Gold filigree was inlaid into the wood and glittered in the lamplight. They were beautiful, but no one looked at them. Through those doors was the Vizier's private study, and access was only permitted by invitation from the Vizier himself.

"You're late," came a harsh whisper from behind Sophie, making her jump. "Again."

"I am not late," she said defensively, turning to see the very person she expected but had hoped she wouldn't have to see today. Ina. She was a fellow apprentice who was always trying to push Sophie around because she was only half Zo'rahni. "The Vasalii said 'mid-morning.' Is it not mid-morning?" she reasoned sweetly, trying to keep the sarcasm out of her voice. Within the family, the Vizier was referred to as the Vasalii, since the title meant the head of the household. The apprentices would also call him master, though that title was used less often.

The older apprentice wrinkled her nose in distaste. She flicked her long black braid over her shoulder in apparent irritation. "I don't see why you get special treatment," she scoffed. "The rest of us have been here since dawn."

"I was up late working on my studies." She knew that she didn't need to justify her actions to Ina, but the snide remarks rubbed Sophie the wrong way. They were supposed to be family, but the other apprentice always treated her with contempt. Most of the others just ignored her if they didn't need something, but Ina went out of her way to criticize her. "If you have a problem, talk to the Vasalii yourself."

Ina scowled. Sophie knew she wouldn't dare bring up something so trivial to the Vizier, especially not when he had been the one to call on Sophie. The other apprentices kept their gazes averted, either intentionally ignoring the two women or wrapped up in their own projects. A slave in a long white dress hurried past them, carrying an armful of scrolls to the room that was glowing with a green light.

She and Ina glared at each other until Sophie sighed. "Look, I've got some work to do before the Vasalii gets here. Can you please save the lecture for later?"

Her scowl deepened, but Ina said no more and walked

to the back of the room, shoving Sophie's shoulder as she passed. Ina settled into a table in the corner of the room, pulling a book off the shelf and laying it flat to read.

Sophie rubbed her arm and fought the urge to glower at the other woman. She knew Ina had multiple reasons for not liking her, but did she have to be so confrontational? Sophie shook her head and walked over to a table, far from where Ina was seated. She reached into her bag and pulled out a roll of parchment, the research she had been working on the previous night. After smoothing the papers out on the table, she examined her writing. Surely, the Vizier would be here soon.

After an hour or so of huddling over the table, Sophie leaned back in her chair, rubbing her neck with one hand and stretching out her back. She risked a glance over at Ina, who was too absorbed in the book she was reading to take notice of her. Sophie looked back down at her work. She'd crossed out a few lines and written notes in the margins. Thick tomes were stacked on either side of her paper. There wasn't much more she could do without testing her theory in the lab. She looked down at her hands. Ink smeared the tips of her fingers and the side of her palm on her right hand. She focused and flicked her wrist lightly, expending just a little bit of power. The ink disappeared, evaporating from her skin.

The door to the library creaked open for the first time since Sophie had entered. All the apprentices looked up from what they were doing and, upon seeing the newcomer, stood, bowing their heads in reverence. A tall man with long red- and gold-embroidered robes entered the room. His long, black hair was pulled back in a loose tail and his skin was the golden bronze of a typical Zo'rahni. With his high cheekbones and muscular frame, he looked to be no older than thirty, though they all knew he was much older. Even so, he was very handsome.

He was also one of the seven rulers of Zo'rahn.

Warm honey-colored eyes scanned the room, an impish smile playing at the sides of his mouth. "I've told you before, there's no need for that here. We're family after all," he said in his deep, melodic voice.

Sophie suppressed a smile of her own. He said that to them every day, but none of them were foolish enough to be so informal with the Vizier. It was true that most of the people here were blood relatives of some form to the Vizier, except for her, of course, but she had never seen even the highest members of the family fail to show him the proper respect.

"Please, continue your work. I have a few items to take care of, and I'll be busy the rest of the afternoon." The apprentices bowed their heads in acknowledgment and went back to what they were working on. The Vizier strode to the far end of the room and placed a hand on one of the doors leading back to his study. He paused. "Sophie. Ina. I'll need your help today."

Sophie was just settling into her chair once again, but stood at the sound of her name and rushed to the Vizier's side along with Ina. They might not have liked each other very much, but the Vizier's needs came before any personal quarrel they shared. He pushed open the ornate doors leading to his study and gestured for them to follow.

Lamps beyond the door flared to life the moment the Vizier stepped inside, illuminating the room's contents. Books, bottles, and various items were piled on tables lining the large room. It was more like a lab, where many projects were undertaken. Unlike the library behind them, the floor was bare, save for a silver circle set into the stone in the very center of the room, runes carved into the delicate metal. That circle was used for ritual magic, an area of the arts that Sophie hadn't had a chance to try yet. Parchment lay on almost every surface, scribbled with notes in the Vizier's own neat handwriting.

The lab was cluttered, but everything had its place. This was where the Vizier worked on his personal projects when he wasn't busy with the Council or his various duties governing the province. He rarely let anyone in here, not even the servants to clean. Sophie looked around in wonder, every item was a different undertaking that the Vizier, one of the most powerful wizards in all of Lanis, was working on. Everything in this room was a wealth of information and power, the likes of which she could only begin to fathom. She'd been here a few times before, but every time she stepped into it, there was always something new to discover.

The Vizier gently placed two fingers on the small of her back, bringing Sophie's attention back to him. She looked up into his eyes, and he smiled warmly at her. Sophie felt her face grow hot again and looked away quickly.

"There are a few leather-bound journals in the other room," he gestured to a door on the left that she'd not noticed before. "Go retrieve them and bring them here. Ina," he said, glancing at the older girl, "assist her. There are quite a few books."

Sophie and Ina both bowed at the same time and said, "Yes, Vasalii," in unison. Sophie turned and walked to the room that the Vizier had indicated, Ina following closely behind her. The door opened to a hallway, lamps floating over their heads like the ones in the other room. One by one, they lit as the two women approached. While Sophie had been in the lab before, she had never been in this room.

She had assumed that the Vizier's lab consisted of the larger room that they had been in with small adjacent rooms for storage, but it appeared to be far bigger than she'd imagined.

The hall ended at a large metal door. There were no ornate carvings on this one, just iron fittings hammered into the frame. It looked heavy and old, like it hadn't been opened in a very long time. This must be the room the Vizier had referred to since there were no other doors down this hall. Sophie glanced at Ina, who stood next to her, but the older woman just scowled at her. "Well," she snapped, gesturing for Sophie to get on with it.

Sophie wanted to shake her head in exasperation but didn't think the consequential lecture would be worth it. She reached out and touched the door, pressing her hand against it. The dark metal was cold against her fingertips.

Her eyes widened and she drew her hand away. For the briefest moment, she'd felt something from beyond the door. Something like... a heartbeat? Sophie glanced at Ina again, but the other apprentice just glared back at her. She must not have felt it. Had Sophie imagined it? She placed her hand back on the door and pushed. It was as heavy as she thought it would be, and she had to use her shoulder to get the door to budge. The hinges groaned in displeasure as it slowly swung open.

The room beyond was large, perhaps the same size as the library, but without all the shelves. The mage lamps above their heads flickered to life, and Sophie could see that the room was mostly empty, covered with a fine layer of dust. There were a few tables on the far wall, but otherwise, the stone floor was bare. Sophie spotted a pile of books on the table farthest from the door. Those must be the journals.

She stepped inside, scattering motes of dust that had gathered near the door. What was this room used for? It looked like no one had been in here for years. Sophie looked back over her shoulder as she crossed to the tables, leaving prints in the dust. Ina remained by the door, looking around at the room, her expression bemused. She must not have known this place existed either.

There were a couple of neat stacks of journals, maybe thirty in all, sitting on the table. They, too, looked like they hadn't been touched in years.

A small metal object that Sophie hadn't seen from the door rested next to the journals. It was about the size of her hand and was an unusual shape. Thin sheets of metal were folded together in what reminded her of a seashell pattern, though round on the sides and flat on the bottom. Sophie had no idea what it was, but it looked as if there could have been something inside.

"Hurry up," Ina scolded, making Sophie jump. She had been so focused on the object that she had almost forgotten the other apprentice was watching her. "The Vizier is waiting."

Sophie threw a glare over her shoulder and bent to pick up the journals. She wouldn't be able to carry them all by herself, but it didn't look like Ina actually intended to help, so she could just move the rest with magic. A levitation spell should be more than adequate.

As she reached for the journals, her fingers brushed the metal object, and she felt that strange surge of magic again, the same that she had felt when she touched the door, but stronger. She drew her hand back. It had startled her, but it didn't feel malicious. In fact, she felt a strong desire to examine the object more closely.

Sophie checked over her shoulder. Ina had finally

stepped inside as well and was looking at some of the other tables. She wasn't paying attention to Sophie at all. She hadn't felt it, whatever it was that this thing was emitting.

Sophie picked up the object quickly, while Ina's attention was elsewhere. It practically vibrated with energy. It didn't even feel like metal, it felt warm and alive in her hand. Somewhere in the back of her mind, a small voice cautioned her about picking up magic items that she knew nothing about. This was the Vizier's workshop, and she had no idea what she was holding, but her burning curiosity pushed those thoughts away. With only a moment's hesitation, Sophie reached out with her senses, brushing her magic up against the item in her hand.

As soon as her power touched it, it began to move. It shuddered delicately and slowly opened, the folds pulling back in a liquid motion, almost like the petals of a flower. Inside was a roughly cut crystal set into a metal base. Was the crystal the source of the artifact's power? Or was it merely a part of the whole? Sophie ran her finger over the crystal, its edges coarse under her touch, but nothing happened. She could feel some of the power coming from it, but she had no clue what it did or how to activate it.

"What are you doing?" Ina said, her tone making it clear it wasn't the first time she'd asked the question. She put a hand on Sophie's shoulder and tried to turn her around to see what she was holding.

The moment Ina touched Sophie, the crystal flashed, and a white light blinded Sophie. She shut her eyes tightly and felt a surge of power, stronger and wilder than any magic she had ever felt before. It rippled through every inch of her body, making her skin tingle. It was a strange feeling, completely foreign but welcoming at the same time. The power called to her like the soft whisper of a lover, and

Sophie reached out for it, allowing her mind to touch that seductive energy.

As soon as she reached for it, the unknown power rushed into her. The energy mixed with that of her own, and Sophie felt an overwhelming need to draw in as much as she could. It made her feel stronger than she had ever been before. She wanted to bask in the warmth of this power forever, but somehow, she knew that there was a limited supply. Soon it would be gone, and this feeling would end. She needed to savor it while she still had time.

Too soon, the feeling started to fade. Gradually the storm that had whipped up inside her head quieted. Sophie opened her eyes.

Ina was on the floor in front of her. She lay crumpled like a puppet whose strings had been cut. Her body was unnaturally still, like she was...

The object slipped out of Sophie's hands and clattered to the floor, forgotten in her shock. She sank to her knees beside the other apprentice. "Ina? Ina?!" Sophie grabbed her shoulders and shook her, but she didn't stir. "Ina, wake up!" Her skin was ashen, and she didn't appear to be breathing. Sophie turned her over and, with shaking hands, pressed two fingers to the older girl's neck to try to feel for a pulse.

"Help!" she screamed, sight blurring with tears. She blinked to clear her vision and concentrate, but panic surged through her. Did that energy she felt earlier have something to do with this? Had she caused it by picking up that object? She couldn't find a pulse. There were no signs of life from Ina at all.

Sophie released Ina's body and scrambled away until her back met a wall. She wiped the tears out of her eyes and screamed for help again. Hurried footsteps echoed from the hall, and, a moment later, the Vizier stood in the doorway, slightly out of breath.

His eyes darted first to Sophie, huddled on the floor sobbing, then to Ina's still form, then finally to the artifact on the ground, which had rolled away from where Sophie had dropped it. The metal folds had closed around the crystal inside, and it was in the same rounded shape as before.

The Vizier looked stunned, and, for just a heartbeat, he stood motionless in the doorway. Then he sprang into action, rushing over to Sophie first. "Are you all right?" he asked, kneeling beside her. One of his hands brushed her cheek, wiping away a tear. "What happened?"

Sophie shook her head. She couldn't meet his eyes. She didn't want him to know what she was increasingly certain she had done. "I– I didn't know what it was. I wasn't trying to hurt her." She cried harder, covering her mouth with her hands. "I'm sorry. I'm sorry..."

He placed a warm hand on her head to comfort her and, seemingly satisfied that she was unhurt, turned his attention to Ina's still form.

The Vizier held a hand over her chest, and Sophie felt the surge of magic as he extended his senses to the other apprentice. Sophie couldn't see his face as he worked and didn't dare move. After a few moments, the sensation of his magic faded, and he closed his hand into a fist. He shook his head, still turned away from her. "She's gone."

Sophie's hands trembled as she reached out and grabbed onto the sleeve of his robe. It had only been seconds since Ina had touched her, hadn't it? The Vizier was the most powerful wizard she had ever known. Surely, he could save her. "Can't you do something? She hasn't been lying there long." She sniffled, unable to help herself. "Please, do something."

The Vizier turned back to her. His jaw muscles were clenched, and he looked frustrated. Impatience laced his voice as he spoke. "Sophie, you know magic cannot bring back the dead. If I could do something, I would." He took a deep breath and seemed to calm himself. He placed his hand on hers, and she let go of his sleeve. "Tell me how this happened."

Sophie glanced over at the artifact. "I just wanted to know what it was. I didn't know it would hurt her," she said, covering her mouth with her hands again to stifle another sob.

The Vizier reached over and picked up the artifact. "This?" he asked, pulling Sophie's hands away from her face. The look in his eyes was desperate. He held the object out to her, and she tried to flinch away from it, but the Vizier held her in place. He was strong, much stronger than she was. "What happened when you touched this?"

She was startled by the ferocity of his tone. "It was warm," she said, voice still shaky. "Then it opened when I tried to use my magic to sense what it was." Sophie looked away from his intense stare, and her gaze settled on Ina's body, lying forgotten only feet from them. "There was a flash of light when Ina touched me, and I felt... I felt..."

As she said the words, she tried to puzzle out what the artifact had done. She didn't want to think about what had happened, but her brain began piecing it together all on its own. She'd felt power rushing into her, felt it flowing into her from an unknown source and filling her up, like water on a parched throat. Oblivious to all else, she drank it all in until there was nothing left to draw from. The bottom dropped out of her stomach, and she knew what she'd done. It had been Ina's power she'd felt. Life energy lies at the core of all magic, and she'd drained *all* of that energy out of Ina.

No, that was impossible. The only way to draw the life out of someone like that was through a ritual spell, and the caster would have to physically murder their victim to achieve the effect. Sophie's eyes jerked back to the artifact. That must be it. The crystal inside had allowed her to draw out the life force of another human. She'd effectively murdered Ina by stealing her power without trying to. Sophie's stomach churned, and she felt like she was going to be sick.

The Vizier must have read the changing expressions on her face. He stared down at the artifact for a moment, then back to the body. Sophie could see him putting together what had happened for himself. She felt it when he reached out to her with his power, brushing her own, sensing the difference in her. He stared at her, and she could see the calculation in his eyes. She saw the exact moment he put it together. "You took Ina's magic," he said slowly.

"No," she whispered, but there was no conviction in her voice. Her stomach heaved, and she tasted bile in her mouth. "I wasn't trying to hurt her. I didn't know what it did."

He gazed down at the artifact, his eyes distant. "I've never been able to get this to do anything. I could sense the magic radiating from it, but it's been dormant ever since I acquired it twenty years ago." He looked down at her again, but now his expression scared her. "But there is something about you that it reacts to. Now I finally know what it is capable of."

The Vizier had always been a kind and benevolent teacher to Sophie. Strict sometimes, but not unjustly so and always willing to listen. She had respected him as both the head of the house and as a wizard, but she had never seen him like this. This expression twisted his features into something cold and foreign. He was hungry for the power the artifact held. Sophie tried to pull away from him, but he held her wrist in a vice-like grip.

He stood and pulled Sophie to her feet with him. "We have a lot of work to do," he mused, looking down at the artifact again.

Sophie looked back at Ina's body as the Vizier dragged her out of the room, all but forgotten by their master. "I'm so sorry," she whispered as the door shut behind her, hiding the corpse and her guilt with it.

TWENTY-NINE

Sophie awoke with a start, the events of a few months ago still fresh in her mind. She was lying somewhere soft and comfortable, with no memory of how she'd gotten there. Her head throbbed and swam as she rose up onto her elbows, finding it difficult to sit up. When she was finally able to manage it through the pain, she looked around. She was lying on a bed with white linen sheets in a small room she didn't recognize. There was a single chair in the room, in the far corner and a chest at the foot of the bed. The walls were bare, and there was a window to her right with the shutters open, letting sunlight in.

Slowly, the memory of what happened right before she passed out came back to her. She swallowed hard, suddenly feeling nauseous. *No, that couldn't have happened.* But what else could explain why she had woken up here? There was just too much going on right now to think about that. Get out first, then figure out what was going on.

Sophie pushed herself into a sitting position. She was alone in the room. Whoever had brought her here must have thought she would be sleeping for most of the day or that she wouldn't try to escape. She could try the door first and if that didn't work, there was the window. With no one watching, it should be easy for her to escape and get back to her friends.

Sophie swung her legs over the side of the bed and felt an unfamiliar weight on her left leg. Confused, she looked down and felt the bottom of her stomach drop.

A thick metal band encircled her ankle, almost smooth except for a barely visible seam down the back. There were a few spots of rust, but otherwise, the metal gleamed in the sunlight. Hands shaking, she reached down and touched the metal, feeling the magical energy pulsing through it. A slave anklet. Someone had put a slave anklet on her.

Sophie slipped two fingers under the metal band and attempted to pull it off, but it wouldn't budge, it was already locked and sealed. It was too tight to simply slip off over her foot, and she doubted it would be as simple as having someone cut it off. She reached out with her magic, but as soon as her will touched the energy of the device, its magic lashed out at her, making her head pound even harder. Her vision blurred before gradually coming back into focus. She panted from the pain, clenching her teeth down on the scream that came clawing up her throat.

"That won't work," came the rough voice Sophie had heard at the warehouse, making her jump. The Spider materialized seemingly out of nowhere, dropping the invisibility spell he must have been using. He leaned against the wall by the door, watching her. "Do you know what that is?"

"A slave anklet," she said through gritted teeth, fighting down the involuntary impulse to retch. Her eyes immediately tracked to the iron ring on his finger. That must be the link to the anklet. A sudden, sharp pain made her groan. It felt as if her head was trying to break open like an egg. Sophie lay back down on the bed and closed her eyes, taking deep breaths through her nose. "A *magical* slave anklet," she said hoarsely once she found the will to speak again.

The Spider chuckled. "Yes. It compels the wearer to do their master's bidding. The more you struggle against it, the more painful it will be. And don't even think of trying to take it off or you'll experience a very painful backlash of energy."

"I noticed," Sophie retorted. She cracked her eyelids open ever so slightly and peered at the window. If she made a run for it, he'd catch her before she reached it, that was if he didn't overwhelm her on the spot using the anklet. She couldn't use her magic to get the anklet off, but maybe she could still use it to get away from him somehow.

He must have guessed what she was thinking. The sardonic grin never faded from his face as he calmly and clearly said, "I command you to not use your magic or try to escape."

Sophie felt the anklet's power as he gave the command. Tentatively, she reached out to her magic, prepared for some backlash from the anklet, but the magic felt far away. She reached for it again. Her power always came when she called on it, but now she couldn't touch it, like vapor slipping between her fingers. It took all her willpower not to cry out in terror.

She took a few deep breaths. It wouldn't do any good to lose control of her emotions. She needed to stay calm and figure out how to get away from the Spider and find her friends. Surely, the others would be trying to find her. She refused to think about what had become of Khalil. Yes, he and Eolisti would both come for her. If she could keep this man talking, that might buy them enough time to help her.

"Where is Joel?" her stomach clenched at the mention of his name, but she needed to know what happened.

"You mean the Vizier's spy? Why, he left as soon as he turned you over to me, payment in hand."

"No," Sophie said, trying to shake her head, but that hurt too much. She wanted to deny it, to scream at the Spider that he would never do that. Everything that had happened that morning still felt like a bad dream, but she remembered. The memory of his voice drifting to her as she'd lost consciousness echoed in her mind. Joel, her friend and companion, had betrayed her.

"Khalil," she began, trying to refocus her thoughts. "What did you do with Khalil?" As the question left her lips, she both needed and feared the answer.

The Spider sneered. "Your would-be guide? By the time the Soulless are finished with him, I doubt there will be anything left to mourn over." His reaction seemed incongruous with his confident words. It took him a few moments to compose himself, but then that lazy grin fixed on his face again. "He really should have accepted my offer. It would have been a very profitable arrangement. Better than a painful death."

Sophie clenched her fists and fought back tears. She glared at the Spider, who gazed blandly back down at her. More than anything, she wanted to hit him, though she knew it wouldn't do her any good. In all likelihood, it would provoke him to punish her with the anklet, but it would still be so satisfying.

He chuckled again, seeming to take immense pleasure in her pain and impotent anger. "It's time for you to go back to Zo'rahn, mageling. There is no one left to help you, nowhere else to run."

His words held such gravity and confidence that, for a moment, she began to despair before she remembered that there was still someone on her side. Eolisti was still out there, but would she even know what was going on? What would she do when no one came back to the inn? Khalil couldn't be dead. She wouldn't believe it. The Soulless were terrifying, but the Spider didn't say he'd seen him die. He could still be alive. Would he and Eolisti come for her?

She decided for the second time that she had to do everything she could to slow the Spider down and give her friends enough time to find her. "Why are you doing this? Why would the Vizier hire someone like you instead of using his own people?"

He scoffed. "I don't owe a traitor like you any answers." The Spider's grin faded, and he narrowed his eyes coldly. Sophie swallowed. "Enough of your prattle. No one is coming for you," he said firmly. "Get up."

Sophie felt her limbs moving, even though she struggled against the anklet's control. There was that crippling pain again, and, even though she wanted to resist, she found herself standing in front of the Spider, glaring up at him.

He scowled back down at her. "It's time for this job to be finished. I've wasted enough time on you already." The Spider grabbed her arm and shoved her toward the door. There was nothing she could do to stop him.

THIRTY

Sophie stumbled onto the cobblestone street as the Spider pushed her out the door of the inn. She shot a glare back at him, then looked around at the street. The sun was still high in the sky. Children still played and people went about their business. No one paid them any notice as the Spider pressed a hand to her back in a way that would seem gentlemanly to any observers, but with a force that propelled her forward, compelling her to keep pace with him. He'd made her don a long, linen dress, much like what the townswomen around her were wearing, and a shawl that covered her hair and most of her face. As certain as he claimed to be that her friends were dead, he still didn't seem willing to accept any risk of her being recognized.

He leaned down close to her ear in a familiar manner.

"Do not speak to anyone else unless I tell you to," he whispered, activating the anklet with his words. She hadn't been planning to ask anyone on the street for help since she assumed he would kill everyone in earshot if she tried something so overt, but the command angered her all the same.

Instead of taking the main road, the Spider led Sophie into an alley across from the inn. Once they reached the next street, they turned right, walked a little way, and turned into another alley. He never took her down a main road for more than a few steps before heading down another backstreet. It was difficult to get a sense of where they were with all of the winding and backtracking they were doing, but eventually, Sophie could see the ocean in the distance between a few of the buildings. They must be getting closer to the docks.

Looming above some of the other buildings, she could see the top of a large warehouse. It didn't look like any of the other structures she had seen near the docks, but Sophie had seen buildings like this before in Tanzar. It was a dry dock where ships were built, or more likely in a place like this, repaired. As they wove through the streets, she became more and more confident that the large building was their destination.

"Why are we going there?" she asked without thinking.

"Why? So that you can be reunited with your family, of course," the Spider purred, a note of satisfaction in his voice.

It was difficult for her not to roll her eyes. She was still afraid of him and what was to come, but most of that fear had turned to anger. Instead, she set her jaw and scanned the surrounding buildings and alleys. Maybe she should scream and make a ruckus. There weren't many people around, and if her friends were trying to find her...

As if in response to her thoughts, there was a flash of sunlight on metal, and it felt like her heart leaped up into her throat. Had it been her imagination? She could have sworn she had seen the gleam of Eolisti's hair and shield. Sophie risked a glance back at the Spider. He didn't seem to have noticed.

No, it had to have been Eolisti. She couldn't afford to think otherwise. Sophie looked around again. They weren't that far from the large building now. There wasn't much time. Once the Spider had her out in the open, it would be nearly impossible for her allies to get the drop on him. She had to do something to distract him. She had to act. Now.

She stepped to the side and faced him, putting her back against a wall. She wasn't trying to get away from him— the anklet wouldn't allow her to do that—but she wanted to be far enough away from him that he wouldn't be able to push her along anymore.

Before she had gotten fully out of his reach, he snatched her arm and pulled her back toward him. He stopped walking and glared at her, his eyes narrowed.

"What do you think you're doing?"

Sophie ignored the question. "I think I've realized something about you," she said, loudly enough for her voice to echo in the narrow roadway. She knew it was a gamble, but she had to try something.

"When you attacked us before you were so angry. I wondered why you hated me so much when I'd never even met you before. I mean, you're obviously of Zo'rahni descent but"—she made a show of looking him up and down—"you're not *from* Zo'rahn, are you?" His hand clenched on her arm with bruising force, but Sophie did her best to ignore the pain and stare up into his dark eyes. He scowled down at her, and she could almost feel his anger boiling up.

She had been grasping for anything to get a rise out of the Spider, and it looked like she hit the mark. Sophie could tell that she'd hit a nerve. She smiled at him. "You would think someone as strong as you would be part of one of the ruling families, or at least recognized by the Viziers, but I've never heard of you before. Why is that?"

He was shaking. Sophie wouldn't have been surprised if he'd started foaming at the mouth. "You—"

She cut him off before he could order her to stop. "I think it's because your Zo'rahni blood is too weak, and that's why you hate that a half-breed like me is *treasured* by so powerful a family. You do the bidding of the Viziers, and they call on you when they need something, but they don't *really* respect you. You aren't even a person to them."

Pain shot up her arm from where he held her, and she fought not to wince or cry out, but he wasn't using the anklet on her. Out of the corner of her eye, she saw something move, and it spurred her on. "You're like an animal, only called upon to do your master's bidding," she hissed. "Then they send you away, and you wait until they call you again. A loyal, obedient—"

Apparently, she had gone too far. Pain exploded in her abdomen as the Spider drove his fist into her stomach. Sophie gasped and doubled over, and her captor let her arm slip out of his grip as she slid to the ground. Sophie choked and tasted bile at the back of her throat. She pulled the shawl back from her face with one hand and clutched at her stomach with the other, trying to gasp for air. It was a good thing she hadn't eaten recently. Otherwise, she would have thrown it up onto the cobblestones.

As she lay on the ground, still reeling from nausea and pain, the Spider knelt next to her. He reached out and took a fistful of her hair, wrenching her head back and forcing her to look up at him. Her vision was blurred with tears, but she could still see the rage in his features.

"You should know your place, mageling," he spat. "Who are *you* to question *my* loyalty?" He let go of her hair and stood, looming over her. A wicked grin played on his lips as he watched her struggle. "Get up," he said ruthlessly.

The skin where the anklet touched tingled and Sophie tried to comply, but she coughed and heaved, falling back to the ground. Pain shot through her, worse than it had when she'd tried to touch the anklet, worse than anything she had ever felt before. It was like every inch of her was being set on fire, searing her flesh and reaching into the very core of her bones without actually burning her. Her back arched, and she screamed in earnest. The Spider didn't seem to care about her making noise anymore. He let her scream until the pain finally started to ease.

"I said, *Get. Up.*" The sadistic pleasure in his voice was unmistakable. Another wave from the anklet hit her, and she screamed again until her throat was hoarse.

The Spider stood over her, watching her writhe in agony. He was too distracted to notice as Khalil came up behind him and swung a wooden board at his head. There was a resounding *CRACK*, and the Spider crumpled to the ground.

Sophie's screams subsided as the pain started to fade again. Khalil leaned over her and put his arms under hers, gently lifting her to her feet. The lingering effects of the anklet completely vanished once she complied with the Spider's last command. She swayed, and Khalil put one arm around her, leaning her up against him so she wouldn't fall back to the ground. "Are you all right?"

Sophie opened her mouth to speak but felt the tingling sensation from the anklet again. She snapped her mouth closed and nodded into Khalil's chest. Her stomach still hurt, and she shook with the effort of standing after what the anklet had done to her, but as far as she knew, she was physically uninjured.

Eolisti darted out from between two buildings, drawing her sword. "We should kill him," she said, looking down at the Spider's unmoving form.

"We're not killing anyone," Khalil snapped. "We need to get out of here before he regains his senses."

With a tremendous effort, Sophie lifted her arm to point a shaking finger at the Spider. Pain surged through her as she gasped out, "Ring..." then clutched at Khalil's shirt, trying not to scream again.

"He put a slave anklet on her." Joel's voice rang out as he emerged from the same place Eolisti had. "There should be a silver ring on his right hand that controls it."

Sophie eyed him warily as Eolisti searched the Spider.

After a moment, Eolisti held up a plain silver ring, inspecting it in the sunlight. "Is this it? It doesn't look like much."

"It's not supposed to," Joel said. "It's supposed to be inconspicuous. From what I've heard, the anklets are mostly used for transporting and breaking slaves. Or for slaves that can use magic." He looked over at Sophie sheepishly. "I'm not sure how to take the anklet off though..."

Khalil held out a hand. "Give it to me." Eolisti stepped toward them and placed the ring in Khalil's outstretched palm. "Can you stand on your own?" he asked Sophie.

In answer, Sophie pushed away from Khalil and stood up straight, only wobbling once before she found her balance. Her skin felt tender and sore, like she had a bad sunburn, and though her stomach still hurt, she felt her strength coming back.

Khalil placed the ring on the middle finger of his right hand and touched it to his forehead. He then knelt in front of her, reaching his hands out until they brushed her left leg. His fingers trailed slowly down until they reached the edge of the linen dress. Sophie felt her cheeks heating with the delicate way he touched her skin, searching for the anklet he couldn't see. She looked over Khalil's head at Eolisti. The Anai was digging around in the satchel the Spider had been carrying.

"Asshole," Eolisti muttered under her breath as she pulled a small cloth bag out of it and placed it into a pouch on her belt.

Once Khalil's fingers found the anklet, he gently tapped the ring against it. Sophie felt a tension that she didn't know was there break, like the cracking of an eggshell. There was a soft snapping sound and Khalil stood, holding the anklet in his hand. "These are made in Alkhazai," he said in explanation and took off the silver ring, putting both it and the anklet into his pocket. "It will need to be disposed of properly."

Sophie felt the energy rush back into her as soon as the anklet came off. She reached out with her senses and was relieved to be able to feel her magic again. "Thank you," she said with a sigh.

Khalil nodded once then said, "We need to leave. Now."

The Spider groaned from where he lay on the ground, and Sophie's heart raced. He was starting to come around.

With one arm supporting her, Khalil rushed them back between the buildings Eolisti and Joel had emerged from. Before Eolisti followed, she turned and kicked the Spider hard in the side, then made a rude gesture at him as he grunted in pain. She sprinted after them, and they emerged onto the next street over. People were talking and glancing over in the direction they had come from.

Their group stepped aside when a few men came close,

but no one stopped to question them, instead running down the same alley they had just come out of. After they'd passed, Khalil led them through another alleyway across the street. Once they were off the main road, he paused to let the others catch their breath. Sophie was breathing hard and still hurt from both the anklet's magic and the Spider's strike. She was grateful when Khalil helped her lean against the wall and gave her a waterskin to drink out of.

"Check to see if there is anyone following us," Khalil instructed Eolisti. The Anai nodded and moved to the entrance of the alley, peering out into the street. Sophie had a sudden feeling of déjà vu, that was exactly what Joel had asked her to do before she had been drugged.

"Sophie," came Joel's voice from beside her. She glanced over at him as she handed the waterskin back to Khalil. Joel watched her closely, a pained expression on his face.

"I was wrong to hand you over to the Spider. No reason that I had justifies betraying you, and I... I'm sorry." He looked down at the ground. "I know you probably hate me, and I understand if you can't forgive me." He clenched his fists at his sides. "But I will see you safely out of the country."

Sophie stared at Joel. If he was apologizing openly, then Eolisti and Khalil must have already known that he'd betrayed her to the Spider. He seemed genuinely sorry, but she wasn't quite sure that she believed him. Before she could respond, Eolisti walked back over to them.

"I don't see anyone following. It looks like quite a few people are gathering where we left that bastard," she said, referring to the Spider.

"That doesn't mean there isn't anyone looking for us. We should move." Khalil held a hand out to Sophie, and she took it, pushing herself off the wall against which she'd been leaning. Sophie glanced back at Joel, who was turned slightly away from her. They would have to talk more later.

The pain was starting to recede, and she was able to run on her own, only holding on to Khalil's arm for support. They hurried out of the alley and wove through the streets, heading toward the other end of the docks. Where the Spider had been taking her was apparently the furthest you could get from where ships actually docked and still be considered part of the port. Sophie glanced back over her shoulder at the dry dock. She could still see it over the tops of the other buildings, but it was fading into the distance, and she wondered who had been waiting there to take her.

"There!" Eolisti's voice brought her attention back to where they were going. The Anai pointed to a ship that was moored to the very last dock. It was smaller than other ships she'd seen loading cargo in Zo'rahn, but it was still sizable, with three large masts. She could see men moving around on the deck, and one of the sails began to unfurl. On the side of the caravel, the name *Westwind* was stenciled in gold and red paint.

Men and women working on other boats or carrying supplies watched them as they passed, apparently puzzled by their haste to make it down the pier. Once they reached the *Westwind*, Khalil directed them toward a ramp that connected the boat to the dock.

"About time," called a deep, surly voice from the deck. A fair-skinned man with curly blond hair cut close to his head peered down at them. "We were getting ready to leave without you."

Khalil nodded up at him. "Thank you for waiting, Captain."

The captain scowled. "Well, don't just stand there, get them on the ship." He disappeared from view.

Khalil gestured toward the ramp, and Sophie and Eolisti began walking up it.

"You all go on. I'm staying." Joel's voice came from behind Sophie. When she turned around, he was standing on the dock, making no movement toward the ramp.

"If you stay, Spider and his men will find you and kill you for your betrayal," Sophie said before she could think about her words. She may have still been suspicious of Joel, but that didn't mean she wanted him dead. "You can come with us and start a new life, away from all of this."

Joel shook his head, a sad expression on his face. "I have to go back for my sister. I can't leave her here." He laughed, and it sounded pained. "I didn't even have a chance to say goodbye before I left. It's my responsibility to make sure she's safe."

Sophie glanced at Eolisti, and the other woman met her eyes. The Anai shook her head, then darted toward Joel, wrapping her arms around him in an embrace. He looked stunned as she released him, then without a word, she turned around and ran onto the ship. He watched her go, a look of bemusement on his face.

"Joel," Sophie began, searching for the words she wanted to say.

He approached her and placed a hand on top of her head. "I hope you find the life you are looking for, Sophie."

Her eyes welled up with tears, and she threw her arms around him. He smelled of campfire smoke and sandalwood, and it reminded her of nights she'd spent listening to his stories in the desert. It didn't matter what he'd done. She still cared about him, still wanted to thank him for being there for her and helping her throughout this journey. Too many people had been hurt helping her. She didn't want him to be another one.

He held her back for a moment then said, "You need to get out of here. Go on, I'll be fine."

Sophie pulled away from him and wiped away a tear, then turned back toward the ship and the waiting Khalil.

"Take care of them," Joel called up to Khalil. The other man nodded to him and turned to follow Sophie onto the ship as she passed him.

There was a low thud, and Joel grunted behind them. Khalil grabbed Sophie's arm and pulled her to him, covering her with his cloak. She looked around wide-eyed. "What's happening?" She glanced over her shoulder at Joel and felt the bottom drop out of her stomach.

A thick wooden shaft with black fletching stuck out of his side. Blood stained his clothes from where the bolt had hit him and trickled down his tunic to drip onto the dock. He looked dazed, not yet comprehending the reality of what was happening.

"No, no, no!" Sophie tried to stand to go to him, but Khalil grabbed her arm.

"You need to get out of sight," he hissed, pulling her toward the ship's deck.

"No!" she cried, trying to pull away from him. Another crossbow bolt hit the ramp a few feet from where they were standing. Joel's dark-brown eyes met hers, and she felt her chest tighten at the look on his face. Hot tears ran down her cheeks. *Joel.* She tried to take a step toward him again, but Khalil would not let her go.

"Take care of them!" Joel repeated, putting more emphasis on the words than he had earlier, then dove behind a barrel that had been left on the dock. A crossbow bolt sank into the planks where he had been standing. He threw a look at them over his shoulder. "Khalil, what are you waiting for?!"

Khalil nodded at Joel's words then rushed up the ramp and onto the ship, dragging Sophie with him. Sophie struggled against Khalil as he pulled her up onto the deck. "I can heal you! You don't have to do this!" She half screamed down at Joel, still crouched behind the crate.

"I'll try to buy you more time!" he called back as another bolt thudded into the barrel he hid behind. Sophie could see men moving down the docks now, swords drawn. People jumped out of their way as they came closer to the *Westwind*.

"We need to leave NOW!" Khalil shouted at the nearest crewmen.

The captain called out orders, and two men rushed forward to pull the ramp onto the ship. A third drew a long saber from where it had been sheathed on his belt and cut the rope tying the *Westwind* to the dock. The ship immediately lurched away, and Sophie stumbled as sailors dashed around her, trying to unfurl the sails. Once she regained her balance, she pulled her arm out of Khalil's grip and ran over to the railing.

The tide was with them, and the *Westwind* was moving away from the docks with increasing speed. She could see Joel where they had left him. The men chasing after them had reached the *Westwind*'s newly vacated berth, and Joel's sword flashed as he tried to fend them off. She wanted to help him, but with the ship rocking back and forth with the waves, she couldn't be sure she wouldn't hit Joel instead of whoever was attacking him. Was there anything she could do?

Sophie saw the flash of sun hitting steel, and in a panic, she raised one hand, sending out a burst of energy. She missed, and another crossbow bolt embedded itself deep into Joel's back. He let out a strangled cry, and the man fighting him pushed him back. Joel lost his footing and fell.

"No!" she screamed again and sent another wave of nearly invisible energy toward the docks. The boat rocked violently and sent the blast down into the water, only succeeding in splashing seawater up onto the men.

An arm wrapped around her from behind, and Khalil picked her up, hauling her away from the edge of the ship and out of sight of the docks.

"Let me go!" she shouted in a half sob, kicking her legs. "I have to help him!"

"You need to get out of the open," he said firmly, carrying her under the ladder that led up to the helm. He pinned her to the wall, holding her arms so that she couldn't move back over to the taffrail. "Joel made his choice. Don't throw his sacrifice away by being reckless."

Sophie slumped in defeat. She knew Khalil was right, she'd known it when she'd looked into Joel's eyes. He'd chosen to say and fight. To give them a chance to escape. She wanted to go back for him, but that would mean that she and everyone on the *Westwind* would be caught. The Spider, or whoever was waiting for them, would kill everyone on board to get to her.

As much as she hated it, there was nothing she could do for Joel.

"Khalil!" the captain's voice rang out, tense and panicked. "We're going to need that mage!"

Khalil released her, and they climbed the ladder to the helm. The captain gave her a sharp look, then motioned back toward Nobarum. Sophie followed his gaze to the docks. They were enough away that she was barely able to make out the people standing there. Her eyes flicked over them, then settled on the one man standing at the edge of the docks. A slightly larger man with black hair, a goatee, and black robes.

Her eyes widened, and she took a step backward. It had been nearly eleven years since she had seen Iseul, but she remembered exactly what he looked like. He was the man who'd taken her away from her mother and father, the man who'd torn her family apart.

He hadn't changed much. He still stood in the same way, with his legs spread slightly farther apart than a man might normally. His black robes stood out in the sunlit afternoon. Most of the men and women in Nobarum wore white or tan, so he looked oddly out of place. He was surrounded by men, presumably the ones who had been fighting Joel. Fear bubbled up in Sophie's stomach. She'd heard rumors that one of the reasons Iseul went out and tested children was that he didn't have a lot of talent, but if that was the case, why would the Vizier send him alone? Why would he not send two or three of the family's wizards?

Sophie walked toward the edge of the helm. She could feel energy gathering and knew he was casting a spell. Would the rumors about him prove true, or would his vast experience threaten to overwhelm her as the Spider's had?

Iseul raised one hand toward the ship, and small spheres of orange flame flickered into life, floating around him like oversized fireflies. Suddenly they streaked toward the ship, growing more massive and more deadly as they raced through the air.

Sophie had already begun to weave a shield spell. She poured her anger at the man standing before her into it, making it that much stronger. She spread her fingers and willed the spell to split, creating multiple smaller patches of solid air and energy that the miniature fireballs crashed into and then exploded several dozen feet from the *West-wind*'s wooden body. She shielded her eyes from the flashes of light and could hear some of the crewmen whooping behind her as their ship sailed on unscathed. Sophie allowed herself a brief smile, caught up in the emotions of the men around her.

If the blocking of his magic had inconvenienced Iseul, they were too far away for her to tell. He raised one hand up over his head, and Sophie felt a surge of power wash over her, gathering momentum. The air above them crackled with energy. Clouds rushed in, turning the sunny afternoon sky as dark as night as they roiled above the *Westwind*, churning faster and faster. Sophie didn't know what spell Iseul was using, but she could feel the strength of the gathering power, and it frightened her. She had always been taught that magic was about focus and control, but this was primal, unrestrained power.

She threw her arms skyward, willing her power to form a shield above the ship. Sophie had never attempted a shield big enough to cover such a large area, but she managed to get it in place just as the first bolt of lightning streaked toward the deck with an ear-ringing thunderclap.

White light seared her eyes, almost making her lose her concentration, and she barely managed to hold the shield. The air around her vibrated with electricity as she felt another surge of power building. Sophie shut her eyes tightly and turned her head away. She took her fear and anger and rage and poured all that energy into the spell, willing it to hold, willing it to keep them safe.

The flash of light was visible even through her eyelids, and the sharp crack of thunder shook her to her very core. She swayed on her feet and felt hands touch her shoulders, steadying her.

"I've got you," came Eolisti's voice, barely audible over the ringing in her ears. "Just keep that shield up!"

Another three strikes of lightning hit the shield at once. Sophie felt beads of sweat trickling down her neck as she pushed more power into the spell, drawing off some of the nervous energy and fear of those around her. Eolisti held her firmly in place, and she was sure that if the Anai wasn't there helping her, she would have collapsed onto the deck by now. It was taking every ounce of strength and will she had to hold the shield.

Another blinding flash of light and thunder echoed all around them. Sophie felt her shield fracture at the impact, and her heart skipped a beat. She glanced around at the sailors standing on the deck watching the lightning strikes with morbid fascination. They were all out in the open. They didn't know what was coming.

"Run!" she screamed at them, not knowing if they could hear her. "Find cover!"

Thunder clapped and Sophie's shield broke. Chaos erupted as lightning struck the center mast, sending pieces of wood flying in all directions. The impact sent her tumbling back into the taffrail. Men screamed in pain and fear as the impact threw them around the ship like dolls. Smoke curled from where the lightning had struck, and flames licked up the broken mast, threatening to set the other sails on fire. Those who were coherent enough to think scrambled for water to put out the fire while others attempted to pull their comrades to shelter.

Sophie gripped the taffrail and pulled herself to her feet, watching in horror as men scrambled to put out the fires. Many were bruised and bleeding, and some of the sailors lay on the deck, unmoving. She searched around for Eolisti, but she couldn't spot her in the confusion. The clouds above them flashed, and Sophie knew another strike was imminent. She thought about the death of her friends and the pain she had put everyone through. They had come so far only to fail at the very end.

No! A small voice screamed in her head. *No! This is not the end!* And with one last surge of effort and will, Sophie cried out, lifting her hands over her head and forming one last shield spell. It flickered to life, fueled purely by her own stubbornness. As lightning streaked down again, she angled the shield, pouring all of her hope and desperation into deflecting the strike and sending it back toward the shore.

The bolt of lightning missed the docks, hitting the water in front of where Iseul stood and sending a wave splashing up onto the platform. She saw him stumble and fall as the water hit him, washing him along the docks. Would that be enough to break his concentration?

The captain shouted something to his men, but she couldn't hear well enough to make out the words. Sophie's legs buckled, but she was so tired she didn't even feel it when she hit the splintered deck beneath her. All of her fear and rage and grief had been spent on that last spell. She heard another shout somewhere near her and then footsteps. Her vision blurred, and for a second, she could see shapes moving around her. She vaguely heard voices, but they were muffled over the ringing that lingered in her ears. Then with a sigh, Sophie closed her eyes, and everything went black.

CHAPTER

THIRTY-ONE

The *Westwind* was far out to sea by the time Sophie regained consciousness. She found herself alone in a dark cabin. As she tried to sit up to get her bearings, she knocked something off the bedside table and sent it clattering to the floor. Moments later, the door flew open and Eolisti rushed in, asking where it hurt and how she could help.

Sophie realized it hurt just to move. Her entire body was sore, and she felt ravenous. The Anai told her that she had been asleep for two full days. They had been afraid that she might never wake up.

Eolisti helped her get out of bed and dress, gave her some fruit to eat, then took her out onto the deck. Sophie found it difficult to walk by herself at first, but it seemed to get easier the longer she was on her feet. While they walked, Eolisti filled her in on what had happened in the aftermath of the attack on the ship.

Her gamble had worked. Once the wave hit the docks, the sky had begun to clear, and they were able to put enough distance between the ship and the shore with the

311

two remaining sails to be safely out of range by the time Iseul recovered. They'd found Sophie lying by the taffrail, and Captain Alvar had ordered that a cabin be set aside for her so that she could recover. Someone, usually Eolisti or Khalil, had kept a constant vigil in case she woke. They hadn't been able to get very far very fast with the ship as damaged as it was, so they'd sailed along the coast to the next port town north of Nobarum and brought on supplies to fix the ship. After some hasty repairs were done, they set sail again the following day and were already well into the Silver Sea. The men worked around the clock fixing the *Westwind*, and there was still a lot to do, but nothing that couldn't be done while they were moving.

The sun was high when they emerged on deck. The *Westwind* was surrounded by water as far as the eye could see, reflecting the shimmering sunlight in its gentle waves. Some of the sailors that Sophie recognized were setting planks and hammering nails into the damaged ship.

Overall, they were lucky. While the main mast had taken the lion's share of the damage, it hadn't broken completely or fallen, and the men had managed to save the sail. The wood was charred and black where the lightning and subsequent fire had struck, but with some quick thinking, they'd wrapped most of it with rope to secure it. It wouldn't hold forever, and that sail couldn't be unfurled, but they were still able to traverse the sea with the other two sails until the main mast could be replaced.

Sophie spotted Khalil helping with the repairs, nimbly climbing up and down the rigging and securing damaged ropes and tying down damaged parts. The sun gleamed off shining gold hair, and Sophie recognized the Anai that she and Eolisti had been talking to back in town—the one that Eolisti had disappeared with for a night—talking with some of the sailors. Her eyes slid over to Eolisti beside her, who was grinning shamelessly.

"His name is Elindiir. He's an envoy from Nemethy who was in Omer for business." She held up her hands and shrugged. "He told me he was sailing west the same day we were leaving, but I didn't know he'd be on this ship until we were already here." Her eyes sparkled. "He promised to tell me all about the Anaiian courts of the west. Maybe I'll even get to go to Nemethy."

Sophie covered her smile with her hand. It sounded like Eolisti had no intention of going back to Elasariin anytime soon.

When the men noticed Sophie was up and walking around, many of them put down what they were doing and approached her. They thanked her for saving the ship and their lives, and she felt a stab of guilt. If she hadn't been on the *Westwind* in the first place, they wouldn't have been in danger, but she accepted their gratitude as gracefully as she could. Two men had died during the attack and had been laid to rest out at sea before she'd awoken. Sophie didn't even know their names or what they looked like, and it was difficult for her to accept that two more people had died because of her.

"How are you feeling?" Khalil asked, having made his way to her after the small crowd of sailors around her had dissipated. His hood was down, and he was wiping the sweat off his brow with a towel. His eyes were the same cloudy white gold that she had seen before, but out in the sun, they looked less menacing and more... him.

"Fine," Sophie said, smiling up at him. It might be selfish to think it, but she was relieved that he and Eolisti were safe. "Just a little weak."

Eolisti put a hand on her shoulder. "I have something to

show you later." She grinned at Sophie's look of confusion and winked. Then Eolisti turned in Elindiir's direction and sauntered toward him.

Later, when Sophie was alone in her cabin and the sun had set, there was a knock at her door. She opened it to find Eolisti holding a small drawstring bag and bouncing on the balls of her feet. Sophie stepped aside to let her in, and the Anai sat on her bed, immediately opening the bag and digging around in it.

"What is that?" Sophie asked, closing the door and joining her on the bed.

"Just what I took from that Spider guy."

It took Sophie a moment to process what Eolisti had said. "You stole his money?"

Eolisti scoffed. "He deserved it. Bastard," she growled. "Anyway, there was something with his stuff that looked odd." She pulled a large green emerald out of the bag. "It looks like a normal gem, but I don't think it is. There's something off about it."

Sophie felt her breath catch in her throat. "That's a communication gem."

Eolisti flipped it up into the air and caught it nonchalantly. "A what?"

"A communication gem. It's a gem that is enchanted to correspond to one similar to it. Gems are typically paired, so that information put in one gem is sent to the other. There are tablets that they fit into, and when you carve your message in the wax, the other paired gem stores the information and your message will show up once the receiver puts their own gem into a tablet," Sophie explained.

"That sounds like a lot of work," Eolisti said, flipping it up again and snatching it out of the air.

"Well, you can also use it to send a message that's purely sound, but it doesn't retain the information once the receiver listens to it."

Eolisti looked at her. "So, this gem..."

"Is probably paired to one the Vizier owns, since you got it off of the Spider," Sophie finished.

The Anai looked down at the emerald in her palm. "Do you have to have magic to use it?" She looked up sharply. "Could he have been spying on us the entire time?"

"That's not really how they work," Sophie assured her. "The sender has to consciously relay information, and the receiver can't activate the gem that's not in their possession. And no, you don't have to have magical ability to use the gems. It just takes focus and knowing how to activate it." She shivered. "Like when Khalil activated the slave anklet to remove it. There was no magic involved on his part, but he'd obviously dealt with them before."

Eolisti nodded. "So, you can tell this guy to go roll around naked in a hill of fire ants?"

"I... don't think that's a good idea."

The Anai shrugged and tossed her the gem. Sophie caught it and peered down at it. "Well, that's up to you, I guess," Eolisti sighed and stood. "Being on a boat is boring." And with that, she strode to the door and left, leaving Sophie to contemplate the gleaming, green emerald on her own.

Sophie found it difficult to sleep. She lay in her bed, staring up at the ceiling for most of the night, alone with her thoughts. She held the emerald up in front of her face, feeling its edges in the near-complete darkness. What should she do with it? Should she send a message back? A final goodbye? The Vizier would be angry, whatever she did. It would be dangerous to communicate with him. After all they had been through, it wasn't worth it.

She sat up. "I need some air," she muttered to herself and pulled a light, airy dress over her head. With the emerald still in hand, she left her cabin and made her way up the stairs into the night.

When Sophie emerged on the deck, neither moon was out, but the stars shone brightly in the night sky. A few of the sailors were on deck, but the ship seemed mostly still and quiet. The rest of the men must have been asleep. Captain Alvar was nowhere to be seen, and a man that Sophie was pretty sure was the first mate stood at the helm. He nodded to her, and she waved back to him.

Khalil leaned against the taffrail to her left, and Sophie approached quietly so as not to disturb him. The breeze ruffled his dark hair.

"Can't sleep?" he asked without turning toward her.

Of course he knew she was there. He really was something else. "No." She smiled to herself. "I guess I've slept enough." She looked down at the gem in her hand and then out at the ocean again.

Sophie made her decision. She leaned over the rail and let the emerald slip out of her hand, dropping it into the dark water below. She felt an overwhelming sense of relief, but also of sadness. The last tie to her old home had been severed.

"What was that?" Khalil asked, face still turned out toward the sea.

Sophie shook her head. "Nothing. Just a relic from my past. I think it's time I moved on for good."

He nodded, and she could see a smile tugging at the sides of his lips. Sophie leaned on the taffrail with him and looked out to the sea, the stars sparkling like diamonds on the black water. Somewhere across that endless expanse, she would be able to build a new life for herself, with the help of her friends. They had all sacrificed so much for her. She would do all that she could to make sure that their suffering was not in vain. There was much to do once they landed in the west, but getting across the Silver Sea could take weeks. There was plenty of time to plan her next steps later.

There was still a long journey ahead of her, but for now, they were safe, and that was all that mattered.

About the Authors

Accountant by day, writer by night, Vivian Bricker has been penning fantasy stories since she was old enough to pick up a book. She lives near Denver, Colorado, with her husband and three dogs: Hiro, Kalli, and Mira. Free time is hard to come by, but when she has a few extra hours, she likes to paint, practice archery, and run tabletop roleplaying games.

@VBrickerAuthor

Karen Nobles also lives near Denver with her husband and their giant rescue dogs, Stella and Hugo. In order to keep her babies in the luxury they deserve, Karen spends her weekdays chained to a desk writing contracts. In her free time, if she isn't writing, you're likely to find her training to kick ass at the local gym, exploring the wild mountain forests near her home, or dreaming up new adventures—for her characters and herself!

brickerandnobles.com

www.ingramcontent.com/pod-product-compliance
Lightning Source LLC
Chambersburg PA
CBHW032336310726
48973CB00007B/1744